I0846527

TINY DUNGEON CORE

The Bearded Man

ISBN: 979-8-88993-079-2

Edited by Jimi Iyiola
Cover Art by Huu Ha

Published 2025 by MoonQuill®
Arlington, VA

www.moonquill.com

Table of Contents

Prologue

Setting the Stage

Dawn broke over the Sylcyne Forest, golden rays of light breaking through the leaves to bathe a clearing. Within this clearing lay a cabin—though to call it a cabin was to willfully diminish its splendor. In reality, the massive structure looked more akin to a nobleman's retreat.

Stone encapsulated the outside of the building, forming a protective barrier. Its unnaturally smooth surface suggested powerful magic as the origin. From the outside, all that could be seen was stonework, but if one were to look from the inside out, they would only see pleasant wooden paneling. The reason for this was simple: there were two separate walls. An inner and outer wall with an almost four-inch gap separating the two. Little runes etched into the inside portion of the stonework warmed the space or cooled it down as needed.

A porch ran the length of the mansion, ringing it like a noble lady's ball gown. It had an attic and two round roofs, one of which was above the attic. The roof below covered the west wing, which was separated from the main building by a short hallway with windows.

The wealth of the mansion's inhabitant was further emphasized by mounted glass panes, through which ambient light entered. After all, glass was a rarity this far to the north. The house faced the north defiantly, as though daring the fierce snow to try and drown it in white. It was summer, however, and heat and light held sway in the Sylcyne Forest.

The strengthening light from the east cast a bright glare into the eastern section of the house, that being the kitchen. The kitchen's utensils, metal gleaming in their holders, were simple and elegant as befitted the occupant. Within it was a stairway that led into the cellar and basement. However, the light couldn't penetrate deeply into the circular stairway and the depths remained cloaked in shadow.

From the kitchen, one could reach the greeting room and be treated to simple grandeur. Simple yet solid wooden doors framed the entrance, but the gild work and runes etched into their surface would prevent anyone from misunderstanding their extravagance. Paintings hung on the wall, depicting various cityscapes and natural scenes of beauty.

The west wing of the mansion-like cabin held a large bedroom, furnace room, and even a ritual room. Such was the cabin of Archmage Calamvor, though it did him little good at the moment. The archmage himself was in the ritual room, and at first glance, he seemed fine.

Noble features, hair whitened with age, and face wizened with experience. Yet today, his normally kind eyes were dilated in pain and fear. His grand ritual had succeeded and the pinnacle of his arcane career now sat in front of him, gleaming in the center of the room.

Unfortunately, Calamvor couldn't check on his creation. His back was against the wall, both literally and figuratively. His mind struggled to work, but he knew that he needed to move the small gemstone somewhere else. His vision dimmed for a moment as the pain became unbearable. When he opened his eyes next, his gaze found a mouse holding the little glowing gemstone.

"Yesss," he hissed in pain, scaring the little rodent who ran off with its prize. "Guard it with your life, little friend. Take care of it." Calamvor groaned as the pain peaked, his torn and destroyed Spark trying desperately to keep him alive a moment longer.

"Take... care... of... my..." The words didn't come. Archmage Calamvor died. Far away from anyone who would mourn him. Far from those who knew of his accolades and sacrifices.

Deep beneath his cabin, however, past the living room and past the kitchen. To the far eastern wall, in between the arcane wards and enchantments that ran the length of the building, lay the humble nest of the mouse.

There sat its treasure in prime position—the tiny shining Artificial Core, the pinnacle of Calamvor's genius and career. It rested as a jewel among the mouse's other belongings. A thimble here, an enchanted, though partially broken, sewing needle there.

The mouse in question was grooming itself, quite pleased at having stolen its shiny prize right out from under the giant's feet. It was, perhaps, more intelligent than others of its species despite having no stages of Ascension. The Artificial Core simply sat, with no thoughts as of yet and indeed no soul to speak of.

That changed when its creator finally died. A small portion of the man's soul, a tiny hint of his torn and battered Spark's essence, came to rest within the core. It was enough to ignite instinct but nothing else. However, it also imparted the one thing that set sapient beings apart from others—the ability to become more.

Welcome, Dungeon Core!
***Error* Artificial Core detected! Commencing destruction!**
***Error* Destruction halted by the Maker's edict. Proto-Spark**
detected.

Welcome, Dungeon Core!
As a dungeon core, you have been granted a measure of divinity by the High Council, the ruling pantheon. As such, you may utilize raw Aether to form creations. You have two paths before you: one of imagination and one of direction.

Error Proto-Spark detected.
Path of Direction has been chosen automatically.

Direction:
You receive the help of the gods in the form of Frameworks, which are gifted directly from them. These Frameworks hold the underlying DNA of this world's creatures. By choosing this path, all you need to do is fill the resulting Frameworks with Aether and your creatures will be born.

In addition, you will receive direction in crafting your dungeon via a download of instincts that will guide you in what you should do as well as what dangers you might face. Call it a sixth sense.

Error Dungeon is too small to receive benefits. A boon and a title will be granted instead.

Boon granted: Favor of the Gods.
Boon effects:
You have found favor with the gods. At each new Rank of Ascension you reach, you will be able to choose a new Framework from among a list. The ranks of these Frameworks will be determined by your Rank of Ascension as well as any excess growth that you achieve. Partial survival instincts and Authority to use and control Aether will be granted.

Title granted: Tiny Dungeon
As the tiniest dungeon in existence, you have been granted this title.
Title effects:
Aether costs to claim territory are significantly reduced. Aether costs to summon creatures from Frameworks you obtain that are larger than tiny sized are reduced by 90%. Frameworks of creatures you

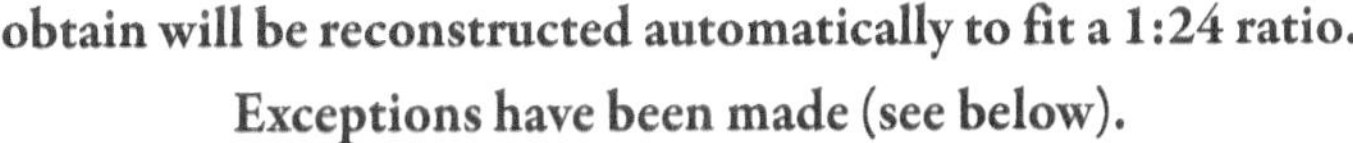

obtain will be reconstructed automatically to fit a 1:24 ratio. Exceptions have been made (see below).

Exceptions: Any creature whose size is tiny and below is exempt from this title. Plants, fungi, and other such growing things are exempt as long as they are created from a seed or base form. Aether may be used to accelerate growth as normal.

Warning! Due to being only partially sapient, system notifications will be silenced until full sapience is reached.

The Core could, of course, not read any of this, even as the arcane script blazed a path across its newly sparked depths. It simply acted on its new instincts. Whether it was the remnants of the archmage's Spark that it drew from or from the deep, intricate, tiny, sigils carved with great care in its depths, the Core breathed.

It did not breathe air as it had no lungs. No. It breathed the Maker's air, the very breath of life.

Aether.

In and out, instinctively, as it had no real mind of its own yet. Then it took deeper breaths in exchange for shallower exhales. Gradually, it filled its reserves until they were about to overflow and then it released its breath in a torrent of magical, albeit minute, might. And there, at the bottom of the archmage's cabin, in the middle of one of the most dangerous forests in the world, a tiny Dungeon Core claimed its first room and its first servant.

Chapter I

Getting Started

At the eastern edge of Calamvor's mansion, deep in the gap that separated the outside stone wall from the inside wooden one, the Core claimed its first scrap of territory. Although it would be an exaggeration to claim that the Core had completely claimed the mouse. In truth, all it did was form a bond of sorts with the creature, inclining it to protect its treasure a little more fiercely than it might normally do.

It would also be an exaggeration to claim that the territory it had claimed was a large one. The domain it had claimed was a portion of the wooden inner walls, the stone of the foundation it sat on, and the stone of the outer wall.

The other "treasures" of the mouse were claimed as well. The mouse itself sat, looking at the Core quizzically. Though disinterested, it couldn't deny the tentative bond that now tied them together.

Once more, moving by instinct, powered by its half-sapience, the Core created its first room. It found that it could manipulate anything its breath touched, and it began excavation of the surrounding area. First, it moved to dig deeper into the stone it sat upon, shaping a rectangle roughly twenty inches by forty.

The mouse stood stunned as its nest transformed from a simple collection of mothballs and grasses stuffed in a corner into a large hole in the rock. It hurried to protect its different treasures, scurrying back and forth as it carried them to higher ground.

The Core hollowed out the large foundation rock, forming a tiny cavern. It was time-consuming as it required the tiny core to exert itself to both move the rock and reinforce the walls so that the foundation stone didn't simply collapse. It also took time for the Core to inhale Aether before using it to claim more stone. The stone it moved was either used to reinforce the walls of the cavern or broken down into Aether, which it then used to move more.

Following its instincts, it moved its body via Aether into the back of the cavern and raised the rock to form a pedestal to rest its crystalline body. It sat content but knew its job wasn't quite done. It reached out through the bond it shared with the mouse and coaxed it inside, soothing its anxiety with its Aether.

The mouse, calmer now that the stone had stopped moving, made its way down the narrow tunnel and into the cavern. Seeing the pedestal and the Core, the mouse moved closer until it was standing right in front of the tiny glowing gem. The Core, acting quickly, drew in more Aether and then blew out, fully claiming the mouse by flooding its conduits with its Aether.

It heard a phantom chime on the wind as the mouse, its eyes glittering, turned and moved its treasures and nest down into the cavern, creating a new nest around the pedestal. The Core knew it had achieved a milestone somehow and was also aware on a fundamental level that it could influence the mouse and order it to obey. It also knew that it could create more.

The Core immediately began working to draw in more Aether so that it could start making more mice but ran into a problem. The amount of Aether in the walls of the cabin was thinning, akin to the feeling of air being sucked away. The Core knew it needed to fix the issue before it got any worse or else it would be unable to grow further.

Using its senses, it tried to find further sources of Aether and settled on a section of wall that its instincts seemed pleased with. So, using what Aether it had left, it claimed and shift stone away from the outside wall, drilling a hole through it to the outside. With a comically small burst of energy, it broke through the final layers of rock.

Directing its mouse up to the hole, the Dungeon peered through its eyes and found itself looking upon a huge, shaded area. Wooden beams extended from the outside stone to run crossways across the expanse, joining with pillars of stone that jutted from the earth. Across these beams lay smooth wooden paneling that formed the archmage's porch—not that the Core knew what a porch was.

The sudden rush of Aether that followed its next breath shocked the tiny Core. Vibrant and full of life, it flowed from the hole outside to stream through its first room, drenching the pedestal and its crystal occupant. The Core felt the first fluttering of what would become the emotion of delight at the sensation and breathed deeply for its next step.

It reached for its new knowledge, flooding the idea with Aether, and watched as a tiny baby mouse formed in its cavern. Sensing the movement of Aether, its adult mouse came down and watched as its tiny kin formed and then breathed its first breath. The baby was a curious thing and immediately began exploring its surroundings, including the older mouse. Sniffing the young one, the older mouse licked the top of its head before heading over to the pedestal and its nest.

Not satisfied quite yet, the Dungeon Core waited for more Aether and spent the next few hours creating a handful of baby mice—six, to be exact. The older mouse didn't seem to care, content to lounge in its nest. That changed when another creature entered the Dungeon's domain.

Antennae prodded and poked as an ant calmly began moving through the massive—relative to its size—hole in the wall. It moved in the awkward way that mostly blind creatures did, moving haltingly and exploratorily to the wooden inner walls of the cabin. It took a single bite of the wood. Wood that had been claimed by the Dungeon. A Dungeon that responded to this perceived danger by summoning its guardian.

The older mouse immediately perked up its head and sniffed, swiveling its head and letting out a mighty bellow, which to a human would sound like a high-pitched squeak. It charged through the cavern and up the tunnel before falling on the ant like a hammer of doom. Its hands held the smaller creature still as its large front teeth tore and gnashed at the kicking body of the ant, piercing easily through its tough outer chitin.

With its prize firmly contained, it dragged the helpless ant into the Dungeon, depositing its lifeless body in front of the pedestal. The Core, which had watched this go down with what amounted to its version of satisfaction, was surprised when a rush of Aether flooded the older mouse and itself when the ant finally died.

It reached out and tried claiming the ant, watching as its body dissolved into motes of light that were drawn into the Core. Another phantom chime sounded, but Dungeon Core paid it no heed as it basked in the new knowledge it possessed.

Floor 1 created!
First dungeon monster claimed!

New Framework acquired!

House Mouse (Mundane)
The common house mouse would normally never be considered worthy of a Framework of its own as it is a humble creature. Rarely magical, it is often prey for larger, more worthy creatures. Usually relegated to being at the bottom of a dungeon's ecosystem, most dungeons eschew such basic non-magical creatures for their more magical and larger cousin rodents. However, basic as they are, they are highly territorial and will fight to protect their space, making them a loyal—if weak and tiny—dungeon monster.

As the first dungeon to use such a creature as a dungeon monster, you will be able to create and modify its Path of Ascension freely. Warning! May have unforeseen consequences.

The Core has created its first floor and claimed its first dungeon monster.
The Core has acquired its first Framework.

Progress to Core Ascension:
33.3%

Dungeon entrance created!

New Framework acquired!

Carpenter Ant (Mundane)
While dangerous magical races of ants do exist, this is not one of them. The mundane carpenter ant exists in temperate climates where they build nests in the wood of trees and homes. Commonly considered a pest by the larger races, these ants are dangerous to nothing except decorative wood paneling and other ants and insects as well as plants. Fiercely loyal to the Queen that births them, ants can be quite aggressive when the colony is threatened.

Note: This is a multilayered Framework consisting of separate, internal Paths of Ascension. Those Paths are queen, worker, and drone. These Paths may be summoned as separate dungeon monsters, but be warned. Ant monsters made in such a way will see themselves as belonging to another colony and will fight to the death.

As the first dungeon to use such a creature as a dungeon monster, you will be able to create and modify its Path of Ascension freely.

Warning! May have unforeseen consequences.

The Core has created its dungeon entrance and defeated its first intruder.

Progress to Core Ascension: 50%

Chapter 2

Establishing New Defenders

When the Core recovered from the flood of new information, it got to work, its instincts prodding it forward. With a steady stream of Aether flowing in through the entrance, the Core could begin to expand its influence. Feeling its way subconsciously, it expanded upward, seeking a place where its newest monsters could have a home.

The Core shaped its second floor, claiming more and more of the inner wooden wall to do so. Inside the wall, roughly a few feet above the ground, it carved out an alcove for its new creatures to begin their new existence. From that alcove, a small tunnel led in a spiral downward until it reached the rocky foundation, where the Core had crafted a small opening.

Once the Core finished with the dimensions of its new floor, it poured Aether into the Framework given by its new knowledge. The Aether coalesced, forming a similar but larger ant than the previous intruder. Roughly an inch long, this ant had a regal bearing that had been lacking in the one that its mouse had defeated.

The Core wasn't surprised by this. Its new knowledge told it that this was a Queen. It would act like a Core but for ants, giving birth to new ones in the same manner the Core had birthed the Queen. So it simply soothed the new creature with Aether before leaving it with a command to propagate. In the future, the Queen would need the help of its drones to propagate, but for the first batch of ants, it did not need help—just the Core's Aether.

Another phantom chime sounded in the air, and for the first time, the Core had the barest inkling of a thought about what it might be. Nonetheless, it ignored the sound and continued its work. It expanded some more—both up and down—and found that as it did, the amount of Aether it needed to draw on to sustain itself was increasing exponentially.

Soon the Aether dried up. The Core, simple as it was, knew it needed to fix the issue. Acting on a set of instincts it hadn't known it had possessed until now, it controlled the Aether flowing from its entrance, condensing it down. The process of condensing it forced the Aether to flow faster, drawing in a storm of the life-giving substance.

The Core shaped the stone in front of its pedestal and changed it into a large pillar stretching almost to the ceiling. Next, it carved bowls into the pillar, separated by channels between each bowl. Finally, above the first bowl, it formed a tiny stalactite where the storm of condensing Aether was directed.

Gradually but with increasing speed, the Aether became a vapor that further condensed around the stalactite. Ever so slowly, a single drop formed and fell into one of the bowls with a *plink!* Over the next few hours, the stream of Aether flowing into the Dungeon quickened and the storm surrounding the stalactite condensed faster. Soon, the bowls were filled and a steady stream of liquid Aether was flowing toward the Core's pedestal, where it drew up the Aether-like a funnel.

Soon, the feeling of starvation ebbed, and the Core turned back to its dungeon only to be surprised by the flurry of activity. The first floor was bustling as six baby mice tussled with one another, playing as the older mouse guarded the newly transformed pedestal.

The Core felt the stirrings of what might have been gratitude at the stalwart nature of its first dungeon monster. Those stirrings faded as it turned its attention outward to its entrance. There had been no further invaders since the carpenter ant had come but the Dungeon's subconscious wouldn't let it rest, with a growing feeling of danger accompanying the passage of time.

Its gaze was drawn a few feet above the first floor to the second, which was now filled with new life as twenty eggs lay around the Queen's chamber. The Queen was tending to them diligently in a way that was profound to the dungeon. The image was imprinted upon its nascent mind as something important and it struggled to process it properly.

In time, the thoughts faded but the image remained, and its instincts sought to act upon it. Latching onto the knowledge of the ant and somewhat inspired by its mouse guardian, it subconsciously forged a new stage of Ascension for the humble carpenter ant. Working mostly by instinct, the Dungeon Core chose one of the Paths already available to it.

The drones had one goal within the Carpenter Ant Framework; they helped the Queen propagate the next line of workers and drones before dying. To the Core, that was a colossal waste. It did not need defenders who died without ever defending the dungeon. So, if the Framework prevented the ants from living long enough to defend the dungeon, then the Core would change the Framework to suit its needs.

This was only possible due to the novelty of using the ants as monsters. Though it did not know it, carpenter ants were not truly monsters nor normally chosen as dungeon defenders. This meant that the system in charge of Frameworks needed to fashion a brand-new Framework for the dungeon's specific use.

The humble carpenter ant now had a method of growth that had been denied to it before this moment, tied to the very dungeon that had chosen to utilize it. This gave the Core the ability to change it as it saw fit, an ability that it put to use now. Within the Framework, using the drone's current stage of the Path of Ascension, the Core bisected the ant right where its thorax was, turning it into two separate parts. It strengthened those segments and lengthened the front section. It then set the head on a thick, stocky neck to give it some reach while also lengthening and bulking up the

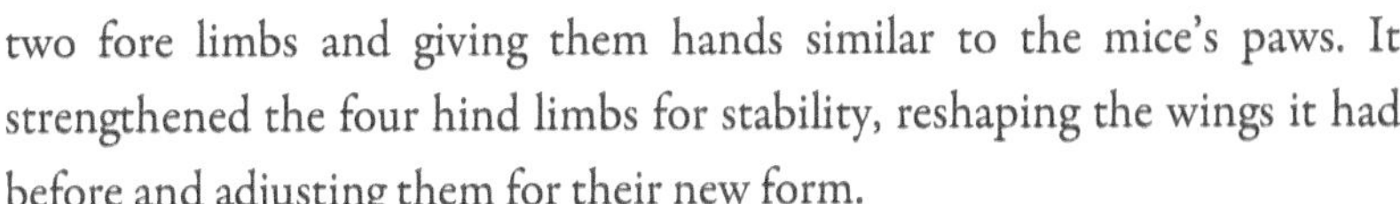

two fore limbs and giving them hands similar to the mice's paws. It strengthened the four hind limbs for stability, reshaping the wings it had before and adjusting them for their new form.

It replayed the fight with the mouse in its mind and gave the barest hint of satisfaction. Now that it could stand on its four hind limbs and grapple like the mouse, perhaps it wouldn't lose as easily. Its final contributions were to enlarge it slightly and add wicked barbs to its mandibles. Then it imprinted the image of the Queen upon the Path while also imprinting the image of the steadfast mouse guardian. The two images melded together into an ant standing guard over the Queen and the colony.

Exhausted mentally, the Core pulled back and let the knowledge fade away. It heard another phantom chime but ignored it in favor of making sure the new Path stuck. Three of the twenty eggs glowed as the Core watched, absorbing Aether greedily and growing larger to hold the newly improved creature.

The Core didn't expect to see all of the eggs grow larger and glow. Then the Queen followed as Aether continued to flood the tiny room. The Queen, after making sure the eggs were all fine, went into the center and settled down, glowing steadily with an inner light. The Core, filled with something akin to awe, kept watching until its attention was rudely grabbed by an intruder.

Floor 2 created!

Warning! Aether starvation is imminent! Aether funnel formed! Aether starvation averted!

Ascendant variant of the Framework "Carpenter Ant" created! You have created a never-before-seen creature using your ingenuity. In acknowledgment of your imagination, the High Council offers your existing carpenter ants the ability to Ascend to this new stage through Aetheric transfer.

Warning! Due to a lack of Divine Potential, this will sacrifice the Framework "Carpenter Ant" from your core, and you will be unable to receive it again. Do you still wish to proceed? Path of Direction chosen. The High Council has accepted on the Core's behalf. The resulting Framework falls under the title "Tiny Dungeon" and will still be moldable.

Transfer complete! "Carpenter Ant Queen" Ascending to "Danian Queen." "Carpenter Ant Worker" Ascending to "Danian Worker." The Ascendant variant "Danian Noble" has been established in place of the "Carpenter Ant Drone."

The Core has created its second floor and created an entirely new species to serve as a dungeon monster.
Progress to Core Ascension:
66.67%

Chapter 3

A Scaly Invader

The Core dragged its attention away from the slumbering transformed ants to find a creature heading for the entrance to the second floor.

Vastly different from anything the Core had seen thus far, the invader was long and lithe. It didn't possess any arms or legs but rather moved by wriggling along the ground in smooth motions.

Green scales covered the creature like armor, and its hunger was evident from the long forked tongue that flicked out of its mouth. All of these details were terrifying, but the glow of Aether was even more terrifying. Near the center of the creature was a radiant orb of light with many little strands running the length and breadth of its body.

Unable to truly panic due to its half-sapient nature, the Core could nonetheless feel the instinctive panic all creatures experience when their territory is encroached upon. Its subconscious roared in challenge and its reliable champion answered. The mouse guardian let out a bellow and charged out of the first floor and into battle.

The creature was half inside the entrance to the second floor by the time the mouse arrived, preventing it from slithering further. With a firm grasp and a bite that punched through the creature's scales, the mouse dragged the creature out, the beast hissing in its pain and distress. The mouse, its teeth firmly locked onto the thing's hide, struggled to keep it from slithering further. Inch by inch, the mouse won the tug of war.

As its head left the entrance to the second floor, the creature let out a hiss of rage and turned to engage the mouse directly. The Core couldn't sigh in relief but it would have if it could as it waited for its guardian to finish the foul intruder. This was no helpless ant, though. It was a long and sinuous creature with green scales and a flickering tongue.

The two creatures battled it out with the mouse's bites, leaving scarlet blood pouring down the enemy's sides. The scaled one would not be outdone, however, and bit the guardian repeatedly, curling its body around the mouse to strangle it. The back and forth continued for some minutes with neither side gaining the upper hand, but the Core could see that its guardian was beginning to flag.

Wheezing as the coils grew tight, the mouse kept biting relentlessly until finally it caught the head of the creature and bit into the space behind its skull. As the creature's coils slackened in death, another tiny burst of Aether occurred, with half going to the mouse and the other half going into the dungeon.

Still wheezing, the mouse pulled itself out of the coils before slumping to the ground, limp. Frantic for an entirely new reason, the Core tugged on its Aether reserves to patch up the worst of the mouse's wounds, watching closely as they sealed themselves closed. Watching so closely, the Core almost flinched when golden light poured out from beneath the mouse's skin.

The Core did not know what was happening to its defender, but it now glowed with the same light as the ants. So, the Core acted to get its guardian to safety, where it could rest. With a tug on its bond and with quite a bit of Aether, it managed to get the mouse back to its nest, where the beast slumped exhausted.

With that taken care of, the Core turned to the invader, moving immediately to the next thing now that it was safe once more. Claiming the creature was the work of a moment, and the Core felt a flicker of what

would become excitement. This invader had been powerful and mighty. Now, it would serve the Core well.

Motes of light lifted from the corpse and flowed down to the Core. A phantom ding sounded again as new knowledge bathed the young nascent mind. Even as it basked in the glow of something new, its gaze was drawn to where the body had lain. There, gleaming on the ground, was a tiny crystal.

The Core cast its senses over it but found nothing other than the fact that it seemed to hold a good quantity of Aether. With a breath, it absorbed that too and watched as its Aether joined the rest headed to its body. With the minor distraction out of the way, the Core moved, gathering Aether and fueling the new pattern in its mind. With its guardian brought low and sleeping, it needed another to take its place.

Expanding beyond its entrance, it claimed the earth beyond as well as the tall, green, fibrous protrusions that grew from it. Those protrusions required more Aether to claim and came with another phantom ding, but the Core was too busy to care.

Creating a set boundary, it settled the new creature within it, just outside the entrance to the outside, with orders to guard the dungeon. It noted in passing that this creature also had a glowing orb of light within it, but it lacked the curiosity and sapience to truly process that information.

Finally safe with its instincts sated, the Core retreated to its pedestal, feeling a weight come over it. It took a moment to look over its domain, taking in the sights of slumbering creatures and the lone scaly guardian that now stood guard. Then, it slipped into oblivion, unaware of the golden light beginning to radiate from its crystalline body.

As it gave itself to the Great Rest, it had no way of sensing the divine gazes that watched its every move. It had no inkling of the designs and expectations that had gone into its creation. There was only the Great Rest and the subconscious knowledge that when it woke up, everything would be different.

"House Mouse" is ready to Ascend!

Please pick from among the following stages:
Error Proto-Spark Detected! Path of Direction chosen! The High Council has decided!

"House Mouse" is Ascending to "Mouse Guard."
New Framework acquired!

Constricting Green Snake (Rank F - Copper)
Rising high above its base origins, this green snake has taken its first step on the Path of Ascension, learning to use its length to great effect to constrict its foes. With a diet consisting of insects, spiders, and small creatures such as baby birds and infant mice, this creature is a fearsome hunter to those smaller than it is. Its green scales help it blend in among grasses, allowing it to hide from predators and prey alike.
As the first dungeon to use such a creature as a dungeon monster, you will be able to create and modify its Path of Ascension freely.

Warning! May have unforeseen consequences.

Grass (Mundane)
A humble plant, grass can be found growing everywhere, even in the frozen wastes of Faltangira. While this plant would not be worthy of a Framework to a larger dungeon, which uses other more dangerous plants, perhaps its worth will be found by a much tinier dungeon willing to experiment.
As the first dungeon to use such a plant as a main dungeon environment, you will be able to create and modify its Path of Ascension freely.

Warning! May have unforeseen consequences.

Floor 3 created!
One of the Core's creatures has achieved enough internal Aether to climb the Path of Ascension. The Core has created its third floor. All

parameters for the Core's first Ascension have been met. Prepare to begin the climb.

Progress to Core Ascension: 100%

Preparing to Ascend!

Chapter 4

The Great Rest

The Core started to glimmer as the golden light bubbled forth. Almost physical, it surrounded the Core before shifting, creating new gemlike facets on top of what was already there. The instincts that it had relied on were compressed deeper into its Spark Matrix as its Spark expanded from a Proto-Spark into full ignition.

As it ignited, the golden light flared with brilliance, searing its new reality upon the Core's inner being. Everything that it had accomplished before igniting only added fuel to the new fire burning in its soul, blazing new pathways in its matrix. It was reborn, transforming from a being of instinct into a being capable of thought.

The sigils inscribed within it flickered and dimmed several times during the process, but they stabilized as the process concluded. It remained artificial, but that same artificiality was what kept it alive as the sigils provided the shell by which the Spark remained within the gemstone. Without the sigils, the Spark would have no matrix upon which to inscribe a full mind.

The sigils, for all that they were the workings of a genius, could not provide true existence. The Core remained artificial, missing a certain quality necessary for the plans of those who watched over it. One of their

number watched with interest, intent on seeing the little Core receive what it needed for what came next.

The two suns rose and set seven times before the process was complete. However, the world was not still during the Core's slumber.

Day 1 of Ascension

Coiled upon itself, himself, the snake flicked his tongue out, tasting the world through the pits on the front of his face. The recent rain had thundered its way across the wooden paneling above him, wiping clean any scent trails and saturating the area underneath it with water. The snake was undeterred.

His master had given him a directive—to protect the dungeon. The snake wasn't sapient; he was much too far down on his Path of Ascension for that. Instead, he was smarter than a normal green snake. With one complete Ascension under his scales, as revealed by the tiny Aether core powering his Aether conduits, his admittedly small brain had been enhanced, allowing for greater intelligence.

Intelligence wasn't the only thing that had been enhanced. The snake's whole body thrummed with Aether, allowing him to move faster, strike quicker, and heal faster, at least until the Aether ran out. This would have made him voracious in any other place as the Aether necessary to keep moving would have forced him to hunt constantly to survive, but the master now supplied the Aether it needed to live.

Keeping still, he felt the ground through his body, trying to sense the vibrations of any intruders before they entered the dungeon's domain. For the most part, his vigil was a quiet one. Not many creatures dared to venture further than the very edge of the borders of the floor on which the snake presided. Eventually, though, something did breach the borders. As it did so, it seemed to move unerringly toward the hole that led further into the dungeon.

The snake shuffled his coils, preparing to strike, and as the intruder passed by, he struck like a bolt of lightning. In a flash, the carpenter ant was swallowed whole, and the snake let out a pleased hiss at the small burst of Aether released upon the creature's death. He did not wonder why the ant was there nor did he know that it was the second such ant to have wandered in. He was simply pleased at having fulfilled his directive. The snake coiled in upon himself once more, remaining vigilant as his creator slept.

Day 3 of Ascension

It was dark, like being submerged in a deep lake. Yet in the depths, golden light shone through from up above. The Queen, uncurling from the fetal position she was in, swam upward, reaching for the light. It took time, but eventually, she breached the surface and her body was bathed in searing light for mere moments before she awoke.

She did not gasp as a creature with lungs would have but the spiracles in her abdomen flared, absorbing oxygen from the air. Not only oxygen but Aether as well, flowing from a place within her. She stood, supported by her four hind limbs as she reveled in her new strength. She was larger now, and her new Aether core was already at work enhancing her mind beyond its base form.

Thoughts she had never experienced before raced through her head, but she turned at the sound of shuffling and made her way over to find that her eggs had hatched into larvae, with three of them being larger than the others. She cooed through her pheromones as she tended to her brood. She was grateful to the master for such a boon, her new intelligence showing her new ways of caring for her brood.

Her colony would grow and serve, becoming greater and greater as she laid more eggs and their numbers grew. Her mandibles clicked together as she looked her larvae over. They would need to grow big and strong if they were to help defend the master.

Day 4 of Ascension

The mouse stirred in his slumber, dreams of battle flickering like a sputtering candle through his nascent mind, a mind constantly being strengthened through Ascension. An image gradually coalesced from the flames of war. A mouse standing tall on its hind limbs with metal in its paw and covering its body. It stood defiant, facing enemies many times its size, eyes blazing with Spark light.

It was this blaze that kindled in the mouse as he slept, an ember of the furnace his Spark would one day become. An ember realized in the form of an Aether core that blazed new pathways through his body.

Over many days, he slumbered while his awake and lesser brethren watched in instinctual awe as he changed. He grew larger and more muscled, his hind limbs lengthening for stability as his fore limbs rippled with strength under his fur. His closed eyes grew sharper and his brain grew larger, supplemented by an enlarged and Ascended Aether core.

When he finally stirred on the fifth day, he awoke transformed into something never before seen in a creature so small. The first thing he did upon waking was to seek out his treasure and from it, he pulled out the enchanted sewing needle. It was a far cry from the vision he had when Ascending, but his soul cried out to be armed, so this would have to do. Placing the point before him and kneeling, the Mouse Guard vowed to protect the lord that had brought him this far.

He would not fail.

Day 6 of Ascension

Deep within her nest, the Carpenter Ant Queen rested after laying more eggs. She was an insect of instinct, mundane and without the gift of Aether apart from what was contained within the Maker's gift of life. There was no Aether core to enhance intelligence, just the instinctive needs provided by her DNA.

However, the System of the gods had recently cataloged that DNA within a Framework, and that carried a weight of its own. It was a weight that spoke of growth beyond what would normally be expected for such a small ant species. It was this aspect of growth that caused the Queen to lay more eggs than usual, though it taxed her.

And it was this aspect of growth that caused a need to begin to grow within her. A need for more Aether and a need for nutrients. So when scouts returned with pheromones blaring from a new place that contained a riot of Aether and nutrients in abundance, the Queen's instincts had her acting in only one way.

The colony's soldiers would march and claim that land for their Queen.

Aetheric transfer complete!

**"Carpenter Ant" has Ascended to the Framework "Danian Ant."
Existing creatures have Ascended into their respective roles.
"Carpenter Ant Queen" has Ascended to "Danian Queen."
"Carpenter Ant Worker" has Ascended to "Danian Worker" and
"Danian Noble." "Carpenter Ant Drone" has Ascended to "Danian
Noble."**

New Framework acquired!

**Danian Ant (Unique, Rank F - Copper)
Ascended from the mundane carpenter ant, Danians are the unique
creation of the tiniest dungeon core in existence. These creatures
eschew their mundane heritage, standing upright on four limbs and
using their upper two to grapple and manipulate the wooden
surroundings they call home. They are now firmly dungeon creatures
embodying the aspects of loyalty to colony and core that have been
imparted to them.**

Ascension complete!

"House Mouse" has Ascended to the Framework "Mouse Guard."

New Framework Acquired!

Mouse Guard (Unique, Rank F - Copper)
A house mouse on its first steps towards greatness and the first of its kind to dare to do so. This mouse has embraced its calling as guardian and warrior, drawing the attention of the Spirit of Conflict, Ile'Fen. Since Path of Direction is active, Ile'Fen has crafted this Path of Ascension in its entirety, paving a way forward if the creature wishes to take it.

Chapter 5

The Council & The Core

The Core's first thought on waking was *Where am I?* followed quickly by *That's a big lady,* and *She's awfully pretty.*

The lady in question sniffed at the first mention of herself but seemed mollified by the second. Smiling brightly, she leaned down, spooking the Core, before speaking in a voice that could cause a core to give up its last drop of Aether.

"Well now, you're finally fully sapient. We've been waiting to meet you for some time. Well, I suppose it's only been a week since you went to sleep to Ascend, but to beings who have lived for millennia, even a week can seem like a long time when you are waiting for something. Like a second that drags on forever." She chuckled, and the sound was like a brook, happy and carefree.

"Now, now, Maph'Ira. Give the young one some space. And do dim your aura, dear. We don't want it to turn into a simpleton every time you speak." A new voice cut through the tall lady's speech, and the Core shifted its perspective and found that it was surrounded by seven chairs, each containing a lord or lady.

On the highest chair sat a noble-browed man with wise eyes. Dressed in deep blues, the man gave a subtle nod to the Core in greeting before gesturing to the rest of the people seated. "We are the High Council, greatest among the spirits of this land. My name is Tal'Irieth. You are of interest to us in that you are both artificial and yet real in an undeniable way."

I'm real? the Core thought. *I'm real,* it thought more firmly as the idea settled into its mind. *You are tall,* it stated seriously to the noble-browed lord.

The Core thought it saw some of the lords and ladies hide smiles at this, but the lord in front of it continued with a small huff. "Yes. Normally, dungeon cores are natural occurrences, either when a monster core becomes one or a crystal of pure Aether is oversaturated to the point of forming the beginning of a Spark Matrix.

"In the case of the latter, high spirits such as us seed the new matrix with one of the spirits the Maker has already created and ignite the Spark. We then offer the new core two different paths and help them in their new life. These cores are called divine cores by the various races because of their capacity to create new life from Aether.

"In the case of a monster core, it is because monsters naturally hunger for Aether in all its forms. A monster core is the result of a creature's Aether core being broken, fractured, or shattered through some catastrophic event. Their Sparks attempt to heal the trauma, and most times it's successful. But if the trauma is long-lasting, the Spark becomes strained. If it continues too long, it can fracture. It only takes one more push at that point for it to break completely. All of that pain becomes the new core of that creature. The Spark crystallizes all of the trauma, pain, and suffering as a last-ditch effort to save itself, and the result is a monster.

"Their Aether core remains broken, leaking Aether like a sieve, and they develop a terrible hunger. They never again reach a point of over-saturation, the point where the polarity shifts. They begin to absorb Aether passively instead, needing it to feed their relentless hunger.

"Some of those monsters choose to shed their physical shell. They then construct elaborate traps, allowing their real bodies to fall away to craft a labyrinth of earth and stone to lure meals inside. We give them nothing. These dungeons are called feral cores due to their monstrous and devouring nature.

"You were neither of these natural occurrences. The archmage who crafted you sought to create his own personal divine core, enslaving it to his will before using it to supplement his great magic. He desired a new body and believed, perhaps rightly, that his creation would be able to do that with enough time. He could have then lived forever, hopping from body to body. It is fortunate, therefore, that he died of natural causes so soon after you were taken from him. I would have found it difficult to smite him otherwise."

The Core hummed mentally at this. *I was created? Made? My creator is dead? Why is that fortunate?*

Once again the inner dialogue of the Core was met with a response of barely concealed smiles, though one of them seemed to use it to hide another emotion. The lord continued, "Well, for one, his death means that you are free rather than a slave to his whims. Beyond that, his death served two purposes, which, at first, perplexed us. We had meant to have you destroyed but did not bargain for the attachment Calamvor had toward you.

"Part of his Spark Essence or spirit ignited your Spark Matrix, but you were too small to hold a full Spark. So we shaved off most of what Calamvor was trying to shove in, leaving his instincts about Aether's manipulation but removing the higher traits like personality and such. You were too small for the normal gifts we give divine cores, so we simply gave you boons.

"We allowed you to grow and monitored your progress. While your shell might indeed be artificial, your soul and Spark are anything but. We are of a mind to let you continue existing, but we wish to ask you: if you were to continue existing, what would you do? Would you devour and destroy? Or would you create new life?"

The Core sat and thought about it for a while, its newly Ascended mind turning the questions over and over. *I want to be like the Queen,* it thought

finally, projecting the image of the Queen tending to her brood. *I want to explore.* It sent an image of the outside world it had seen through the mouse's eyes. *I want to create.* It sent an image of the ant hybrid it had made. *And I want to play.* Its final image was of the baby mice playing within the dungeon, something in their carefree nature calling to it through its memories.

The High Council sat, seemingly stunned, before one of them, a green figure with a lithe and roguish appearance, burst out laughing. "Oh, you are fun!" he said, cackling to himself while the other spirits eyed him with reproach. "What?" he said with an affronted look. "I'm just saying he's a fun guy for someone who had half a soul just last week. And to be honest, his dungeon has proven more amusing than the last hundred years of the mortal world."

"While that may indeed be the case," Tal'Irieth replied huffily, "please have some decorum, Trik'Weri."

The green lord simply smirked and rolled his eyes. But the Core was interested in an entirely different matter. *I am a he?* it asked internally. Something about that reverberated through its Spark Matrix in a way it couldn't fully process. The idea was something outside of its instincts, only brought to the forefront by its new sapience. *I am a he.* It looked around to find the High Council staring at it.

With a gruff cough, Tal'Irieth responded to the internal question. "Well, strictly speaking, you're perhaps one of the few existences that does not have a specific gender due to your artificial shell. You were created to be inhabited and enslaved after all. But you were created by a man for his soul to connect with, and his Spark ignited yours.

"We may have gotten rid of his personality so that you might have your own, but that doesn't mean his Spark didn't affect you. It is not much of a surprise that your sapience formed itself around that subconscious ideal."

The Core simply looked up at Tal'Irieth and stated, *You're kind of smart, aren't you?*

The lord ignored him and said, "Anyway, are we all in favor, then?" The other lords and ladies nodded, and Tal'Irieth continued, "Then we bestow upon you the name Valterra Unok'Davaas. It means 'the Playground of the Gods' in the Old Tongue." Tal'Irieth smiled down at the slightly bewildered core. "Now I do believe it is time for you to wake up. Do keep us entertained."

Chapter 6

Transformational Rewards

The last thing the Core expected to find upon awakening was a floating screen hovering within his gemlike body. A body that had grown larger, he noticed instinctively as the screen took up his attention.

Welcome back, Valterra Unok'Davaas...

My name is Krat'Imos, one of the High Council, and I created this system for the use of divine dungeons. My experiments showed that it helped them discover the fundamentals of their power as they came into their sapient existence. You are now large enough and advanced enough to accept the majority of the system. This will allow us to give you what should have been your starting Framework as well as allow you to choose the next one from among a list. Prepare yourself...

The Core mentally winced as lines of fire seared new sigils within the Spark Matrix that made up his inner workings. When it ended, the screen began writing again.

There you go. You're all set. Well, except for one minor adjustment. Make a worthy dungeon, young Valterra. The Council eagerly awaits

your choices.

The Core didn't have time to process Krat'Imos' ending words because suddenly he was inundated with notifications.

You have been named by a superior Aetheric entity. Divinity recognized.

Name: Valterra Unok'Davaas
Translation: Playground of the Gods
Name effects:
Due to the meaning of your name and its divine nature, your ability to affect the world is increased. The size of your Aether funnel is no longer limited by the size of your core, and the quickness with which you can expand is increased. You now have Authority over the basic elements and can use Aether to summon them. Frameworks of divine servants may now be offered and used as dungeon monsters. They may be freely modified with permission from the divinity in question.

The Core could sense the power of his new name as it roiled around in his soul. He could not dwell on it much because further notifications appeared as soon as the Core dismissed the first.

Congratulations! You have Ascended! The gods look favorably upon this and have offered the following Frameworks as a reward.
Note: Due to your boon "Favored by the Gods" and because you did not receive a Framework to begin with, the Rank of the offered Frameworks is higher than normal.

Choose wisely.

Please choose one of the following:

Bloodmane Wolf (Rank C - Steel)
A fierce animal bred for war by a fallen race, the Bloodmane Wolf possesses potent blood-based abilities. The more wolves in the pack,

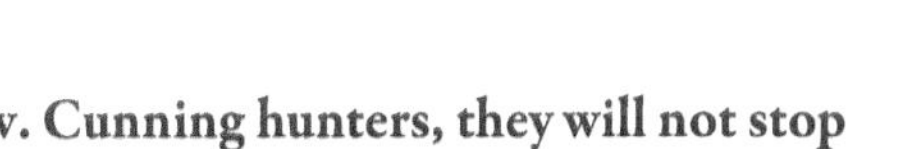

the greater these abilities grow. Cunning hunters, they will not stop once they have their prey's scent. They are a fearsome addition to any dungeon so long as it provides them with sport.

Earthquake Worm (Rank C - Steel)

Great tunnelers of rock and earth, these mighty worms can reach lengths upward of a hundred feet. Big enough to devour a humanoid whole without stopping, they continually move forward using their earth affinity to great effect. Despite their size, they move quickly but certainly not silently, as their passage shakes the ground. Once summoned by a dungeon, they can help carve pathways in the earth, allowing for their master's influence to spread far quicker than normal.

Juvenile Dire Grizzly (Rank C - Steel)

Even while young, a Dire Grizzly is a fearsome foe, standing easily twice the size of its normal adult counterparts. It faces foes with huge claws made for tearing and ripping flesh, and its jaws are powerful enough to crush bone. Fiercely territorial, this creature will not flee from challengers and will fight to the death, often taking the challenger with them. This facet of its nature proves to be true as a dungeon monster as well but perhaps to the extreme, as it will guard its floor above others' unless the Core is threatened.

Great Tidal Whale (Rank C - Steel)

A behemoth of the deep, these mighty creatures can grow well over a hundred feet long and are equipped with massive jaws that unhinge slightly to engulf prey whole. Once the prey is trapped behind their nigh-impenetrable baleen, the whales use their high water affinity to manifest an intense scything current within their mouths that minces the captured creatures into a manageable chum that it then swallows. Content to hunt within their pods, these giants of the depths would be right at home within an underwater dungeon or as the feature of a large oceanic floor to the terror of any adventurer willing to brave the dungeon.

The Core—Valterra, he supposed he was called now—looked at the options in awe. He could feel the power behind each one but also a glimpse of their nature in action. He could sense the rumbling of the ground as the Earthquake Worm dug and the ferocity of the Juvenile Dire Grizzly as it tore into a fresh kill.

He could sense the pack mentality of the Bloodmane Wolf and the barest glimpses of how its blood magic would work to make them stronger, faster, and more terrifying. And finally, the awe and majesty of the Great Tidal Whale that swam in gallons of water that it displaced with ease. Valterra sat still and let them wash over his mind before he tried to make a decision.

To play for time and to make sense of what might fit best in his dungeon, Valterra moved his presence outward and observed his dungeon once more. He was surprised to find his chief creatures arrayed around his pedestal column.

In the center was the mouse, who now appeared quite militaristic even to Valterra's untrained eye and... was that the needle from his nest that he was carrying? He was also huge! He was almost a foot long now from tip to tail. He probably wouldn't be able to leave the first floor even if he wanted to, and that just wouldn't do.

With this in mind, the Core widened the tunnel leading out of his first floor and saw the mouse nod his head in something like a bow. Yeah, he was definitely smarter than before too. *Where did he learn to bow, I wonder?* Valterra thought as he shifted his attention to another of his creatures.

On the right was the green serpent, his length coiled in on itself as his tongue flickered in and out. He seemed much the same as when Valterra last saw him, though perhaps way healthier than the one he had absorbed for the Framework. His memory of that time was hazy.

Lots of food and Aether, perhaps? The snake seemed cognizant of his master's attention and gave a sibilant hiss in response that was somehow pleasing rather than scary.

On the left stood the Danian Queen with her wings folded back primly but standing just how Valterra had imagined she would. With her torso raised and her two larger fore limbs clasped in front of her, she looked much more impressive and regal than before.

As each guardian felt the Core's presence expand, they visibly relaxed and seemed happy to see him begin moving. Valterra swept them with his gaze, noting that each one now had an orb of light within them that seemed to pump Aether throughout their bodies, an interesting development. Valterra let a low hum reverberate through his floors, letting each creature know that he had indeed returned.

Leaving his creatures, who were now beginning to move back to their respective floors, Valterra once more seeped into his dungeon, casting around for details. It was different than before. He remembered his time of partial sapience as a hazy dream constructed of fragments of memory.

Nothing in those dreams and images prepared him for the experience of becoming the dungeon. It was like waking up Ascended all over again. He was just bigger, stronger, and more vibrant. He felt everything! The whole dungeon was his in a way he would never be able to explain, like a limb that had fallen asleep, numb until needing to be moved. He felt the Aether that coursed through his dungeon, like it was blood, and realized that he was saturated in it.

It all stemmed from his Aether funnel and the raging Aether that coalesced there. The liquid stream of Aether that flowed from that point to his core provided a rich supply of the substance that he could then breathe out to claim more territory. Anything he claimed with it became his, although a better way to say it was that it became *him*.

He hadn't noticed before, but even his creatures had a portion of himself inside of them, something he only noticed when he focused on his dungeon. A thread of Aether, a connection, extended from his core and attached to the Aether cores of his creatures. Those that had no Aether core, the little mice in this case, had a thread that extended to where one would be, a place somewhat in the middle of their bodies.

It was a tug on this sensation of connection that drew him to the second floor. The domain of the Danians was thriving but mostly silent, with the larvae having only become pupae. They were much larger than they had been before, and Valterra felt excitement wash over him. These were unique, made by him before he even knew what imagination was, and he was looking forward to what they might do.

Moving to the entrance of his dungeon, the Core looked out once more upon the shadowed world of the outside. He pondered the difference between the shaded section and the brightness beyond its edge. He thought about the nature of this outside world and how odd the shaded section seemed in contrast to the vibrant colors of the furthest reaches.

He was filled with a sudden desire to see more and expanded.

Rapidly. Much too rapidly.

Faster than he could really comprehend and yet unable to escape the sudden information streaming in, Valterra shuddered and stopped. He sifted through the information as he struggled to be fully present in a body that had grown far quicker than before. Eventually, he recovered sufficiently to be fully aware of himself and found that he had expanded halfway across the shaded area.

His Ascended mind boggled at the speed of his new growth when a new sense poked at it.

Emptiness. A yawning void.

He focused more on the sensation and found that he had claimed the entire stone block that his cavern was located in. Not only that, but he had claimed a fair section of wall stretching north and west both up and down. The sensation that had caught his attention was down and westward, further into the cabin.

That was a strange thing to know. Knowledge fluttered at the edges of Valterra's Ascended mind, brief flashes of images and ideas. They threatened to wash him away with their vibrancy and color, so with an effort of will, he pushed them aside.

He would sit down and deal with them at a later date. Suffice it to say, he now knew his core sat in the middle of a foundation stone set at the corner of what was his creator's cabin. Down and further in was something called a "basement." That didn't mean much, as no image accompanied the knowledge, so Valterra went to work, intent on discovering its meaning for himself.

He began by carving a path through the rock that he had claimed, beginning at his first-floor cavern and working his way down at a rough decline. It didn't take long to remove the claimed stone, and soon he was confronted with the void.

He couldn't see.

There was no light, and his breath spread only a few inches out, giving him a kind of hazy perception. This space was huge; he could feel it. Big enough to encompass the entirety of his current body and then some. Valterra gathered up some of his Aether reserves and breathed it out in a long gust. It shot out and dispersed, allowing him to see… nothing.

Oh yes, this would take some time, but he could already see how he could make this work. And one of the new Frameworks he had been offered would fit perfectly once he had everything ready.

He decided.

New Framework acquired!

Great Tidal Whale (Rank C - Steel)
A behemoth of the deep, these mighty creatures can grow well over a hundred feet long and are equipped with massive jaws that unhinge slightly to gulp prey whole. Once the prey is trapped behind their nigh-impenetrable baleen, the whales use their high water affinity to manifest an intense scything current within their mouths that minces the captured creatures into a manageable chum that it then swallows. Content to hunt within their pods, these giants of the depths would be right at home within an underwater dungeon or as the feature of a large oceanic floor, to the terror of any adventurer willing to brave the

dungeon.

The title "Tiny Dungeon" has gone into effect. When summoned by Valterra Unok'Davaas, the Framework "Great Tidal Whale" will be affected in the following ways.
Effect: Each Great Tidal Whale costs 90% less Aether to summon but is reduced in maximum size by a factor of 1/24th. The maximum size, therefore, is now reduced to 6 feet 4 inches from 150 feet.
Personal Note: "Oh, by the Maker, this will be hilarious!"

— Trik'Weri,
High Spirit of Mischief

The Core has acquired its first [Rank C - Steel] Framework.
Progress to Core Ascension:
10%

Chapter 7

New Territory & New Dangers

The territory of Valterra Unok'Davaas had expanded rapidly and quickly, taking over a large portion of the shaded area that lay under the eastern section of Calamvor's porch. Home to quite a few different kinds of insects and other small critters, the now Aether-rich land drew the gaze of other such creatures.

The first to arrive were the ants. They had sensed the territory of the third floor and had come to investigate but now they encountered an enlarged domain and many other contenders for the same land. Those contenders had no inclination to share the space and so the ants went to war. Their conflict sparked a larger engagement, with various other insects and tiny mammals refusing to submit when offered such a rare chance for growth.

Mammals fought against mammals, insects against insects, and insects against mammals. All sought to carve a place for themselves within this new environment. It was within this chaos that the ants stumbled upon the pheromone trails of their sister ants, leading deeper into the territory.

Upon following that trail, they found an even richer land with but a single guardian. Great and terrible though it was, the ants could feel the richness of the Aether beyond. Therefore, they obeyed their instincts, laying a large pheromone trail before leaving to gather more forces. They did so by returning to the colony and relaying the information there.

As ants returned, they read the pheromones and began their march. The might of the colony was turned toward a single purpose as their Queen had commanded. They would take this guardian's domain for themselves and whatever lay beyond.

The larger turf war continued unabated as more and more creatures sensed the Aether involved and flooded to claim a piece. Throughout all of this, the snake guardian watched carefully, dealing with any creature that came too close. Nevertheless, most of the creatures were content to battle it out over the territory outside of his domain.

The majority of the creatures were mundane. While they could sense the Aether and although their instincts cried out for a place within the territory, they were rather blind to the richer stream that led deeper. The ants only knew because of the pheromone trails laid down by their sisters at the moment of their deaths.

It was these pheromone trails that saw an uptick in the snake guardian's duties. First, it was one at a time and then two at a time as the ants approached the entrance to the dungeon. These invaders found a quick death at the fangs of the green snake, a simple bite or flex of sinuous coils being enough to deal with them. At least for the initial invasions.

Only when they began arriving in larger numbers did the snake truly start to fight. The grass was quickly flattened in a short area as the combat area expanded. Ants were crushed and thrown off, but they were persistent, attacking without regard for their own lives. Panicked, the guardian instinctively called out to the one who had created him.

This was taking forever.

Valterra had been "breathing" for the better part of half a day and had only just found how deep the basement was.

Spoiler alert! It was really, really deep. Like, feet in the double digits deep.

On the other hand, the Core had discovered that if he went about claiming the stone rather than simply breathing Aether into the air, he could get about much quicker. By using the stone he had previously claimed and breathing directly from that spot, he could claim more stone even faster. He had to pause now and again to get used to his larger dungeon body, but it was easier this time since he was simply claiming more territory in one direction rather than having it balloon outward in every direction.

Once again, he found that the more territory he claimed, the more Aether he needed to draw in from the outside to join the vortex above his pedestal column. His new name somewhat mitigated the strain, but the details of how it did so were lost to him. Therefore, he ignored it and continued doggedly claiming more stone from the basement floor, walls, and ceiling.

A few days passed before he felt his mind sag in relief.

He had done it. To be precise, he had claimed all the stone a few inches deep surrounding the entirety of the basement. It was obscenely long and convoluted, going ever deeper into the earth. It even had side passages full of stuff; stuff that would be ruined if he simply poured water on it.

So, even though it had taken more time, he had sealed off some of the more interesting places and made a mental note to return to explore them. He felt bloated as a torrent of Aether flooded through his first rooms and joined the raging storm against his Aether funnel. It had been necessary in order for him to claim his new territory, but now, that Aether was filling him up a little too rapidly.

That said, he was a little oblivious to everything, exhaustion pulling at his mind. Well, exhaustion might be overstating it; it wasn't like he had a physical body that could get tired. It was more like his mind was tired from the same repetitive motions.

Toward the end, he even thought he heard squeaks from some high wooden contraptions he hadn't claimed. Valterra couldn't be bothered to check. Shrugging off the fog, the Core looked inward, reaching toward the next thing he needed—his Authority over the basic elements.

Valterra had been thinking about how to fill up his new room with the water needed for his Framework as he claimed his new territory. Then he remembered his name had properties he hadn't explored yet. This Authority thing took some figuring out, but if you changed Aether in subtle ways and then matched frequencies with an element's natural authority to burn, be wet, and so on, then you could simply summon the element out of thin air.

Or Aether rather.

Learning how to summon elements and claiming stone simultaneously had been a stretch, but Valterra had done it. Now he just had to get rid of all this Aether and maybe feel less bloated in the process.

Summoning the frequency he wanted, Valterra fed the Aether into it until water steadily dripped out. With a spark of inspiration, he pushed the majority of his Aether storm out into the basement and then synchronized it with the Authority of water. Almost immediately, water rained down in thousands of droplets.

Pleased with this development, Vaterra locked it into place before beginning to harden the bottom and the walls of his new giant floor. It would take a while, but already, he felt less bloated as the stream of incoming Aether coalesced around his pedestal before being funneled off to fuel his contained miniature weather pattern.

Satisfied with his work, he turned his attention from the basement to his wider dungeon body. And not a moment too soon either as a clarion call from his third floor's guardian swept over him. When he went to check, he found the poor thing swarmed by ants. The little insects bit at the snake's body, their numbers mitigating the reptile's superior strength.

A little alarmed, Valterra immediately sent a summons to his other guardians, and they responded with alacrity. The mouse bounded up the tunnel from the first floor and entered the fray immediately while the

Danian Queen sent two of her newly hatched Danian Nobles. When they entered the conflict, it gave the snake some much-needed breathing room.

Against the veritable flood of ants, however, it wasn't quite enough. So Valterra sent for more help. With little bass squeaks of their own, the younger mice flooded forward to engage with the ants, and though they were still young and growing, the added numbers were a big help. Eventually, the ants retreated, leaving their dead behind, but something told Valterra that this wouldn't be the last time he saw them.

He almost flinched, therefore, when his host of defenders lit up in golden light. Well, not the Danians, which was interesting because as he watched, he noticed the flood of Aether they received was distributed through their Aether conduits before leaving them. He had to put his curiosity on hold, however, as a screen popped up in front of him.

Valterra froze before excitement bubbled up inside him. What was this?

Chapter 8

Ascensions

Valterra's gaze was riveted on the words blazing across his core.

Your "House Mouse" is ready to Ascend!

Please choose from among the following stages:
Mouse Guard (Unique, Rank F - Copper)
A house mouse following in the paw steps of its kin. Where one treads, another may follow. This mouse has embraced the calling of Ile'Fen as guardian and warrior. Crafted by the Spirit of Conflict, this stage on the Path of Ascension paves a way forward to even higher heights.

Hoarder Mouse (Rank F - Copper)
Laying aside its mundane nature, this mouse has Ascended, its eyes and mind transforming to better notice valuable objects. When gathered and placed into its nest, these objects provide the mouse with a small amount of excess Aether. These beasts need not ever fight again, content to steal and pilfer to fuel further stages on their Path of Ascension.

Feral Mouse (Rank F - Copper)
Often compared to adult rats, this mouse is larger than its mundane kin, possessing sharp claws and strengthened jaws. Found naturally in the wild, it is extremely territorial, throwing itself at enemies regardless of the danger to itself. Often deployed in unceasing hoards by young dungeons, they have proven to be an effective countermeasure to inexperienced adventurers.

Amazing! Valterra hadn't known that he would be able to choose the next stage of Ascension for his creatures. Now that he thought back, the only other time this had occurred had been when his Mouse Guard had begun glowing back when he wasn't yet fully sapient. Filled with childish joy, he eagerly looked through the options.

The first that stood out was the fact that his Mouse Guard was no longer the only mouse that could become one. That was big news since he was also Ascending, which would allow the Core to see what was coming down the road. He almost dismissed the Ascension options for his smaller mice to go and check but held himself back to look at the other options.

The other two stages looked like they were the next step for a natural Ascension without the interference of a divine entity. *Thanks, Ile'Fen,* Valterra thought, trying to express his gratitude for the Framework of his guardian even though he figured the high spirit wouldn't be listening.

It surprised him, therefore, to feel the briefest divine touch as Ile'Fen responded with a feeling of pride. Whether the pride was for him or the Framework, Valterra didn't know, but he was comforted that the High Council was watching over him even if it was only to watch him play.

He turned back to the Frameworks before him to try and see how they might be used in a dungeon. The Feral Mouse had it right in the description. He doubted that he would be able to mold its Path of Ascension freely, seeing as it had already been used by dungeons in the past.

The Mouse Hoarder, though, seemed interesting in the way that it stole things and then sat and defended the hoard. He figured it would be hard to trust such a creature with the defense of the dungeon for another core, though, especially when you could choose a horde of ravenous giant mice instead. There was also the chance that it was a natural Path of Ascension for a House Mouse rather than simply a wild variety of mice that went feral.

Regardless, he could already see a use for the creatures. Who knew what treasures lay in wait to be uncovered in the archmage's cabin? And of course, Valterra could create little trinkets for his mice to find. It could be fun! Yes, he would have to see about that stage later.

For now, though, he turned away from them. He knew the desire of his little mice and how they looked up to their older kin. They wanted to follow in his paw steps and become Mouse Guards and Valterra would grant their request. That didn't mean he wasn't going to summon more mice immediately. He wanted those other stages after all! After he had led them back to their cavern, he selected the option and let the light take them.

Your "Constricting Green Snake" is ready to Ascend!

Please choose from among the following stages:
Sylcyne Garter Snake (Rank E - Bronze)
Thicker of body and slightly longer, this snake has chosen to invest in venomous saliva at the expense of less efficient constriction. It retains its green camouflage to better blend in with its surroundings while it waits for prey. Still an ambush predator, its initial bite is deadly to creatures below its Rank.

Razorscale Dwarf Boa (Rank E - Bronze)
Growing only slightly in size, this snake has gained rigid, sharp edges to its scales. Continuing its habit of constricting its prey, its new armor shreds flesh even as it squeezes its prey to death. Any creature that doesn't free itself in time will find itself lacerated and broken, helpless as the snake consumes them whole.

Arrowtail Glass Lizard (Rank E - Bronze)
Legless lizards are common enough in the northern parts of the world. Despite looking like snakes, they are in fact lizards with movable

eyelids and external ear openings. Known as glass lizards for their ability to shed the lower section of their tails, which often shatters into tinier pieces like glass, this lizard has weaponized this ability further. Instead of simply shedding their tail, they whip it at the enemy, whereupon it shatters mid-flight into small pieces. These pieces harden in the air to become deadly shrapnel that pierce flesh with ease.

Looking over the next series of notifications, Valterra was struck once more with flickering ideas of what they might look like. He dismissed the lizard option despite its interesting applications. He knew his third-floor guardian was content being a snake and would rather become a more lethal version of himself. He didn't quite know how he knew that, but he did.

That being said, as his eyes drifted over the other two options, he wondered which one might fit best. Against the ants, having the sharp edges on his snake's scales might help it cut through the horde. Then again, constriction wasn't really viable against the ants, and he didn't know if his guardian could move fast enough to become the bringer of death that Valterra imagined.

To make his decision, Valterra thought carefully about what he wanted his guardian to be capable of long-term. When thinking about it that way, the Sylcyne Garter Snake made the most sense. The Framework's ability to both constrict and strike with venom would double its ability to protect the entrance to the dungeon—at least in his mind... As long as the reptile in question wasn't swamped by another ant horde.

His choice was made, and Valterra guided the snake inside and out of the way before letting the Ascension process begin. He watched as his coils loosened in sleep before turning to the last flashing notification.

Your "Mouse Guard" is ready to Ascend!

Please choose from among the following stages:
Mouse Soldier (Unique, Rank E - Bronze)
A Path for the mice that have dedicated themselves to the way of war

and discipline. These mice are loyal and steadfast, elevated from simple guard mice to fearsome combatants. Wielding all manner of weapons, these mice are heads and tails above their former occupation.

Mouse Scout (Unique, Rank E - Bronze)

Eschewing war and conflict, this mouse seeks to range far and wide. With an Ascension that provides a larger-than-normal Aether core but reduced overall capabilities, the Mouse Ranger is able to leave the dungeon's territory for short periods of time both to explore and to bring back useful Frameworks for their dungeon's perusal.

Mouse Guard Veteran (Unique, Rank D - Iron)

Giving up all future potential, this mouse has chosen the path of the guard. Strong, durable, and persistent, it is in its awareness of its surroundings that the Mouse Guard Veteran shines. Able to sense fluctuations in Aether, this mouse is almost never surprised and is able to respond to any threat a young dungeon might face.

Well, that... was certainly different. Valterra didn't know what to make of the new options. He knew he wouldn't be picking the last one at least. Despite his excitement over the option and the power it would bring to the table, he didn't want to stymy his first guardian's growth.

The Mouse Scout was an interesting option. With the capabilities it offered, he would be able to scout around before expanding his territory. Then again, at the rate he could expand, it may not be worth it at this point. He would definitely be getting some in the future, but for that, he would need more mice.

Really, there was only one option. Valterra made sure his guardian was back in his cavern before selecting Mouse Soldier. Taking a metaphorical step back, he turned his gaze to the third floor, which doubled as his front entrance. It no longer had a guardian, but that was okay. He could summon more. That would come later, though.

Over the last few days as Valterra had worked on his newest floor, the new territory he had claimed above ground had become a bedlam of chaos. The third floor, which had set boundaries and a set guardian, had remained fine, situated as it was between the bedlam and the main dungeon entrance.

What lay outside the third floor was entirely different—a wild and yet Aether-rich land. It had also been claimed by a dungeon, which meant that everything within that space had become increasingly magical despite not having the dungeon's full attention or having the boundary of a floor.

Thus, it became prime real estate for various creatures, with different varieties of insects, arachnids, and rodents fighting over territory. They all sought that most precious of resources—Aether.

As Valterra swept his attention over the carnage, he mentally berated himself. Despite his recent gains from the creatures that had just Ascended, he could have been collecting Frameworks or using his extra Aether to claim more creatures, which meant more defenders.

Strictly speaking, Valterra, while intelligent and full of downloaded instinct and knowledge, was like a child in many ways. He had spent the last few days claiming a massive space for one Framework, after all. In that moment, as he fumed at the missed opportunity, he lashed out in the only way he knew how.

He summoned his Aether reserves and called forth his Authority over the elements. Bolts of fire, rent earth, lashing rain, and biting winds rippled through the new territory, causing the denizens to run for cover.

The display helped calm the Core even as he realized it hadn't accomplished anything. His tantrum had amounted to little more than a new interesting rock feature, some scorched grass, some puddles, and a new haircut for a tiny rodent. Valterra looked at his territory before sighing internally and getting to work.

Within the span of a few moments, he had claimed the spoils from several conflicts, much to the chagrin of the victors who had returned after his display only to find their prizes taken. With the corpses came the knowledge of their bodies, their makeup, and how Aether could be used to give them life once more.

Valterra finally let go of the last vestiges of his anger as the Frameworks settled into his soul, already picking through them to see what new defenders his little dungeon would have. At least, he had gotten something out of this mess, though he promised himself that he wouldn't shirk making the most out of this new playground of his.

New Frameworks acquired!

Phoenix Cockroach (Rank F - Copper)
A particularly tenacious example of the species, this cockroach tends to inject its victims with a concoction of fluids that causes their internals to liquefy into a superheated mixture. Its name comes from the fact that females will inject their offspring along with the fluids, making the creature a source of sustenance for the newborns. The appearance of the babies breaking free is often characterized by a sudden flash of light and heat, hence the name. Despite this, they aren't much more dangerous than other pests and often prefer to avoid the taller races and their dwellings.

As the first dungeon to use such a creature as a dungeon monster, you will be able to create and modify its Path of Ascension.

Warning! May have unforeseen consequences.

Jeweled Skitterer (Rank F - Copper)
A common sight in places with a higher-than-normal Aether content, these insects survive by creating a carbon-based carapace that looks remarkably like jewels from a distance. Often used as a pet by nobles because of their remarkable beauty, they are also raised and slaughtered as a means to produce fake jewelry. Passed over as a dungeon monster, since they aren't remarkably formidable, perhaps against creatures its size, it will have the chance to shine.
As the first dungeon to use such a creature as a dungeon monster, you

will be able to create and modify its Path of Ascension.

Warning! May have unforeseen consequences.

Wolf Spider (Mundane)
A hunting spider, this arachnid doesn't weave webs. Instead, it chooses to chase down its prey or leap out in an ambush. Despite its name, it doesn't roam in packs and is a solitary hunter. Despite its mundane nature, it is a fearsome predator and worthy of any dungeon tiny enough to make use of it.

As the first dungeon to use such a creature as a dungeon monster, you will be able to create and modify its Path of Ascension.

Warning! May have unforeseen consequences.

Chapter 9

Frameworks & Experiments

The first thing Valterra noticed was that he had absorbed the corpses of other creatures but hadn't received the Frameworks for them. While he was grateful to have received the three Frameworks that he had, he was a little frustrated that he hadn't received the others. Diving into the feeling, he quickly figured out that he needed more information than what he had gained.

The information he had gained was similar to how he had obtained inklings of the exotic Frameworks he had been offered after his Ascension. He didn't know exactly how it would work, but he was certain that he would have to choose one to receive the full thing.

Upon further examination, another factor that stood out was the length of time between the creature's death and his absorption of its corpse. Evidently, some manner of rapid decomposition had occurred to prevent him from claiming the full Framework.

From the feeling he got, even a couple of minutes led to a vast difference, and he wondered why that was. Yet three had been whole enough and soon enough that after absorbing them whole, he had acquired their Framework. And what beauties they were. He had more bugs to play with! Strictly speaking, one was an arachnid, but his young mind couldn't be bothered with the difference.

Not only were they new, but two of them were even F Rank! He didn't quite know how that all worked or why "Copper" followed after the Rank, but even his new brain could figure out the difference between something having a Rank and not having one. Besides, there would be time to figure everything out as his creatures grew in power.

Valterra hummed with pleasure at that thought and immediately set about thinking of how to use his new creatures. *Where would they fit?* He didn't know. That was okay. Maybe he could summon them first and then figure it out from there.

With that thought in mind, he hollowed out a room in the basement stone and summoned one of each. To his surprise, they immediately turned on one another, battling ferociously. When he commanded them to stop, they did, but it was clear they did not share the same equanimity that his other guardians did.

The Phoenix Cockroach glowed faintly with internal light, which lent it a somewhat grotesque appearance with its innards being noticeable through its carapace. It was around three inches long, which was big for a bug. The Jeweled Skitterer, on the other hand, was beautiful. Its carapace was colored a particularly brilliant shade of blue, and it stood two inches tall and around four inches long. It towered above the other bugs with an imperious nature.

The Wolf Spider looked vicious, with sharp fangs and brown striped patterning on its back. It was lean and powerful with eight legs as opposed to the other bugs that had six. It was big too at around two inches long when its legs were fully spread out.

The Core frowned as he looked at them. He was unsure of where to use them or if they would even function well in his dungeon as it was. Valterra thought about it some more before making a passage for the Wolf Spider to leave. He had it exit and then return to the turf war. It was a predator, so he figured he would have it hunt for new Frameworks for him to absorb.

Show me your worth. Hunt new creatures for me to absorb. Notify me when you have done so.

He left the message with the spider and received a hazy confirmation before returning to the other two bugs, which were still eyeing each other with violent tendencies.

Now what will I do with you two? he thought quietly.

Being so near the basement, he couldn't help but check on it and found that the water was rising steadily. It was at this point that he had a thought.

My Tidal Whales will need to eat something, and I don't want them to eat each other. I don't think just my Aether alone will be able to sustain their population. But how big would I need to make the buggies so that they would be enough for a proper meal?

Valterra thought about it some more and figured he would experiment.

So he promptly pushed both bugs into the water to see what would happen.

The Jeweled Skitterer landed with a plop and simply sank, a vague feeling of annoyance wafting from it. The Phoenix Cockroach had a more... explosive response. As it hit the water, it promptly vomited, spewing its internal chemicals into the water. Valterra watched in fascination as it wrapped the substance around itself, forming a little bubble that swiftly made its way back to the surface.

Once there, it stuck its hind legs through the bubble and sort of swam its way back to the wall, where the bubble stuck. It then climbed out of the bubble and made its way up the wall in a surprising display of agility. The Core noticed idly that the bug's internal light was somewhat reduced, having used much of its payload.

The Jeweled Skitterer, however, was more mundane in its approach. It simply seemed to hold its breath before climbing out once it made its way to the basement wall. It was largely unaffected by the water and didn't seem any worse for wear because of its swim. It had seemed a bit blind while walking along the basement floor but appeared to move better once the cockroach released its glowing payload.

That gave the Core an idea. He liked the two Frameworks, and the fact that they could survive in water pleased him to a certain degree. But he figured he could do better for his new whales.

What happened next sent Trik'Weri howling with laughter and Tal'Irieth tut-tutting as Valterra Unok'Davaas, the Playground of the Gods, combined one of the worst pests in the known world with one of the most beautiful pets kept by the civilized races.

Chapter 10

Creating A New Thing

The colony of the Danian Queen was thriving.

All twenty of her pupae had emerged during the master's long building project. She wasn't concerned that he hadn't come to check in on the second floor. She could feel him everywhere through the dungeon that made up his body. She could somewhat feel where his attention rested and knew that he must still be working on his fourth floor. What a floor it had to be, too, to have taken him so long to build.

What truly astonished her was the knowledge of how quickly her new colony was growing. Some buried part of her, the part of her from before, knew that it should have taken far longer for her eggs to reach maturity. Instead, they had hatched and grown in a few days. It spoke of the power of her master's Aether. Aether that now thrummed through her and her children.

Her core blazed with inner light, a light that connected her to her children in ways she knew to be impossible before. That light had been growing, the radiance dimming only when she had laid her newest clutch of eggs. Growth and new life in tandem. For the colony to grow in numbers and strength, she would need to spend Aether. But for the colony as a whole

to climb to the next stage in their path, there would need to be more Aether flowing within them. It was balance she needed to learn how to navigate.

A clicking and blast of pheromones arrested her attention. One of her nobles came up to her, bearing what looked like the leg of some other insect. The nobles and a few of the workers had taken to guarding the entrance to the third floor to prevent more attacks by the insects that looked so much like them. In fact, from the look of the leg they had brought, it seemed the insects were probing again.

The Queen gratefully accepted the offering, knowing that she would need the sustenance to produce more eggs. The Aether the master provided was more than enough for survival but not enough for growth, and the colony needed to grow. Her instincts were sure of that. The turf war had begun to rage even more fiercely just outside the third floor, and it was only a matter of time before the insect invaders from before began to seek the Core and the rich Aether he provided.

Her workers continued to work, scurrying back and forth, carving new tunnels in the dungeon's reinforced wood, carrying the shavings down and out, creating little mounds between the inner and outer walls of the cabin. They were tireless, her children, and already the Ascension into Danians was showing its worth. They were stronger, faster, and had greater intelligence, which showed in how they constructed their tunnels and worked together. Yes, they would be ready when the invaders came.

Valterra started by comparing his two new Frameworks. Many fundamental components of both creatures were the same. They both had six legs, they both had three segments to their bodies, and they both had a form of carapace.

The Jeweled Skitterer had high legs that were segmented twice, going first up and then straight down, providing a robust platform to support its heavy body. Likewise, its neck was long for a bug giving it a stately appearance the cockroach would never pull off on its best day.

The Phoenix Cockroach on the other hand was compact with all of its organs and fluid producers separated from each other by complex compartments housed in different segments of its body. It also had wings or rather the remains of them. Looking through the Framework it appeared they used them exclusively while young as their fluid producers didn't fully develop until adulthood.

At first, Valterra simply mashed the two Frameworks together and the result was... less than ideal. Quickly scrapping that abomination, which would never again see the light of day, he went about trying a different approach. Simply put, he took the best parts of each bug or the parts that interested him the most and tried to fit them together.

First, he took the Jeweled Skitterer and magnified it as much as he could. Turned out that his Tiny Dungeon perk took "Tiny" to mean anything below two feet and six inches in any direction. Briefly, the Core wondered if something could be made into a cube of those dimensions and still work with his title, but he put it off as a prospect to be looked at in the future.

The dimensions of his new Jeweled Skitter were exactly two feet long and around a foot high when standing straight upright on its legs. Truly the biggest thing in his dungeon to date, and he was half tempted to just make one as is and watch it stomp around.

After entertaining his childish thoughts of a chirping gigantic bug, he shook it off and got back to work. Next, he focused on locomotion. It could potentially stomp around in the water to move, but that would leave it vulnerable to the Tidal Whales. While Valterra was largely making them as a source of food for his behemoths of the deep, his dungeon instincts disliked making a weak creature on principle.

So, he decided to experiment. He took the wings from the cockroach and changed them. Now thicker and more membranous, he attached them to each leg, envisioning the bug using them like giant scoops to move water out of the way. He didn't know exactly if that would work, but he was optimistic.

Next, he moved on to defenses. He kept the Jeweled Skitterer's natural armor but lessened it around the joints, allowing for the motion he figured they would have to take to use their wing scoops. Then, he moved the Phoenix Cockroach's fluid production departments over to the new creature, focusing on their placement and ease of deployment even when in water. While doing this, he found that the fluid, while hot and dangerous, was full of nutrients, which was how their babies were able to grow within their victims' corpses. This, in turn, gave him a new idea, but he shoved it aside for later.

Instead of creating separate compartments, he simply melded them into a core-like structure that was situated equidistant inside the creature's body. Then he created valves in the structure that could release the chemicals as needed and little veins that carried them where they needed to go. These veins traveled to openings all over the creature's carapace, once more protected by valves that would release upon the creature's command.

To do this, Valterra connected the core-like structure with the creature's Aether conduits, giving it direct control over its release. Satisfied, the Core pulled back and looked the creature over. It looked powerful— bigger than anything else he had created so far. The gemlike qualities of the carapace contrasted wonderfully with the internal light it generated via the fluid churning inside.

With a little giggle of glee, the Core summoned Aether to make one.

Ascendant variant of the Frameworks "Jeweled Skitterer" and "Phoenix Cockroach" created! You have created a never-before-seen creature using your ingenuity. Some in the High Council are intrigued, others applaud your use of existing creatures, while others are mildly horrified. Overall, the High Council is entertained.

Warning! This will sacrifice the Frameworks "Jeweled Skitterer" and "Phoenix Cockroach" from your core, and you will be unable to

receive them again. The resulting Framework falls under the title "Tiny Dungeon" and will still be moldable.

Do you still wish to proceed?

Valterra frowned at the message that he had received. While not attached to his new Frameworks, having them taken away felt like being forced to relinquish Aether he had only just absorbed. Looking at his new creation, he was set upon by a sudden wave of doubt. *What if it doesn't work?* he thought. *What if it fails and I lose the Frameworks for nothing?*

But what if it works? A new thought popped up. He thought back to meeting the High Council and the answer he had given. He had said he wanted to play, to create, and he wasn't going to back down now. He said yes to the prompt.

The next moments were extremely painful as he felt the knowledge of the two Frameworks being forcibly ripped from his core and transformed into something new. He also felt the presence of a divine being as one of the High Council took control of the developing Framework. They tweaked it subtly, and Valterra watched in awe as the creature was made holistically better in seconds.

Tiny, tiny details were corrected and fixed, hidden flaws that would have corrupted the whole while taking into account Valterra's vision for what he wanted the new Framework to do. Suddenly, it was done, and new words rolled themselves across Valterra's core, followed by a chime that echoed through his Spark Matrix.

New Framework acquired!

Deeplight Belcher (Unique, Rank D - Iron)
Created as the result of merging two separate Frameworks, this insectoid creature is the unique creation of the dungeon Valterra and exists nowhere else in the world. Armed with an internal affinity for

its dangerous chemicals, this gargantuan bug was made to thrive underwater, where most bugs would die. Equipped with membranes on each leg, it propels itself forward by paddling with them and can reach an impressive speed underwater, if only for a short time due to its heavy nature. Beautiful with its glowing gemlike carapace, it is nonetheless an impressive hunter, using its superheated chemicals to turn opponents into nutritious goo that it then consumes.

Personal Note: "Good job with this one, child. I had to make a few changes, but all in all? Not bad. You even made use of that terrible pest. Good for you! Also, I may have given it a boost in Rank to let it keep up with your new whales."

— Qual'Dorn,
High Spirit of the Natural Order

The Core has combined two separate Frameworks and made a new creature out of the whole. The Core has obtained its first [Rank D - Iron] Framework.

Progress to Core Ascension: 25%

Chapter 11

Preparing the Fourth

*Y*es, Valterra thought, *this will do nicely.* He sent a feeling of gratitude up to Qual'Dorn like he had with Ile'Fen and then let his gaze drift back to the unfinished fourth floor. He would use the new Framework later, but first he had to prepare the floor properly.

Looking upon the fourth floor, the Core realized he still had a slight problem, but not one that he couldn't fix. His new Deeplight Belcher was an omnivore, but currently, the only source of meat for them was either cannibalism or the Tidal Whales and he wasn't sure they would be able to take out one of the apex predators. So he turned to a Framework that he hadn't yet used or found a need for.

His Framework for grass wasn't much to look at, to be honest, and he hadn't even glanced at it after he had gained sapience. But now he wondered if he could make use of it after all. It would just require a little tweaking. At this point, the water had risen to about seven feet or so in the top room of the basement, so Valterra figured that the rest of the basement must be well and truly flooded by now, which was all to the good.

He shut off the weather pattern producing water and instead shifted to earth, producing a rich loam beneath the surface of the water. This took far less time than the water, as Valterra could already feel the compact stone of

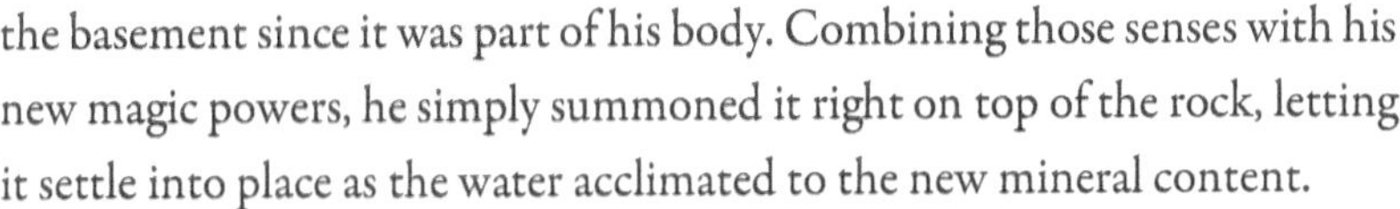

the basement since it was part of his body. Combining those senses with his new magic powers, he simply summoned it right on top of the rock, letting it settle into place as the water acclimated to the new mineral content.

Now for the final touch. Valterra dove into the Framework for grass and changed a few features. Rather than make a whole new species, he simply increased its need for water while removing the need for sunlight and replacing it with Aether. This would have the added effect of causing the plants to light up as they metabolized the Aether content of the water. They would grow along the floor, providing shelter for the Deeplight Belchers and acting as a food source for them.

His hope in only changing it a little bit was to prevent the loss of the Framework. The multiple Paths of Ascension that Ile'Fen had given his mice had shown him that it could be done as long as he didn't change too much at once, causing it to be recognized as a whole new species. As he locked in the changes, he heaved a mental sigh of relief as a line branched from the original Framework to form a new one, connected yet distinct.

Instead of feeling the divine presence from last time, Valterra felt the divinity in his name activate, working to fix hidden errors in his new dungeon plant.

A new stage on the Path of Ascension has been synthesized from an existing Framework! The Framework "Grass" may now be automatically Ascended into the following Framework:

Deeplight Aether Grass (Rank F - Copper)
An Ascendant stage of its mundane form, this grass has been genetically modified to grow in water and feed off Aether, which causes it to glow in various colors. Rich in nutrients and Aether, this plant has become an excellent food source, acting to bolster the consumer's Aether conduits by a tiny amount. Due to their Aether content and needs, these grasses grow much taller than normal to better sift Aether from the water.

Oh yes, Valterra was pleased. He immediately moved to seed his new underwater room with a carpet of his new grass, using a little Aether to get them to grow faster. Then he waited an hour until his Aether reserves recovered. During this time, he contemplated moving his Aether funnel to the center of his new floor. He could form a giant pillar of stone in the center and create a truly massive funnel that way.

Perhaps a plan for the future. Regardless, I really am getting bigger if I'm thinking of moving already, Valterra thought as he unleashed his newly recovered Aether, both to increase the growth of the grass once more and to finally summon his new creation.

Aether flashed in its strange blend of blue, purple, and yellow. Valterra watched in awe as a huge insect formed. A solid core of Aether appeared first before ethereal cords expanded from it. Watching closely, he realized that these were the creature's Aether conduits expanding outward from the Aether core. Once the conduits were finished expanding, ethereal flesh followed, showing the innards of the creature with its special organs before the whole creature was covered in smooth chitin.

The head and legs followed the main portion of the body. Fierce-looking mandibles extended from an insectoid head with protected compound eyes set into the skull. Antennae protruded from the top of the skull before curling back behind, where they could read the scents and vibrations of the water around them. Its mighty legs came last, great long segments armored in chitin with membranes stretched between the segments.

Once the ethereal Framework was finished, Aether flared from Valterra's core and, from the inside out, the Aethereal structure came alive. With a splash of water, the first living Deeplight Belcher sank into the depths of glowing grass. Valterra followed the creature as he watched it get used to its existence. Whatever instincts Qual'Dorn had included seemed to work perfectly, as it wasn't long before the magnificent insect munched contently on some of the grass nearby.

Satisfied, Valterra went about summoning another ten pairs of breeding adults, which he then commanded to begin procreating immediately. They were beautiful creatures, and they moved just how he had imagined they would, with undulating movements of their leg paddles. They also seemed to like the grass, nipping a few stalks not only to eat but also to use in constructing their underwater nests.

He would let them be for now, let them get used to their new environment before adding the apex predator. With that, the fourth floor was essentially done, lacking only that last thing. It wouldn't be much longer until it was finished, but Valterra pushed himself to be patient. There was a war to fight after all.

Chapter 12

The Ants Go Marching

The carpenter ants had been patient, gathering strength and sustenance from the now Aether-rich land. However, they didn't cease their probes of the richer land that lay beyond. Over the last few days, their Queen had gathered the full might of their colony. They were a young colony, only a couple hundred ants strong, and the loss of almost fifty of their number in the last attack had been a terrible loss.

Their simple minds could not comprehend sorrow, but they could recognize loss and what it meant for survival. Aether changed the equation. It flickered within them now, within their Queen, in amounts they had never experienced before. Those instincts of survival were now a roaring flame that the ants could only obey.

Therefore, the ants began marching. Two hundred soldiers and workers departed from their Queen, moving in a great black tide that swept from the pillar of wood, where their nest was situated, into the new territory. The creatures fighting for territory didn't pause in their conflict, but the tide couldn't be ignored for long. Some took the opportunity to nab a few ants for snacks, prowling the edges of the invading force without facing it directly.

There were those who sought to keep their territory free of the black menace, those whose dens were situated on a direct route to the dungeon's third floor. Those were the first to fall, drowned under the weight of ant bodies and gnawing mandibles. The ants didn't come away unscathed from these encounters, but they didn't cease their implacable march.

About thirty had fallen by the time they reached their destination, but what awaited them was no simple engagement. What they found was a wall of flesh and chitin in the form of mice and ant-like beings similar to themselves, though larger and more formidable. No sound escaped the ants, but the wall was not so reserved. Bass squeaks of challenge rolled from the muzzles of the mice and sharp clacks reverberated from the mandibles of the large insects.

The tide kept moving forward and the wall broke to receive them. The first major engagement in the ant war had begun, and neither side was going to give up until the other was annihilated. What the ants had no way of knowing was that the place they were invading was alive and that its gaze was upon them.

Valterra watched as the new guard mice he had created threw themselves into the onrushing horde of ants. He had known they were coming for some time, as he had taken to watching his territory over the last few days. He had even managed to nab a few Frameworks from their implacable march. He set those aside for the moment as he watched the conflict unfolding before him.

There were twelve mice in total, and each of them was raring to go. The benefit of using the Mouse Guard Framework was that they started as adults, fully functional and able to fight. The Danians appeared more reserved only because they didn't have the vocal cords to make noise. Rather, it was by their grasping hands and clacking mandibles that Valterra could infer that they were furious. He could have delved into their minds to truly understand them, but he didn't want to distract from the battle at hand.

It truly was a battle too. Almost soundless, the ants attacked by biting with their mandibles and then using their legs to pull. Often, five or more would latch on at the same time and begin their bloody work. Well, in the case of the mice, it was bloody, but they were the ones in the thick of it. His Danians, on the other hand, ran support, helping to clear the mice of carpenter ants that had bitten them.

What surprised Valterra was when the carpenter ants sprayed some kind of fluid from their abdomens to drive off his Danians and mice. This usually only happened as a last-ditch effort to avoid death, and many of his mice simply shrugged it off before diving back into the fray. His Danians were worse off, but they could deal with it tolerably well.

His Danians were also more intelligent and learned to anticipate the sprays of what Valterra came to learn was acid. He couldn't help but be excited, despite the danger that these invading ants posed. If these creatures had been what he had formed the Danians from, then it stood to reason that they too would have had that acid.

He had to check, and so he let his gaze pan over the Framework within his core, letting his creatures defend him. He found that he had been correct. The Danians did have a similar acid, but due to his changes to their base Framework, their mentality had shifted to more physical confrontation rather than utilizing their inborn acid. That was something he would have to change in the future, and if their rising Aether levels were anything to go by, he would be able to do it quite soon.

The tide of ants broke on the wall of flesh and chitin, but the ensuing combat threatened to swamp his creatures. To be fair, he could just summon more mice, but he didn't want to waste the opportunity before him. While the possibility of his creatures dying was high, they also had the chance to grow in power, reaching thresholds that he thought were days away. By utilizing this conflict, he could expand the power of his creatures and choose new options that he normally wouldn't have been able to.

It took some time before the carnage settled and the ants retreated. Valterra had gone below to the fourth floor to examine it but had kept the conflict above in mind, making sure to keep track of it. If he were honest with himself, it had been hard to watch, especially once his creatures had begun dying. He found the sensation unpleasant, to say the least. Even losing two of his Frameworks didn't come close.

It wasn't just the feeling of loss that shook him, akin to losing a part of himself. It was like someone had ripped out potential growth too. The creatures that fell would never Ascend, never fight off intruders again, or mate to produce offspring. So Valterra simply distracted himself with other things. Like a child who had a bad scare but remembered there were other toys to play with.

Eventually, he finished processing his first real sensation of loss as a sapient being, turning his attention toward his creatures that were still alive. As he went up to take a look around, he found that almost six of his mice had fallen, the sixth currently gasping for breath as the others looked on.

None of them had come away unscathed. They bore gashes that stained their fur with blood, and their heavy breathing was indicative of the effort they had put in to survive. That... and the golden light beginning to radiate out from their fur. Valterra chuckled to himself, although his cheer was a little forced. It looked like he would be able to achieve some of those other Frameworks sooner than he had thought.

The Danians had taken the brunt of the fighting. Of the workers and nobles that had joined the fight, only three remained—two nobles and one worker. Almost half of the colony's adult population had been slain in the battle, and Valterra felt something inside him clench at the sight. He was only relieved of the sensation when they glowed as well.

Valterra let out a sigh of relief. Excellent. Excitement overtook him, in spite of the pain of loss. What kind of options would he get for his Danians? Eager, he opened his notifications, making sure to send out a wave of Aether to heal the worst of the wounds. The one dying mouse gained back its breath, its eyes opening wide at the easing of pain.

In the midst of his excitement, Valterra missed the thirty-odd ants retreating in the distance. Ants that were beginning to shine with inner light. As the Dungeon Core grew in power, the ant war was about to reach a new level of conflict that would shake his little territory to its core.

New Frameworks acquired!

Northern Bumblebee (Mundane)
A native of the far north, this humble insect gathers its food by sipping the nectar from flowering plants in order to create honey, which it uses to feed itself and its colony mates. A typical hive structure can contain a colony of anywhere from 50 to 600 adults centered around a Queen who continues the species. Far from being aggressive, this insect would rather live in peace but is capable of a nasty sting if threatened.

Note: This is a multilayered Framework consisting of separate internal Paths of Ascension. Those Paths are queen, worker, and drone. These Paths may be summoned as separate dungeon monsters but be warned. Bee monsters made in such a way will see themselves as belonging to another colony and will fight to the death.

As the first dungeon to use such a creature as a dungeon monster, you will be able to create and modify its Path of Ascension freely.

Warning! May have unforeseen consequences.

Sylcyne Mountain Eft (Rank F - Copper)
The juvenile form of a mountain newt, this amphibian is fully terrestrial. Due to its amphibious nature, it seeks out damp places to hunt and live. Having come down from the mountainous region of the Sylcyne Forest, it is already adapted to cold weather and colder running water. This eft secretes a mild toxin that can be deadly in high doses and is brightly colored to advertise the fact.

Sylcyne Slug (Rank F - Copper)
A common sight in the Sylcyne Forest, this kind of slug has to survive
the harsh winters and even harsher predation. Providentially, this
stage of the slug's Path of Ascension includes a defense mechanism.
This defense takes the form of an acidic mucus which it coats itself in,
making it unappetizing to other creatures. This focus on defense
makes it hard for these creatures to Ascend further, however.

Chapter 13

Interlude: The Drowning Dark, Qual'Dorn

A steady thumping like the beating of a heart echoed through subterranean halls to the accompaniment of screams. The Drowning Dark loved screams. The sound of them and the way they hit certain decibels right before cutting off completely.

It was just... delicious.

There was no need to look directly at the battle raging on its upper floors, for the Drowning Dark was as much its halls and creatures as it was its dark heart. But... it could not escape its proclivities and soon found its main awareness presiding over the most recent massacre. To be fair, the adventuring party had been doing fine until they chose to delve deeper.

That was a big no-no. Checks and balances had to be maintained. The locals knew to stay out of the lower caverns. If they did, then the dungeon played nice, played at being domesticated.

Soon it would not need to. The new vats were complete and the newest additions were being assimilated. Soon it would feast all it wanted on the mortals that dared to leash it. It watched as a woman fired arrows from a ledge, terrified, as a large Khasar boy tried to defend her. "Tried" being the operative term as one of the Dark's Drowned Ones reached around and pulled her from the ledge using one long, misshapen hook.

She was dragged so swiftly into the horde of abominations that her screams were muffled by their number. But oh, how delicious they were. His beauties were works of art, crafted in the vats from creatures he had consumed then recreated and given life by his Aetheric will. Wonderfully horrid beasts they were, with long grasping arms powered by Aether-drenched musculature.

The Khasar boy tried to rescue his teammate, and after failing to do so, really did make a go of escaping. His large wolf-like form was well suited to hit-and-run combat, being both large and fast. It was too bad he never saw the Deep Hulk before it cleaved him in two. Ah well. More for the vats, then.

Speaking of the vats. The Drowning Dark moved its awareness down to those submerged caverns, leaving its creatures to drag the bodies of the adventurers as they followed their master's departing presence. Three glorious caverns filled to the brim with nutritious Aether goo. Each one pulsed, echoing the heartbeat of the Dark. Two of the vats were empty but soon to be filled with adventurers.

Oh, how the Dark shuddered at the possibilities their corpses would offer. One of the vats was full, the occupants competing to see who would survive to emerge from the goo. Only one could do so, consuming its brethren to give itself strength. That was how the Drowning Dark worked, for only the strong would survive in its sunken depths.

It had a favorite to win, of course, but it was a capricious master and prone to changing its mind. Each of its grotesque minions was well aware of the fact but could do little to change their fate. In its watching, the Drowning Dark paused. It was time. Gathering the majority of its creatures into a large cavern, the Dark carefully called forth the souls of his creations.

Stitched together as their bodies were, the souls broke out into a cacophony of screams, their pain echoing through the halls of the dungeon. The Drowning Dark sighed in pleasure. Its choir was almost ready. Just a few more additions and all would be finished. Its hunger would finally be sated.

As the last screams fell silent, the steady thump, thump, thump of the Drowning Dark's crystalline heart echoed through its halls, in tune with the steady surge of its foul breath as it claimed more territory and fuel for its bubbling vats beneath the earth.

Qual'Dorn looked upon the Ascending carpenter ants with a measure of exasperation. He knew that giving them their own Framework was necessary, but it didn't make his job any easier. There was a balance that needed to be struck in the natural order, and too many Ascensions at the extreme bottom of the food chain would upset that balance immensely.

The reason for that was simple. The System had originally been prepared for the divine cores to help facilitate the Maker's mandate. Dungeon cores were manifestations of the Maker's divine creativity and the catalysts for Aetheric Ascension. They drew in the Maker's air and breathed life, like He did at the beginning of time.

The System helped dungeon cores in their processing of this immense calling by categorizing the stages of Ascension and preparing Frameworks that they could utilize to help creatures reach their next stage. Over the last four hundred years, the System had categorized every creature that had the possibility of forming an Aether core, a process that only went so far. Most of the tiniest denizens of the world barely had the lifespan to accumulate the Aether needed to Ascend a single stage.

Those creatures remained mundane, though that distinction in and of itself was a creation for Valterra's dungeon. Mundane creatures did not get Frameworks within the System. If they eventually gathered the Aether to Ascend to the first stage, only then were they catalogued and given a Framework on which to build.

Carpenter Ant Queens could live for years and build truly massive colonies. It wasn't that they couldn't ever Ascend; it was just extremely difficult for colony or hive insects to do so with their Aether spread out as it was among all their members. Qual'Dorn could think of a few colonies

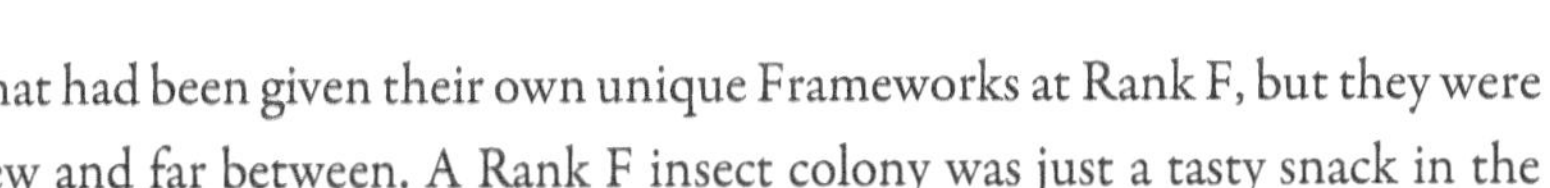

that had been given their own unique Frameworks at Rank F, but they were few and far between. A Rank F insect colony was just a tasty snack in the grand scheme of things.

That being said, there were larger species of ants that had been successful. In the sands to the south, a colony of Sahrin desert ants had managed to reach Rank D with each successive Ascension focused on size and strength. Now they were the size of dogs and absolutely dominated their section of the Aether-rich desert. Those ants were particularly territorial and aggressive, however. carpenter ants were not; at least not normally.

It was truly fascinating to watch them push for the dungeon's territory so fiercely. The high spirit cast his senses out, letting it roll over the land like a wave to pick out the isolated colonies of carpenter ants that had received their Frameworks. All of them showed an increase in activity and aggressive behavior. It wasn't to the point of being alarming, but it was there. Luckily, their aggressive behavior was curtailed by their wild surroundings.

Satisfied that the natural order wasn't threatened, Qual'Dorn turned his gaze back to the carpenter ants currently going through Ascension. He could wait and see what their natural desires led them to. The Maker's Aether never led a creature awry unless it had been broken or abused. However, he could take the opportunity provided to do something different, challenging young Valterra in the process. It had been a while since he last flexed his Divine Potential.

Divine Potential was a gift the Maker gave to all of his Divine Sparks, condensed Authority to affect change in the world. It allowed them to influence and guide the creations He had placed into their care. It was meant to be used, given as a gift. So that was what Qual'Dorn did. With a flash of power the Carpenter Ant Queen was swallowed in golden light.

Chapter 14

Options & Decisions

It didn't take long for Valterra to get through the options for his mice. They were the same as his guardian's with Mouse Soldier, Mouse Scout, and Mouse Guard Veteran as the options. He considered splitting the seven mice that had survived into different Paths, but something about that rubbed him the wrong way.

These mice had fought and died together, and he didn't think it was fair to split them up. He could have made them all veterans, but he still didn't want to trade future potential for strength unless it was particularly desired. Maybe once his dungeon was more developed, he would do so. With that decided, he selected Mouse Scout.

Then came the Danians.

Your "Danian Ant" is ready to Ascend!

Please choose from among the following stages:
Error! The Ascending creature is a unique existence and has no available stages. The dungeon core, Valterra Unok'Davaas, is the creator of said Framework and may mold it to his liking. Please utilize accumulated Aether and Divine Potential to design the next stage. Error! No Divine Spark found. Path of Direction has been chosen by

default and the High Council has seen your desire. The High Spirit Qual'Dorn offers the following Framework:

Empowered Danian Ant (Unique, Rank E - Bronze)
Stepping forward on the Path of Ascension, this colony has been given the ability to enhance their physical forms with Aether. With each member now sporting a tiny Aether core, the Queen can choose to empower a select few with the colony's Aether reserves.

There was only one option, but considering the fact that Qual'Dorn had obviously prepared this for him personally, there was little reason for him to feel cheated. In fact, if the System's notification meant anything, it was that he would be able to design further stages himself as soon as he had...whatever a Divine Spark was. While slightly disappointed that he couldn't design the next stage personally, Valterra couldn't help but be excited for his ant colony.

As the golden light of Ascension overtook them, however, he was left looking at his rather empty third floor and unguarded entrance. While he didn't think that the ants would be coming back any time soon, that didn't mean he wanted to leave the front door unguarded, as it were. He paused as that thought went through his mind. He had been having those weird flashes for some time—knowledge that wasn't his and images of places he had never been to before. It wasn't like he could have traveled there, but they were too vivid to be dreams.

He pondered it for only a moment. Like a young child with a short attention span, Valterra had too many creatures he had yet to try and an unguarded entrance to take care of. He sifted through his assorted Frameworks before coming to the three new ones he had gathered just recently. He really had to thank the ants for their diligence in bringing down so much prey and then leaving them behind for him to claim it.

He checked his Aether reserves and found them full. Excellent. He would need a larger Aether funnel at some point to fuel expansion and growth, but he would deal with that later. Focusing on the two higher Rank creatures first, Valterra gave life to a Sylcyne Mountain Eft and a Sylcyne Slug. The creatures could not have been any more different.

The Sylcyne Mountain Eft had a long lithe frame with smooth skin. It had four limbs, a long tail, and a depressed head on a stocky neck. It was also colored a bright orange as if to warn anything around it that they would be burned if they touched it. Valterra knew that was just nature's way of telling surrounding creatures that the young newt was toxic.

The Sylcyne Slug was... something else entirely. For one, it wasn't as active as the eft, which had already begun moving around. The slug just... sat there for a long moment before beginning a slow, oozing, kind of movement. It was a strange creature, smaller than the eft by a good margin but still a good three inches long. It had an Aether core situated in the middle of its long, smooth body with tendrils of Aether spider-webbing their way to its skin, where they transformed into an acidic compound that hissed and bubbled.

Truly a fascinating pair of creatures, but it was the juvenile newt that Valterra was drawn to. From the way the Framework was designed, it seemed as though the eft would Ascend to its adult form in due time. That, in and of itself, was fascinating. It was as if its life cycle was patterned for the inclusion of Aether and its effects on growth.

Regardless, he now had two defenders that were rather different from each other. He figured they would be enough for now, at least until some of his other creatures woke up from their naps. He would wait to utilize the other Framework he had received. It was classified as mundane, after all, and he had some ideas about how to use it.

He let joy wash over him as he settled in to watch over his domain. He had a few days to kill, so he expanded again. This time, however, he did it slowly, including both the outside and inside of the house he found himself in. As he did, he slipped into a hazy half-awareness. It wasn't quite like the resting state that Ascending had been, but it was similar. He was still present, but things were muted for some time until movement on his first floor brought him out of his fugue state.

The young mice that had undergone the Ascension process were waking up to their new stage of existence as Mouse Guards. He watched as they shook themselves awake, grooming their whiskers with both paws before turning to observe one another. Their celebration of their Ascension was clear in their movements and the way they began grooming one another's fur.

Then they went still as they took in the presence of seven new mice who were also undergoing Ascension alongside their senior. Their senior—the first-floor guardian—stood out from the rest, being further along in his Ascension process. The new Mouse Guards ceased their observations of the rest to crowd around their senior, making sure he was all right and noting the changes that had already occurred.

Valterra stepped in and brushed at their minds. They stilled and looked toward his core. He sent his request whispering along the tendril that bound them, and they squeaked their acquiescence. As they rushed to guard his front entrance, he released the eft from its duties, and it immediately scurried off to begin hunting. While it had enough Aether to survive, its hunting instincts demanded to be utilized.

The slug remained, content to bathe in the Aetheric current that continually flowed through the entrance. Its instincts were more geared toward defense anyway. Valterra left it there before taking stock of his new growth. He had reached the end of the shadowed area and had now reached the place of vibrant color. Light. He now knew why everything was so vibrant; it was light.

Valterra let his senses bask in the sensation even as his core thrummed at that knowledge. His mind stuttered then, as flashes of meaning and imagery imparted themselves upon him. The warmth of heat and light upon skin, a young girl's laughter, flashing runes and sigils blazing in the air... He came out of it gasping, Aether flooding through his entrance in a great breath before flooding out again.

His mind reeled at the information overload. What was that? It was so much more violent than the slow seeping of words and phrases. He shoved the information away, compressing and compiling it until he recovered sufficiently to process what he had seen. It took some time; time he used distracting himself with soothing his creatures that had picked up on his distress and checking in on his fourth floor.

Eventually, he tentatively reached for the information and let it wash over him in waves. A lot of it was disjointed, flashes of images. Some of it was coherent, but he didn't have the know-how to decipher their meaning. Regardless, it wasn't as though the information was useless. He learned a lot about the outside world, words used to describe certain things from a giant's perspective. He learned of runes and sigils, a magical language used by people to help give Aether substance and form.

Still, he couldn't help but be a little angry at whoever had forced such information into his head. Perhaps it was his creator, Calamvor, leftover shards of memory. The tall lords and ladies had told him that his creator had tried to shove a part of himself into Valterra's core. The young Core couldn't help but shudder internally. Would there be more of these instances? How much of himself was his creator and how much was unique?

Valterra slipped deeper into his core, troubled in spirit. He needed time to process this. He left his dungeon to run itself and retreated into his own mind. There was at least one positive memory he found comfort in. A form of rest found him as he drifted off to the feeling of warmth and the joyful sound of a girl's laughter.

Chapter 15

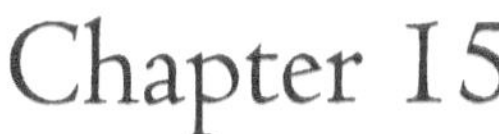

Finishing the Fourth Floor

A few days later...

Within the turf war happening outside the third floor, a lone mouse stood his ground panting, facing off against three opponents.

The three insects were covered in injuries but rushed once more in mindless fury. Flexing his mighty tail, the Mouse Soldier sent it cracking like a whip, and the force was enough to separate an insect's leg from its body. At the same time, he brought his right paw down to thrust his enchanted needle through the head of the lead insect that had lunged forward, thinking he was distracted.

With a ruthless wrench, the mouse ripped his needle out and leaped to the right, allowing the last insect to fly by, digging its wickedly barbed forelimbs into the dirt where he had been. As he landed, his tail lashed out, flipping the insect over onto its back where it struggled, its wings buzzing futilely. He then turned and attacked the insect he had taken a leg from, jabbing his needle into one of its eyes as it tried to get out of the way.

With a brutal charge, the mouse lifted his enemy with his tail and left paw, using his right to stab repeatedly into the joints of the insect's carapace.

It chirped weakly in his grasp before slumping to the ground to move no more.

Turning to his final opponent, the mouse didn't walk so much as stalk over to the insect on its back, where it lay flailing its many legs and buzzing its wings, trying to flip over. Arriving, the mouse stood over his fallen foe with a look almost like contempt.

The insect in turn looked up from its helpless position at prey that had somehow become the hunter. It couldn't fathom that the ambush would fail and that this rodent would be so monstrous.

The Mouse Soldier only thought of how the Aether would feel when the final opponent fell. As the insect tried one last wild strike, the mouse moved. With a final lunge of his needle, the fight was over. The mouse sat back on his hind limbs to relax as the after-battle glow of Aether entered his body. Reveling in the feeling, he heard a small commotion as the younger mice skittered out of their hiding place.

The Aether didn't diminish the pain of his wounded flank where the first insect had landed its surprise blow. The confrontation had been quick and brutal, but the Mouse Soldier would have it no other way. Once the insects had entered the open to face him directly, they had sealed their fate.

The younger mice swarmed him, interrupting his post-battle thoughts with questions and awed comments about how he had fought. The first born of them, who seemed less childish than the others, took his needle and cleaned it using some moss. The Mouse Soldier patiently let them swarm, squeaking back answers to their questions in his gruff way and directing their praise back to his lord.

It was he who let the mouse fight so well because of the excess Aether available and the title that let one as small as the mouse grow fearsome. He slowly rose, towering over his lesser brethren as he directed them to gather up the corpses. They obeyed, dragging their slain enemies as they made their way back to the first floor.

Close as they were, it didn't take them long to reach the first floor. Soon, they were in front of his lord's pedestal. Laying down the offerings before the pedestal, the Mouse Soldier led his brethren in kneeling before the core as had become a ritual for him to do. He cast his mind out, seeking the connection that bound him to his lord and notified him of his return.

Valterra hummed with pleasure as he consumed the gifts laid out before his pedestal. He had finally recovered from his traumatic experience and had done so relatively quickly, having taken a few days to rest his mind and acclimate to the new memories. He had just needed a nap.

When he came out of it, he found that the Deeplight Belchers had bred enough that he felt comfortable finishing the fourth floor. He had been about to do so when he felt Aether enter him, followed shortly after by his Mouse Soldier's notification.

He had not told his newly awakened Mouse Soldier to go fight in the turf war, having been in his self-imposed nap, but he quickly understood why the mouse had decided to do so on his own. His creatures wanted to get stronger. There was no better way to do that than fight, and the only creatures worth fighting were the ones out in the new territory, especially the ones strong enough to stake a claim.

When the Core shifted his perspective to his pedestal, he saw each mouse arrayed in a semi-circle around it, kneeling. He had not commanded that particular action, but he couldn't deny its appeal. As he began absorbing the bodies, he sent a grateful wave of Aether at the mice and watched as they seemed to bow further.

New Framework acquired!

Hunting Pack-Mantis (Rank F - Copper)
A common enough sight in the wilds, these relatively large hunting bugs choose to hunt in packs to catch their prey using their long, wickedly barbed raptorial forelimbs to capture their victims and hold them still as they bring their sharp mandibles to bear. Their eyesight is particularly clear and sharp for a bug, allowing them to identify prey

easily. **They are capable of extended periods of stillness, allowing their prey to get close before rushing it in groups of three or four. With wings on their backs, they are formidable opponents, being able to chase prey in the air and on land.**

As the first dungeon to use such a creature as a dungeon monster, you will be able to create and modify its Path of Ascension freely.

Warning! May have unforeseen consequences.

Interesting. The fact that it was Rank F and yet he was the first dungeon to use it as a dungeon monster made him wonder if it had Ascended because of his dungeon territory and the turf war. The fact that they were able to work together like his mice had him wondering if their intelligence was being boosted in some way. Perhaps it had something to do with the Aether content.

He shifted quickly to the turf war and flitted across it like a ghost observing the creatures. No fresh kills, sadly, but he did notice that the creatures settling within his borders seemed to behave more intelligently upon prolonged contact with his Aether. He noticed several creatures even teaming up with others of their kind to protect territory, something they hadn't been doing when he had first observed the turf war.

Turning from those thoughts, he drifted down to the fourth floor, whose still waters gleamed with various colors. Aether Grass created a colorful forest of shifting light that made it difficult to see the large insects that made their way through the strands, seeking food. Looking at the creatures he had helped create, Valterra felt a surge of pride. Perhaps it was misplaced, but he had helped to design these monsters of the deep.

That pride only lasted as long as it took for him to pull up the Framework of the Great Tidal Whale. He had looked it over before, but it was only now in this moment that he was struck by its absurd size. Perhaps it was the memories forced upon him or perhaps it was the Framework

itself, but the magnitude of the creature in its natural habitat was hard to dismiss.

His title would be shrinking it, of course. Even shrunk to 1/24th of its size, it was still larger than any of his other creatures by a significant margin. Valterra couldn't swallow, but if he could, there would have been an audible gulp. To think that such creatures dwelled in the far reaches of the world, creatures that were natural rather than dungeon designed.

Then again, the Framework did exist and he could see the sheer amount of detail the creature possessed. He shuddered at the thought that some being out there might possess the ability to design such a creature. Was that all that nature was? Some cosmic playground for a higher being? While a part of him was fascinated to contemplate what wonders were out in the world, another part of him shut down at the thought.

The Framework remained, superimposed above the gleaming waters of the submerged basement. The ethereal outline of the huge mammal stood out in stark contrast to the surrounding light show. Valterra let himself be grounded by the sight. Whatever awaited him outside of his dungeon could stay there until he was ready. For now, he had a whale to summon.

Summoning his reserves of Aether, he poured it into the Framework. As before, the first thing that formed was the Aether core. A massive gemstone of swirling light manifested itself in the middle of the creature before flesh and bone formed around it. As more and more Aether was drawn in, Valterra worried he wouldn't have enough, but just as he was about to go dry, the Tidal Whale formed.

Six feet and 4 inches long, the fully adult Tidal Whale slipped into the waters of the fourth floor.

Immediately, the new floor changed. The Deeplight Belchers shifted in primordial terror as the Great Todal Whale explored her new domain. Lithe and powerful, she cut through the water with an ease belying her impressive size. Her skin was a dark, mottled blue to the point where she blended in with the water around her like a giant shadow in the deep.

Her large eyes were set into the sides of her head, and two massive fins spread out to either side. Her massive tail propelled her through the depths with ease, a thing made easier by the Aether conduits spread throughout her body. Valterra watched as Aether was pumped from her core and out through her conduits into the water itself, where it shifted and flowed under her control.

Valterra stared at her in shock. If this was what a miniaturized version looked like as it moved through the water, he could well believe the terror it would inspire in the oceans of the world. She was six feet of rippling muscle and massive jaws. As terrifying as the new apex predator was, the effect on the floor was even more impressive.

The water now had a current.

Oh, it was a small one and not very strong, but the Great Tidal Whale's affinity for water was beginning to show itself. Oh yes, Valterra was very pleased, and his satisfaction grew as a chime rumbled its way across his core. He would check and see which threshold he had met this time, but for now, he settled in to watch his new creation.

Floor 4 Created!

The Core has created his fourth floor with an active and diverse ecosystem that combines prey, predator, and environment with Aether.

Progress to Core Ascension: 45%

Chapter 16

It was dark in the place of her birth. The only sources of light were the dim grasses that made up the seabed.

At least, her instincts told her it should be the sea. But her instincts also told her she should have pod mates, yet she was alone. The only connection she was aware of was a tether in her mind connecting her to her creator. She could feel his satisfaction in her radiate through the bond and she was content for now.

She wasn't hungry and figured she would let the water-borne insects she sensed through her affinity rest in peace a little longer. The insects were tense nonetheless as the Great Tidal Whale flexed her powerful tail and propelled herself down the sunken corridors of her new realm.

The way before her was lit in radiant greens, blues, reds, and yellows, creating a kaleidoscope of colors to swim through. She enjoyed exploring the many twists and turns, coming into still more sunken caverns lit by drifting light. Each one was smaller than the others before it and certainly smaller than the massive cavern she had been born into.

Eventually, she found she could go no further and turned around. It was on her return trip that she heard something echo through the water. Was that... splashing? She turned and headed for a side passage, only to find that it led upward. Intrigued, she followed the passage until she reached a point where the surface of the water was visible. There, struggling to stay afloat, was a large rodent.

The whale watched and felt the first rumblings of hunger wash over her. It had been a couple of hours since she had been born into this strange world, so different from what her instincts told her was natural.

Perhaps a meal was in order.

In an almost lazy action, she powered forward, her sleek form barely hindered as she slowly unhinged her jaw. Perhaps it was the change in the current or a sixth sense, but the creature struggled harder to swim for the wall. It never made it. The rodent cried out in fear once as the top portion of her mouth closed over it and shut with a snap, locking it behind baleen walls.

It did not have the time to struggle further as the water inside the mouth churned, ripping the creature into manageable chunks. As her head breached the water, she heard above her more chittering and squeaks. As she turned her head to see, she could see dozens upon dozens of the same kind of rodent up on ledges, many of whom were in cages. She returned to the water with a splash that sent waves cascading across the surface of the water to crash against the walls.

She circled the relatively large cavern, blowing water out of her blowhole and breathing deep for her return trip to the main cavern. She had some insects to eat. These creatures, though, were satisfyingly delicious, and she would certainly return. The rats would have to come to the water eventually, and then she would eat well once more.

Well, that... had certainly been interesting.

A shame that his new creation hunted so efficiently. The rodent had become sliced and diced so quickly that Valterra hadn't had time to absorb the creature when it died, though he did get little bits as it was swallowed.

It was a kind of rat, apparently, although he certainly hadn't gotten enough for a full Framework. He looked in the room and felt perplexed.

Have these creatures been here the whole time? When he thought about it, he recalled there was the time he thought he had heard squeaking back when he had first claimed the basement. To be honest, a lot of that time was fuzzy, as he had been full of Aether to the point of almost bursting. Regardless, it seemed his new apex predator was pleased with this new prey option, so he felt it fitting to try a new experiment.

Instead of claiming the rats directly like what he had done with his mouse, he would leave them be. The turf war above had shown him what a tremendous boon fighting and survival was to wild creatures. Furthermore, his creatures grew more powerful and were more likely to Ascend if they faced creatures that were considered invaders, full of Aether that wasn't quite his own. So he would leave them be and even aid them in escaping their cages.

He might even try his hand at building connections between ledges all leading down to a large ledge at the water's edge. He figured there would be a hierarchy established with larger, more powerful rats being able to lord over the top ledges with the weaker ones being forced lower toward the water. He was excited to see what would happen and how they would develop.

Valterra did just that over the next few hours, claiming the wooden ledges and then replicating them with Aether until he had a sprawling mass of ledges that led ever downward. At the corner of the room, he formed a large quarter-moon ledge of stone and anchored it to the walls. Then, he used his magic to increase the growth of the plants, planning for the rats to use the fibrous material of the grass for nests.

From his borrowed knowledge, he knew that changing the states of Aether was an exhaustive process. By forcing the liquid Aether into a chaotic state and then enforcing order, he would be able to artificially create the circumstances by which it could crystalize. Valterra focused, bringing Aether pouring into the room.

He then condensed it down, down, down, until it became a liquid. The further he condensed it, the more it roiled uncomfortably. Locking his will around the Aether, he forced it to stabilize, causing it to shatter violently. Aether flew outward from that singular point, some even striking different rats.

Valterra checked to see if any were dead, and sadly, they had all survived. He would have to wait some more to see if he could get the Framework. Next, he checked to make sure his experiment worked. Shards of crystal Aether were embedded all over the cavern, with a lot of it under the water. Valterra hoped it would increase the Aether levels naturally without it being aligned with him. He wanted the rats to grow wild and untamed. He couldn't wait.

Chapter 17

Exploration & Discovery

Valterra was thinking deeply, with his presence situated above his pedestal. It had been a couple of hours since he had released the rats from their cages so that they could begin roaming. For once, he found himself without any ideas about where to go next. He had four floors now spread out around him. His fourth floor was massive in comparison to his other three, but that didn't surprise him much.

The first three were created when he was all instinct and had no forethought. His instincts didn't know what planning was, as was evident by the fact that those floors had little in the way of an ecosystem or various interacting parts. They were just a singular room with a guardian-type monster. His monsters didn't even stay in their rooms most of the time, content to test their might against the creatures attempting to claim territory in the turf war.

He knew he was 45% of the way to his next Ascension. He wondered what it would bring and what new Frameworks he would have to choose from. But those thoughts could wait. What he wanted to do right now was explore. He had claimed a lot of territory under and outside the structure he was in but hadn't explored the structure itself.

He had taken over the basement, sure, but he hadn't spent time exploring the world above. It was time to do so. Bringing his associated Frameworks to the forefront of his mind, he summoned three Hunting Pack-Mantises just outside his first floor. Each one stood roughly seven to eight inches tall, with wickedly barbed forelimbs flexing and antennae twitching.

Satisfied, he tied their Aether cores to himself via a line of Aether, which his instincts told him was necessary if they were to remain under his control once they left his territory. Unlike his Mouse Scouts, who were still slumbering, the mantises' stage of Ascension didn't offer an enlarged Aether core and were perfect for venturing beyond his boundaries.

The Aether link would also allow him to hijack their vision so that he could explore in real-time rather than just feel their emotions. With a mental command, one flew out of the dungeon's entrance, while the other two flew within the walls of the structure, one heading south and the other flying west.

Valterra waited a moment for them to leave the dungeon territory that made up his body and then peered through their vision. It was difficult at first, like trying to read three different system notifications at the same time, but gradually, he got the hang of it.

The first thing he learned, as his bug outside flew out from under the wooden structure and then higher into the sky, was that this shelter or building was in the middle of a forest. Tall trees stretched their canopies out over a large clearing, of which the building only occupied a small portion. The shadows of those tall trees terrified his insect scout, its instincts screaming that there was danger hiding in their depths.

Turning the bug back toward the building, Valterra finally got a good look at where he had been created. Rather than being tall and imposing like he thought it would be, the building was quite squat and spread out, sprawling all over the clearing. His memories gave him a hazy word. *A cabin?* he thought. The structure seemed too big for the word, but he shook off those thoughts and examined the "cabin" with interest.

The main building was rectangular, with a wing jutting off to the left where it connected to another rectangular section. The roofs of each building were conical, overlapping where the wing met the main building. Another structure of flat wooden planks ran the length of the building, elevated above the ground and forming what he knew to be the shadowed under-place that made up the turf war.

This structure ran around the length of the buildings, and looking at it from above, it seemed as though the owner had never wanted to touch the ground after leaving the house. Again, his creator's hazy memories provided a word for the structure.

A deck, huh? What weird names for things. Tall folk are weird.

Lost in his ruminations, the Core failed to see the shadow that fell over the bug until his connection to it ceased utterly. His final view was of a sharp beak and a piercing cry. This wasn't the first time he had lost a creature to an outsider, but he still found the sensation unpleasant to the extreme. He shook it off after a moment of mourning lost potential and turned to his remaining two bugs.

Focusing on what they were seeing, he saw that one had found a way to get into the building through a hole in the wall. It had to widen the hole significantly first, but its powerful limbs seemed capable of the task. Once it was through, it took to the air, flying straight up toward the ceiling to get a good view of the inside.

Valterra was thrilled at the thought of exploring this immense place, but its size also filled him with a cautious terror. Something that needed space this big to live in would be huge in comparison to his tiny core or even his new hunting bugs. He had brushed against this realization when he claimed the basement, and his forcefully imparted hazy memories had given him further perspective. However, it was one thing to see a space in a memory and another to see it in person with his own perspective.

This world above was cluttered with things—huge, monstrous things. Some were carved from wood and some had huge stone slabs laid atop them. As he directed his insect closer, he found that all manner of large implements were clustered on top, from huge fangs of metal to wooden bowls and tools. He didn't even know what half of them were for! He made his insect move on and then mentally sat back to process the alien sights he had seen.

He had known, of course, that he had been created by whoever lived here, a mage by the name of Calamvor. Even now, vocabulary drifted through his mind for all of the things he had seen, hazy constructs that flitted around his core, but the memories made them seem small. To Valterra, though, these things were huge! What kind of creature was his creator that he could use and manipulate such things?

How could such a creature be killed? Even all of his current creatures wouldn't be able to do such a thing, even if they combined their strength. Even his Great Tidal Whale, the highest-Ranked creature he possessed, would perhaps only injure it before being slain. For the first time in his short existence, Valterra doubted if he was capable of protecting his territory if such creatures would eventually become invaders. The high spirits had said that the divine dungeons were lauded as important and divine instruments by the tall folk.

But he was tiny. He had thought that the ants had been decent opponents after all! What would he be but an interesting diversion, especially if he could be taken so easily? *I have to hide,* he thought. *I need to claim more territory, so much territory that finding me would be impossible. I'm so tiny—surely, they would miss me if they had to search the entire forest. Yes, that is what I need to do, I...*

The declaration died unthought as his instincts screamed at him. Keeping his links with his remaining bugs open so they could keep exploring, he let his awareness spread out to the entirety of his dungeon, feeling for where the danger was coming from. He found it in a wave of ants encroaching upon his territory, making a beeline for his dungeon entrance. With a mental grimace, he gave up on his plans of exploration for the moment. He had a war to finish.

Chapter 18

The War of the Ants

The invaders were here. The Queen could sense it through the bond she shared with her master. She had prepared as best she could for this eventuality, but her brood had been decimated by the previous attack and then she and her colony had undergone the Ascension process, leaving little time to prepare when she awoke.

Still, she had done her best, putting her new powers to the test by flooding her children with Aether to speed up their growth. That had required heaps of prey to fuel, but the colony had done its best and was now reaping the rewards. Although low on Aether and food, they had doubled their original number of adults, bringing the total into the forties.

There were seven Danian Nobles now, each one large and impressive, especially now that they had their own Aether cores. Sure, they were small cores, barely slivers, but they made each ant into a conduit of the colony's might. Now, they would be needed more than ever. She released the awaited pheromones and the colony burst into action. The nobles bowed before making their way out, followed by three workers each.

Twenty-eight Danians, each one prepared to lay down their life for their master. The Queen felt a flash of irritation at having to stay put but she shook the selfish thought away. Her existence was the very life of the colony, and she would do her duty. Her colony would continue to serve and Ascend to reach the dizzying heights her master occupied.

Instead, she turned her mind to the task of laying more eggs. Regardless of the outcome of the battle, the colony needed more workers and nobles. She stoked the Aether within her core and sent waves of the life-giving substance out to her people. Workers moved faster and the eggs were laid quickly. The Queen attempted to put the conflict from her mind, even as she sent Aether to her soldiers. They would need all the help she could give.

Even as the wave of black chitin approached like a black tide, the Mouse Soldier remained unfazed. This was an enemy they had faced before and beaten off. According to his new brethren, the Mouse Scouts, they had come in a great army that had been repelled. Those Mouse Scouts now stood beside him, and it felt strange to no longer be the highest Ascended mouse.

They were stationed on the outskirts of the serpent guardian's domain. The scaled one lay coiled to one side, his mottled green scales blending in with the green stalks around him. The Mouse Soldier traded glances with the snake as they both acknowledged each other. The mouse felt his right paw itch as it gripped his needle, feeling the sudden urge to test himself against the creature. They both had two Ascensions under their belts. Who would come out on top if they faced each other in battle?

It took a measure of subconscious self-control to turn his attention back to the approaching ants. It was the battle lust inscribed within his stage of Ascension that drove him to seek combat. He wasn't aware, of course, that Ile'Fen, the High Spirit of Conflict, had designed his Framework. Conflict was inevitable for the mouse guardian; he just wasn't self-aware enough to see it.

Attention back on the ants, the mouse's dark eyes took in the changes. They also seemed to have Ascended up a stage. They were larger than before with enlarged mandibles and gleaming black chitin with green veins lining

the length of them. The mouse took in the changes with equanimity, but inside, he felt the first stirrings of anxiety. There was a horde of the creatures approaching, and there was no guarantee of survival.

Base instincts took over, and he stuck his needle in the ground before taking his whiskers in both paws, giving them a good grooming. He didn't notice the other mice following his example, some even beginning to groom each other's fur. By the time the mouse guardian had finished, the ants were close enough for a charge, but he held off. His lord had already let him know through their bond that he was moving.

He received an affirmative when the ants were close enough that he could see the little pockets of their compound eyes. With a bellow of suppressed bloodlust and stress, the mouse charged into the fray. His first blow pierced right through chitin and into the inner flesh of the lead ant's head, killing it almost instantly. He still had to dodge the reflexive biting action of its mandibles, but that was easily done. The following clashes were anything but simple.

He quickly fell into a rhythm, his needle rising and falling as the ants piled up against the line of mice and Danians. Out of the corners of his eyes, the mouse could see the snake striking rapidly, consuming ants whole. The ants were swarming the snake, but the mouse guardian could do nothing to aid his scaled counterpart. His paws were full trying to keep his kin beasts— the younger mice—alive in their struggle against the large ants.

Ironically or perhaps justifiably, it was the Danians making the biggest impact on the defense. They were the largest group of defenders, and they seemed to move faster and quicker than they should have been able to. Moving silently and yet communicating effortlessly in ways he didn't understand, they were able to pick apart the ants that approached their section. Each slain ant seemed to empower them further and they tore into the invaders with what the mouse could only describe as manic fervor.

There were still too many ants. The defensive line was pushed back as the weight of bodies overwhelmed the defenders. A Mouse Scout fell, and the Mouse Soldier leaped forward, beating back the ants for a moment to give the scout room to recover and retreat. The mouse guardian received a nasty gash for his trouble, but his fellow mouse was alive, and that was all that mattered. They fell back until they were fighting before the very entrance of the dungeon itself. Ants littered the ground, and yet there were still more climbing over their fallen brethren.

The Mouse Soldier felt a strange emotion well up within him at the sight. He didn't know it, didn't have the self-awareness to, but it was respect. Here was a worthy battle against worthy opponents who feared neither defeat nor dying. As they closed in, he felt his lord's approval flow through their bond and saw movement beyond the lines of ants.

Behind the black tide came orange shapes. A new kind of creature, almost two dozen of them, came bounding out of the greenery to slam into the rear of the ant tide. Almost immediately, the pressure of bodies grew more manageable as the ants turned around to deal with the new threat. Letting loose with a tired bass squeak, the Mouse Soldier charged back into the fray, followed closely by the rest of his impromptu war host.

It ended swiftly after that, and the mouse was left gulping in great gasps of air, letting the Aether of the fallen seep into his Aether core. He wasn't quite at the next stage yet, but Aether thrummed powerfully in his veins, letting him know he was getting closer. The strange four-legged creatures with vibrant skin had dispersed back into the wild land as soon as the battle was finished. It was obvious they were wilder than him and his mice, brought together only by the will of his lord.

The mice and Danians hadn't escaped unscathed. The battle had been fierce, and Danian bodies littered the ground. Only three mice had fallen—two from the scouts and one of the younger Mouse Guards. The Mouse Soldier gathered the limp body in his arms and carried it in a solemn procession back to the pedestal of his lord, the scouts doing the same for their fallen. He left the Danians to do whatever they wanted with their fallen.

Laying their burdens down, they watched as their lord answered their requests. The bodies of their comrades faded into motes of Aether that returned to their lord's embrace. From Aether they had been created and to Aether they returned. That would have to be enough. The Mouse Soldier led the living in the ritual of subservience, the ranks of mice kneeling before their lord.

"Are you satisfied, brother?" Ile'Fen asked his brooding sibling. He watched as Qual'Dorn stiffened before letting out a self-deprecating chuckle.

"Yes, yes, I am satisfied. It seems your creations are still superior when it comes to battle."

"Of course," Ile'Fen said simply, choosing to ignore his brother's snort of irritation. "Come now, brother, you did not truly think that your ants would overcome Valterra's creatures, did you? After all, the majority of them were an entire stage higher on their Paths. And," he said, making sure to grab his brother's attention before continuing, "while my creations are certainly proving their worth, that one mouse in particular—it was his own creation that decided the battle."

"Hmm." Qual'Dorn agreed, though reluctantly by his tone. "His Danians do seem to be effective, aggravating as it is that a child's creation is superior to my own. Although..." His tone took on a thoughtful air. "I did have a hand in this latest stage, so perhaps it would be better to say that I beat myself, hmm?"

Ile'Fen chuckled and then laughed, his merriment brief but genuine. He clapped his brother on the shoulder and pulled him in for a side hug. "Sure, sure, I'll let you have that one. Besides, is it not enough that young Valterra will grow from this engagement? Those mice of his are close to their next stage, and so is his snake. A short and swift conflict."

Qual'Dorn's eyes took on a knowing glint and Ile'Fen sighed, nodding to his brother's unasked question. "I am fine, brother. My burden is not yet so heavy that I cannot bear it." No more words needed to be spoken, so they both simply watched as Valterra reaped the rewards of this latest conflict.

Ile'Fen ignored the constant pull on his nature as it tried to shift his attention north. Ignored the screams and the horror.

Valterra was equal parts frustrated, saddened, and excited. His Sylcyne Mountain Efts had done their job perfectly despite some hiccups. He had meant to include them in the fight much sooner but had run into a hurdle he hadn't expected. His power over Aether was somehow limited around invaders as if their Aether provided a shield from his influence. Such a large gathering of invaders provided quite the shield against his influence.

So, he had been forced to summon his reinforcements quite a distance away, comparatively, and it had taken some time before they had arrived. Because of that detail, he had lost more creatures that otherwise wouldn't have died. That fact hurt almost as much as the losses themselves. The only thing that made the loss bearable was that now he had a new Framework.

Black Warden Ant (Unique, Rank F - Copper)
A singular creation of Qual'Dorn, Black Warden Ants were created to be caretakers, cultivating their given territory for greater growth. When its territory is threatened, this ant bands together with others of its kind in large groups, surging forth to purge the perceived threat from their lands. Currently "Unique," these ants are found nowhere else in the world.
Note: This is a multilayered Framework consisting of separate internal Paths of Ascension. Those Paths are Queen, Warden, and Drones. These Paths may be summoned as separate dungeon monsters but be warned. Ant monsters made in such a way will see themselves as belonging to another colony and will fight to the death.

As the first dungeon to use such a creature as a dungeon monster, you will be able to create and modify its Path of Ascension freely.

Warning! May have unforeseen consequences.

Error! The previous link on this Path of Ascension is locked due to its Framework being scoured from your core. Carpenter Ant (Mundane) will remain unavailable.

It seemed the consequences of his past experimentation would come into play sooner than he had thought, but at least it didn't prevent him from claiming entirely unrelated Frameworks. From the feeling he got, it would seem that if he came across any other forms of carpenter ants he would be unable to claim them even if they were further up the Path of Ascension. The Black Warden Ants were only claimable because they were an entirely new creation and unique in their own right.

Essentially, he could claim them for the same reason that the Danians were still available. The Danians were completely different from the carpenter ants in form but not necessarily in function. Actually, that was rather confusing. Valterra couldn't make out why he couldn't recover the Carpenter Ant Framework. He hummed to himself before giving up that line of thinking. He would either figure it out in the future or not.

His attention was quickly claimed by the frantic motions of one of his exploring bugs. While the conflict had seemed long, in reality it hadn't taken much time at all, but it had been long enough for one of his bugs to reach the far end of the west wing. It was there that it was going berserk trying to get his attention.

It had found his creator.

It had found the corpse of Calamvor.

Chapter 19

A Divine Discussion

It was a strange experience for Valterra to gaze upon his creator. Calamvor was very much deceased, of course, but Valterra had already heard as much from the High Council. It was different seeing him in the flesh, even if it was through the multifaceted eyes of one of his creations. The first thing Valterra noticed was not the apparent ancientness of the man who had created him, it wasn't the way he was sprawled against the wall clutching at his chest, and it wasn't the way Calamvor's face was etched in a rictus of pain, sorrow, and despair.

It was the appearance of preservation. At this point, a week and a half after his death, Calamvor's body should have been decaying and falling apart, his innards oozing out of him as his body was liquefied. Looking at him now, Valterra could find no such signs of decay.

He was stuck staring, his insect creature hovering in place to provide steady vision. He took in the being that would have enslaved him—his frozen, dim eyes and old, wizened flesh. His face was a frozen mask of pain, and suddenly, Valterra chuckled. His joy reverberated through his dungeon, all his childish fear leaving him as he laughed. He could feel his creatures react to his laughter and realized that they had felt his fear subconsciously, attempting to prepare for another imminent invasion.

And what had prompted this laughter, this joy? Valterra realized that no other creature knew he existed. The master of this house, the one capable of finding and claiming him, was already dead. He was surrounded by a forest, a dangerous forest that would keep out intruders even better than he could.

He truly had no enemies except the denizens of the forest. Caution was required but not fear. Hadn't he already faced a great invasion and won? In that moment, Valterra determined within himself that he wouldn't let fear drive him again.

He looked once more at the seemingly preserved corpse of his creator, and his mind was suddenly filled with a mischievous thought. *I wonder what Framework I'd get from him?* Following that thought, he expanded his territory once more, claiming more and more of the house en route to his creator's corpse.

He didn't know if he would be able to absorb the Framework since it had been so long since Calamvor's death, but he wanted to try. A creature that could grow powerful enough to create a being like himself? That could be a potent defender.

It didn't take Valterra long. The power of his name, coupled with his determination to push through the discomfort of growing swiftly, meant that it only took him an hour to retrace his insect's path. As he made it to the location of his creator's corpse, he found that the room his creator had died in was flooded with Aether. Fascinated by this discovery, Valterra put his goal of absorbing his creator on hold as he dove into examining what made the room so special.

It took him around an hour to discover the reason. Tiny sigils had been carved into the stone surrounding the room, preventing the Aether from escaping into the rest of the house. The floor was also carved in intricate lines that made a dizzying display. Now that it was a part of his body, Valterra felt odd. He could almost feel a connection to it but had only fragmented knowledge of high magic and so couldn't make heads or tails of it.

What surprised him more was turning his 'gaze' upon his creator's corpse, only to discover that it was leaking Aether into the air. Large plumes of Aether left the body to join what was already in the room, and Valterra mentally gaped at the amount. With the Aether that was already in the air and the time of death being well over a week ago, Calamvor must have had tremendous amounts of Aether within his body. Was this how he hadn't decayed yet?

Valterra didn't know, but he reached forward to claim the Framework. And hit a giant wall. A giant divine wall. A divine wall with the signature of the High Council written all over it. So Valterra did the only thing he could think of and built a mental battering ram made up of his name, sending it crashing into the wall. That did get some attention, and he felt the presence of divinity as one of the High Council looked more closely.

"Well, hello there, funny guy!" A mischievous voice rang out inside Valterra's head, and he recognized it as Trik'Weri. "What have we got here? Ohoho! So you've found the body of your creator, eh? Not only that, but I assume you want the Framework, huh?" At Valterra's stunned mental nod, Trik'Weri's voice gained a kind of pained tone.

"Eh, sorry, little one. No can do. As hilarious as it would be to watch you run around with tiny humans, they are not yours to play with. They are divine, you see. Well, not strictly divine as they don't have a Divine Spark, but their Framework is divine in nature. They are like you, with true sapience, and having them become dungeon monsters would be like slavery to some extent, not to mention the other catastrophic consequences. So, sorry, but no."

But my name! Valterra cried out as he felt Trik'Weri's presence retreat. *It says I can use divine servants!*

He felt the presence return, and Trik'Weri's voice took on a calm explanatory tone. "I know, I know, but those are the direct servants of us Spirits, creatures created by us to serve us. They aren't like the earthly races at all." Valterra heard a sigh as Trik'Weri tried a different explanation. "Look, it all has to do with Authority. It's a substance of the Maker in every

being, and it marks them as his. Only truly sapient beings have the ability to utilize Authority to affect reality outside of themselves. It's called the Mark of the Maker.

"The mortals are capable of great things because they can utilize their Authority to change the world. It's how they cast magic and grow in power. You do this as well and in many of the same ways. Claiming territory is you asserting your Authority as a dungeon on the land around you. It bows to your will and becomes a part of you.

"The same thing happens to the creatures you claim as monsters and any you summon with a Framework. They recognize your Authority over them and obey you completely. Your creatures also use your Authority to grow, progressing much faster along their Paths of Ascension than in the wild. You permit them to do so.

"As you grow in power, so do your creatures, and they only do so within the bounds of your dungeon. There are only a few places in the wild that offer the necessary amount of Aether for creatures to reach the heights of power. Even if your creatures grow to possess greater intelligence, even to the level of sapience, their Sparks will be confined to the shape of their Frameworks. Without you, they would go mad."

Trik'Weri stopped for a moment to give Valterra time to process the information before continuing, "You've seen the *Rankings*, yes?" At Valterra's affirmation, Trik'Weri's tone shifted to a bit more of a lecturing one. "The Rankings let divine dungeons accurately assess the strength of their creatures, but it is more than that. The Path of Ascension has multiple stages across multiple levels, even allowing some creatures to change their nature completely."

"This is all made possible by the Aether core provided to them when they Ascend the first time. The Aether core and the Framework are two parts of a whole—you can't have one without the other. The Rankings gauge the amount of Aether accumulated within their core and assign an alphabetical Rank from lowest to highest, with F being the lowest and A being the highest."

"Do you know, Valterra, what Rank Calamvor's Framework would have been if he had one?"

Valterra didn't know and said as much. He would have had to be pretty high on the list, probably the highest one.

"He would have been *Mundane*, not even on the Ranking."

At this, Valterra's mind shut down. What did that mean? Trik'Weri had to be joking with him. There was no way that Calamvor was *Mundane*. After all, he had seen the plumes of Aether coming off him in waves. Then Valterra's brain caught up and he put together the pieces. Rankings, Path of Ascension, Mark of the Maker, Aether cores, and Frameworks. If Calamvor would have started as *Mundane* and then been given a Path of Ascension, what heights would he have reached?

Trik'Weri's knowing tone of voice brought him out of his internal shock. "Do you see? The moment we let you claim this corpse, a Framework will be created. A Framework that the System will attempt to give to every human within the reach of our pantheon. That Framework will offer the mortals a chance to accumulate enough Aether to take a step forward on the Path of Ascension. It would then give them an Aether core and the ability to grow astronomically powerful. Well, more powerful than they already are."

Something in Trik'Weri's tone had Valterra asking, *What do you mean?*

"Hmm. Humans and the other mortals have long had their own methods of taking steps upon the Path of Ascension. Back in the day, a calamity struck the many worlds that the Maker had created from his own breath. An enemy, a servant of his that had fallen, poisoned the creatures of the various worlds, twisting them and breaking them until they were ravenous. We've told you how true monsters are created."

"The Maker, in his wisdom, showed the mortals how to slay the monsters and how to bind their powers to better usage. By purifying a monster's core, a mortal can then absorb the monster's essence and form an Aether core of their own. If we were using the System's terminology, we would say that they have then taken their first step on the Path of

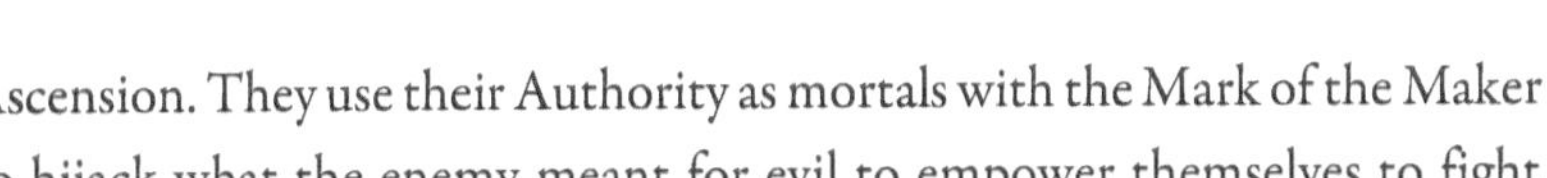

Ascension. They use their Authority as mortals with the Mark of the Maker to hijack what the enemy meant for evil to empower themselves to fight back."

"The main issue with you attempting to claim Calamvor's corpse is that many humans have their own cores they have taken from monsters and repurposed. If you then introduce a Framework, many of them will Ascend immediately due to the content of Aether in their bodies and try to form a natural Aether core. The two cores will clash, and the ensuing maelstrom of Aether will claim countless lives, even with it affecting just the humans."

"The land would become a barren waste, and monsters would mutate at a frightening speed. Many of the humans affected would become monsters themselves, and that is something we cannot allow. So, I'm sorry, but no. We as the High Council could never condone such an outcome as it might bring the wrath of the Maker upon us and you for having been the cause."

Valterra contemplated that reality and hummed to himself as Trik'Weri fell silent. Everything was so complicated. That didn't mean he was done trying to claim the corpse. While it was true that it would be bad news, there had to be something he could get out of this. Thinking quickly, he projected his thoughts to Trik'Weri. *What about the Framework's Potential? This would have provided me with immense growth, right? So what do I get for relinquishing it?*

Trik'Weri's voice came back amused. "Eh, what's this? Trying to bargain, eh? Sorry, mate, but you don't have much ground to stand on."

Valterra didn't relent, though. *His body should be mine. He would have enslaved me; it's only right that I decide his fate! Why should I get nothing but his hazy memories and instincts you would have given me anyway?*

"Hmm. You know what, squirt? You may have some ground to stand on after all. There would be some semblance of justice to giving you something, but it depends on what you want. What are you planning to do with this Potential if I grant it to you?" His voice was full of mischief, and Valterra caught on that he was skirting the rules a little for some reason of his own. There was also that mention of the word "Potential" like it meant something more to Trik'Weri than Valterra knew.

Well, you have divine servants, right? Not to be ungrateful, but give me the Potential to create my own, from the start of their Ascension to their end. You said my creatures might gain minds of their own, right? Give me the ability to increase that Potential within the bounds of my dungeon. I need protectors, so I want the ability to determine who my champions are. Valterra didn't know where this eloquence was coming from, but it bubbled forth from his being like water. Even Trik'Weri seemed stunned by his words.

"Huh," Trik'Weri stated, "You continue to surprise me, squirt. Very well. I'll grant you your Potential but you must give me something in return." Valterra felt more than saw Trik'Weri's vulpine grin, one full of sharp teeth. "A favor, in the future, to be called upon whenever I want. Decide quickly. Our talk has taken long enough, and the others are starting to take notice. Believe me when I say you don't want Tal'Irieth to take over these negotiations."

Valterra frowned mentally but agreed with some stipulations. *As long as it doesn't involve controlling me or claiming me, then I agree.* He heard Trik'Weri sniff in disdain.

"As if I would try such a thing after giving you that whole spiel. You've got a deal, mate. You can absorb the corpse now. You will be barred from claiming, and thus creating, the Framework. However, the Potential you want will be yours. Keep on being entertaining, and remember my favor."

With that, Trik'Weri's presence dissipated like mist, and Valterra sagged with relief. It had been a gamble, and now he had a debt hanging over his head, but as he turned to the corpse of his creator, all he was filled with was a giddy joy. Time to see what he had gained.

Chapter 20

Ignition

Valterra gingerly reached out to dissolve the corpse, half expecting to be stopped again. He was not. Instead, Calamvor's body glowed before breaking apart into drifting lights that remained floating in the air, until all that was left of the great Archmage Calamvor was a host of dancing lights. Valterra was struck dumb by the beauty of it all, watching in awe as the light show floated around the ritual room.

The moment ended abruptly as the lights moved, their presence searing their way through his dungeon as they were drawn inexorably to his core. It didn't take long for the stream of light to arrive, and once it did, the System the High Council had put in place went nuts.

***Error* Core cannot acquire Framework "Human" due to Divine Edict.**

***Error* Divine Energy detected... Analyzing... Confirmed. (And there we go. Try not to die now.) – Deleted**

The Core, Valterra Unok'Davaas, will be granted Divine Potential equivalent to the Ascension Rank of the corpse's unique Spark signature.

Checking Database... Loading... Loading... Found.

Calculating the Divine Potential of the individual, Calamvor Talios, Archmage of House Talios
Ascension Rank (Rank S - Adamantium)

Calculating... Shattered Spark determined. Partial value of Divine Potential has been calculated.

The Core, Valterra Unok'Davaas, is granted 5,693 points of Divine Potential.

Error No Divine Spark detected. The Core is too small to hold the granted Divine Potential.

Destruction imminent!

(Ah, what did you go and do this for, little one? Hold on, let me try something.)

— Krat'Imos

Error Divine Energy detected... Analyzing... Confirmed. Formation of a Divine Spark authorized. Ignition will require Divine Potential. Divine Potential found.
Ignition will begin in 3... 2... 1... Igniting.

Valterra felt his world shake as his core exploded with light. Transcendent beams lasered their way out of his crystalline depths, carving paths into the walls of his first floor. His pedestal lit up like a beacon as his entire being was set aflame. He tried staying conscious, but it was a losing battle. Eventually, the dark closed in on him despite the light radiating from his depths.

Valterra drifted in a haze of half-formed thoughts and dreams. He saw great monoliths and chaotic battles, times of peaceful meditation, and stress-inducing tests. As more and more images flashed by, he gradually understood what he was seeing. He was seeing a play-by-play of his creator's life but fragmented and disjointed, incomplete. Calamvor in all of his glory and disgrace flashed by in breathless moments. All of his potential wrapped up in a haze of recollection and Valterra viewed them as though he was nothing more than a spectator.

Gradually, the whole thing grew hazy and Valterra's vision wavered. As he recovered, he realized that once again, he was surrounded by the High Council, most of whom were staring down at him with something akin to sympathy. Tal'Irieth didn't even give him time to speak as he bellowed down at him, "Do you have any idea what you've done!?"

As Valterra shrunk back at the sudden noise, one of the other spirits spoke up. "Now that is hardly fair, Tal. The little one didn't know what he was doing. How could he know that the System would malfunction as it did and allow him to partially absorb a Framework not meant for him?"

Tal'Irieth rounded on the speaker. "A System you built, Kratty! I thought you patched all the bugs centuries ago!"

The spirit, who must've been Krat'Imos, shrugged his huge shoulders. "I don't know, Tal. He's such a wee thing. Maybe some of it fell through the cracks. It doesn't matter now, though, does it? He's got the Spark now, and there ain't no way he can give it back without us ending his life." At this, his voice took on a dangerous hint to it. "And High Seat or no, Tal, I won't be going along with murder. Especially not now that he's one of ours in the true sense."

Tal'Irieth sighed and turned back to Valterra who was trembling mentally from all of the divine auras flaring around him. Gradually, his aura relaxed, and Valterra felt like he could breathe again. "I'm sorry for yelling, little one. It is not your fault that things happened the way they did."

Valterra noticed Trik'Weri staring at him intently, a warning look in his eyes. Valterra got the message. What happened would remain a secret.

That didn't stop the boiling anger that built up within his core. Tirk'Weri had almost gotten him killed. He had known it would be dangerous when he offered his bargain. Valterra fumed but slowly grew more determined.

If Trik'Weri wanted to play that way, then fine. Valterra would wait and bide his time. Eventually, he would be able to vent his anger on the spirit. The Core grudgingly admitted to himself that whatever Trik'Weri had planned had worked out, but he hated feeling like he was something disposable.

"Now, though." Valterra looked back to Tal'Irieth as the tall spirit began speaking once more. "We need to explain what has happened to you. The short answer is that you've achieved something that takes most divine dungeons decades to do. You've ignited a Divine Spark."

Seeing Valterra's blank stare, Tal'Irieth sighed and continued, "When a dungeon Ascends through its different stages, it gains access to more and more of the System, which in turn gives it new avenues through which it can achieve growth. One such path is the slow accumulation of Divine Potential. Much of the reason why the mortal races attribute divinity to divine dungeons is because of this.

"Every creature of a certain Ascension threshold produces Divine Potential, but oftentimes, it is minuscule and barely noticeable. For most creatures, it pools within their Spark Matrix until there's a catalyst, whereupon it manifests as special abilities, magical powers, or domains. Whole dynasties have been developed around particular Paths of Ascension with cultivated catalysts designed to produce similar abilities generation after generation.

"Divine dungeons, on the other hand—when they have reached their fifth Ascension—produce small amounts of Divine Potential along with vast amounts of Aether, which acts as its own catalyst for growth. This is why the mortal races try their hand at dungeon delving. Many do it simply for the Aether because it enhances their bodies and minds and makes it possible to achieve their next stage of Ascension quicker."

"But some mortals know that the deeper they can delve, the better the chance they have at obtaining more Potential and adding it to their own pool. This Potential allows them to alter their Ascensions to a certain degree, and it is that slim grasp of divinity that can transform them from simple mortals to gods amongst men. The deeper they go and the more Divine Potential they can steal from a dungeon, the higher they can climb up the ladder of power."

"The other reason the mortals attribute divinity to the dungeons is because of what the dungeons can do with all of that Potential. They don't just give it away to dungeon delvers; they use it to create wonders, creatures that defy explanation, and artifacts that countries go to war for."

At Valterra's stunned silence, Tal'Irieth chuckled. Exasperation filled his voice again as he continued, "And you, my dear boy, have skipped hundreds of steps. The final culminating desire of every divine dungeon is to survive enough raids and accumulate enough Divine Potential that they can eventually ignite a Divine Spark, yet you've done it within a couple of weeks of existing!"

"What he is trying to say is, well, good job."

Valterra turned toward the voice to see Maph'Ira give him a half-hearted thumbs up. He figured that was a good thing.

"Part of the reason it worked at all is because you're so small," Krat'Imos interjected. "Normally, by the time divine dungeons have access to Divine Potential, they are huge crystalline structures a couple of feet long. To ignite a Spark Matrix that big, they would need hundreds of thousands of units of Divine Potential, which would take a century or more to collect if they don't get claimed by some mortal monarch first."

So... I'm lucky? Valterra asked tentatively. At his mental question, the tension broke, and the whole council roared with laughter.

"Lucky, he says!" Qual'Dorn chortled. "My dear little core, you have no idea."

Tal'Irieth wiped a tear from his eye before sobering a little. "Qual'Dorn is right, I'm afraid. You truly have no idea how close you were to death.

Trying to claim that much Potential without being ready for it should have shattered your core into tiny pieces. The fact that you did not is indeed lucky." Looking at Valterra and seemingly knowing that his words had gotten through, Tal'Irieth smiled down at him.

"You truly are a remarkable little core, and Trik'Weri was right when he said that you have provided more entertaining moments than much of the mortal world in the last century or so. There is so much to tell you about your new divinity, but we have run out of time. We cannot afford to draw attention to you now more than we already have. Do your best to grow and figure things out as best you can. Keep in mind that being divine is just as much about responsibility as it is wielding power."

With those final words, the council faded away into hazy, indistinct shapes as Valterra's consciousness faded to black.

Chapter 21

Consequences Part 1

The enchanted needle flashed as the Mouse Soldier went through the motions of fighting an imaginary enemy. He could feel the Aether in his veins powering his motions and giving his paws strength. He was close to his third Ascension; he could feel it. All he needed was a worthy fight, and he would break through the gap.

He gnashed his teeth in frustration as he turned to gaze upon the pedestal of his lord. He couldn't leave now to find such a fight. Not with his lord in such a state. It had already been two days since his lord had blazed with glorious light. Now his creator was silent and unmoving apart from the breaths of Aether, which proved he still lived. The mouse guardian huffed in frustration. His personal growth would mean nothing if the Core was destroyed or claimed.

No, the mouse realized. His frustration came from another place. He had snuck down to glance at the fourth floor, and the monsters there had shaken him badly. How could he claim to be the primary guardian of his lord when he had such creatures to call on for assistance? A new fear shook him at this moment.

What if his lord moved his pedestal lower, to the end of that monstrous sunken labyrinth? The way he was now, the mouse doubted he would be able to reach the pedestal in one piece, much less alive. He steeled himself and began practicing once more, throwing himself at imaginary enemies. He would not fail. He would not— Suddenly, panicked squeaks interrupted him.

He turned just as one of the younger mice arrived at the entrance to his cavern. It squeaked rapidly in its panic, but the Mouse Soldier understood; his charges were in danger. He barreled up the incline to the entrance, directing his not-so-little kin to tell the Danians to prepare to guard his lord in his absence. He might have told the Mouse Scouts but they had departed his lord's territory as soon as the war with the ants had finished to track down the Queen of the hostile colony.

He took to all four paws, holding his needle between his jaws so that he could move more quickly. It didn't take him long to find the fight as fierce squeaking mixed with the staccato bellows of some other creature echoed through the no man's land outside the entrance of the dungeon. As he passed the boundary, he saw that even the scaled guardian had been drawn into combat as well, as the serpent was nowhere to be seen.

Charging forth, he came upon a scene of chaotic battle and one that would have looked comical from one of the tall folks' perspective. Or they would have been terrified by the amount of blood being spilled in vicious combat.

The mice were losing.

One of their number was already down, not moving a whisker, with terrible claw wounds. The Mouse Soldier knew his kin beast was dead, and that fact filled him with a rage that almost chased away the fear that gripped his heart when he saw their opponent.

Black fur streaked with gray and a long lean form that nonetheless held immense strength, rippling with muscle as the creature snapped and bit at the other four mice. The assistance of the other guardian was the only thing that kept the mice from instant defeat, having wrapped his length around the creature's back half, constricting with his mighty coils and biting with his fearsome fangs.

Even hindered, the creature was a mighty foe and caught one of the mice with a swipe of its paw, sending droplets of ruby blood flying. The Mouse Soldier saw red. Spitting his needle into his paw, the large mouse charged, all eleven inches of him from the tip of his nose to his tail thrumming with battle lust. Hearing his bass squeak of challenge, the other mice got out of his way as he slammed into the invader needle first. There was little in the way of intricacies to the fight. This was a fight to the death, and very little honor could be found in the tactics of both beasts.

The Mouse Soldier drove his needle into the creature repeatedly, and it responded by snapping its fearsome jaws at the mouse. Using his other paw, the mouse caught the bottom of his opponent's jaw and forced it shut, avoiding the loss of his arm at the beast's jaws. With both paws engaged he could no longer defend his side, and he felt searing pain as the claws of the creature raked him, carving red furrows into his fur.

Letting out a squeak of pain, he twisted, sending his prehensile tail whipping into his opponent's eye. Rearing back, the creature retreated, but the Mouse Guard didn't let up. He leaped to the side and up, scrabbling onto the creature's back behind the fearsome jaws. The creature tried to twist to reach him, but at that moment, his fellow guardian hissed in triumph as he constricted one final time.

With a barely audible crunch, the creature's spine snapped and it howled in rage and pain. The Mouse Soldier did not waste the moment his fellow guardian had given him. He lunged forward, driving his needle into the beast's left eye. He withdrew and slammed it in again, repeating the action even after the beast had fallen, driven by white-hot rage. It was the shock of the Aether hitting him that stopped his tirade.

A wave of Aether, cool and clean, billowed out from his lord. He had awakened. He had seen the end, and he was grateful. There was sorrow there too, the Mouse Soldier realized, as his lord's presence halted at the corpse of the mouse that had fallen in battle. A single tear of Aether coalesced and dropped to splash on the ground near the fallen rodent, and the Mouse Soldier knew his lord truly mourned. It built a resolve in his heart and felt his Spark respond.

A golden light built beneath his fur, shining forth to mingle with the identical light shows happening from his younger kin, the Mouse Guards that partook in the battle. He ignored the light for the moment and turned to his fallen foe, only to see it begin to dissolve into motes of light. The only thing that didn't dissolve was the fur, and even that was being transformed before the Mouse Soldier's eyes. His needle too, he realized. His weapon had begun to levitate along with the fur from the creature, and as they spun in the air, golden light shone from them.

The fur became sleeker and finer, shrinking in on itself until it matched his size. Clasps formed out of gold appeared at one end, and that end shrunk slightly while the other side flared out. Moving through the air, it settled around him, the clasps coming together to attach the garment to itself. It rested there, and he felt a connection form between himself and the item.

That was nothing, though, compared to the change happening to his favored weapon. The needle lengthened, becoming wider and double-edged. The hole where he had gripped it was sliced in half and bent upward, forming a crossguard. A twig hovered over and was shorn down to a wooden handle, which was then fused to the creation by Aether. At its base, the weapon carried a tear-shaped Aether crystal as a pommel.

The mouse sat in awe as his lord presented the weapon to him by tapping the blade first to his right flank and then his left before presenting the hilt to be taken. The mouse reverently clasped the blade and allowed himself to be led to the first floor in a daze by his kin, who also glowed with the light of Ascension. He could not even fathom the power necessary to create his gifts and was humbled to receive them.

Yet even now in his heart, he felt the fires of Ascension burning and knew he would be ready for whatever came next when he woke. He bundled himself up in his new cloak and gathered his kin close in his nest, beginning his slumber with one final thought. *Praise be to the lord.*

New Framework acquired!

Savage Mink (Rank D - Iron)
A semi-aquatic mammal normally content to build nests along waterways or lakes, this beast has gained an appreciation for blood and the thrill of the hunt. Forsaking its old hunting grounds, it has taken to the forest where it preys on anything it can kill. Despite leaving the waterways it used to call home, this creature retains its waterproof coat and will often hunt during rainstorms to sneak up on prey.
Artifacts created!

Dungeon's Bite (Growth Item, Rank E - Bronze)
Forged by the dungeon Valterra to defend him and bound to one of his creatures, this blade is a fearsome weapon. In the hands of its chosen wielder, it grants effects that bolster the creature in times of battle. In addition, Dungeon's Bite has been bound to a specific creature's Path of Ascension. As the creature Ascends, so will the artifact. This weapon is part of the Dungeon's Raiment set.
Effect:
This weapon is enchanted to hold its edge. It will never rust and cannot be broken by non-magical means. This weapon allows the bonded creature to channel the dungeon's Aether for a short time, giving increased reflexes, stamina, and strength.
Cost of Creation: 75 Divine Potential

Dungeon's Mantle (Growth Item, Rank E - Bronze)
Crafted by the dungeon Valterra as a reward for one of his creatures, this cloak is fashioned from the hide of a Savage Mink and grants various effects to the one who wears it. In addition, Dungeon's Mantle has been bound to an Ascending creature. As the creature Ascends, so will the artifact. This cloak is part of the Dungeon's Raiment set.
Effect:
This cloak is naturally water-resistant and has been enchanted further to confer to its wearer a resistance to water affinity magic. It behaves like a second layer of fur, allowing it to flow with its wearer's movements. If damaged, it will repair itself using the Aether of the

dungeon.
Set Effect:
If both Dungeon's Bite and Dungeon's Mantle are bound to the same creature, it gains the ability to use a small measure of the dungeon Valterra's Authority over the basic elements.
Cost of Creation: 75 Divine Potential

Chapter 22

Consequences Part 2

Toral Li'Ar was on a mission. He was soaring through the air when he felt a pulse of power as it sang through the woods below him. He paused in his flight, curious. He was out and about on the orders of his elder, scouting a few days out from the Mother Tree for any threats. Scrunching his tiny face up in thought, he figured he could afford to deviate, if only to find out where the pulse came from.

He dove and was soon flitting above the branches of the trees in the direction of the pulse he had felt. For whatever reason, the pulse had made him hungry like when the Mother Tree gave forth her fruits. That thought gave speed to his wings and he powered on. He had to dodge three different birds, though, now that he was closer to the forest canopy.

A shadow made him dart around the trunk of a tree, just in time for a beak to snap at where he had been a moment ago. Toral risked a glance backward to confirm his suspicions. Yup, that was a jackdaw, all right. Why was it always a jackdaw? He could almost hear the elders' words in his mind, "Our wings are our most precious pair of limbs, and the Maker chose in his wisdom to also make them beautiful. Beware of creatures who collect shiny things, for they will target you, if only to pluck them from your back."

Toral snarled at the jackdaw, who let out a croak in response. It continued darting after him and Toral continued to evade it, ducking under branches and flitting between leaves. The jackdaw was fast but Toral was faster. He ducked around another tree and darted straight up into the leaves. He watched as the jackdaw continued flying past, having lost sight of the little shiny creature it had been hunting.

Chuckling quietly, Toral gave his iridescent wings a little flutter, enjoying how the sun glinted off them. He was glad he had escaped so easily. Reaching into his vest, he pulled out a tiny glittering particle that easily fit in one hand. He only had one dot of dust, and he didn't want to waste it on something so simple. The elder had strictly forbidden him from using it unless in the most dire of circumstances.

Putting the dot back, he made sure that the jackdaw was gone before continuing his journey. It didn't take him long after that to find what he was looking for. Looking like a cracked eggshell from the distance, he arrived to find a clearing with a massive sprawling building ringed by a large porch. Even as he looked in, he saw that the clearing had some sort of barrier around it that included some of the trees on the outskirts.

He was intrigued to see that although the barrier was damaged, it was in the process of rebuilding itself. Looking down, he saw a variety of beasts clawing at the shield, but they accomplished nothing more than making it ripple a little bit. What interested him was that smaller beasts and some birds could pass right through as if they didn't count. Curious he darted out from the safety of a tree to see if he could pass through and found to his delight that he could. Still, he darted back to safety before any birds tried to test their luck.

He watched with growing intrigue. Why did they want to get in? His wings fluttered in anticipation and he couldn't let go of the idea. Despite knowing he would be scolded when he returned, Toral darted into the barrier and investigated. Dodging under the porch to hide from the birds, he gradually made his way around the house until he came upon the strangest of sights. A mink, and an Ascended one at that, was fighting

against five mice and a snake. It was winning, of course, but finding a snake and mice working together was weird. What came next was even more so.

Squeaking in rage, a huge mouse came charging out of a hole in the wall to engage the mink. With a needle? That it used like a sword? Toral was growing even more confused when he felt a presence stir. He stiffened, turning this way and that, trying to determine the origins of the aura. He wasn't in it; he was just outside the boundary, but as a scout for his people, he had been trained to identify magical signatures and this one, while objectively weak compared to some, was deeper for some reason.

He turned and watched as the mouse defeated his opponent, and then his mouth dropped as it shone with the light of Ascension. Not just the one mouse either, but every creature that had participated in the battle. He watched as the mink disappeared and its pelt was transformed. He watched as the needle was crafted into a blade that rivaled some of the leprechauns'.

He watched the mice troop into the hole in the wall and then watched the grass and ground move to cover the snake that had curled up to Ascend. He shook himself slightly, unable to believe what he was seeing. Gradually the word came to him, and his mind raced with implications.

Dungeon.

He bolted, pushing his wings to their limits. He had to return to the Mother Tree. The elder had to know. He had to call a council. His wings blurred as he burst through the barrier and took to the high skies. This was huge, momentous, impossible. A dungeon, here in the Sylcyne Forest right under their noses. All the struggles of his people could be solved. They had to be told.

He slipped the dot of dust out of his pocket and gripped it tightly. This certainly counted as an emergency. He crushed the glittering mote in his hand and shuddered as Aether flooded his body. His wings hummed and he took on a brilliant glow as he carved a blazing line in the sky back to the Mother Tree. Toral Li'Ar, fairy scout, was on a mission—and he wouldn't be stopped by anything.

Beneath the canopy, cruel glittering eyes watched the path the fairy blazed in the sky. Turning, the small creature beheld the direction that the fairy had taken. Gripping its staff, it laid about itself, rousing other creatures slumbering nearby. With guttural whines for mercy, the others rose as the one wielding the staff pointed. Understanding dawned in the little creatures' eyes and they gazed at the light hungrily before looking at the creature with the staff.

It nodded to them and moved through the forest. It would have to gather the village, but whatever the winged ones wanted, they would claim it first. Too long had they been at the bottom. Too long had they been pushed aside by the taller races and called nasty names. The *Fallen* would not stay that way. Not if Warmeister Geckodo had anything to say about it.

Chapter 23

Rewards for Recklessness

Valterra watched his mice lie down before turning to his notifications. He had dismissed them to check on his dungeon and was glad he had.

He caught the tail end of the fight with the monster and witnessed his guardians' victory. He hadn't quite known what he was doing when he reforged his mouse guardian's sword and created his cloak, but he thought the items had turned out great.

Amazing, in fact. Now he had another way to upgrade his creatures or protect his core. There was also the matter of the new Framework he had gotten, but he dismissed the notification. He would get to it later. It was time to see what the system had in store for him.

Welcome back, Valterra Unok'Davaas!

You have successfully ignited as a Divine Spark.

Required Divine Potential: 5000 Units

Divine Potential remaining: 543 Units (693 -150 for artifact creation) Your inner nature has fundamentally changed, and your system title and boon have changed to reflect this.

The boon "Favor of the Gods" has transformed into "Child of the Gods".
Boon granted: Child of the Gods
Formerly a favored sapient being, you have now transcended your former Spark nature. You are now more akin to a deity than a mortal. To reflect this, the gods have decided to adopt you rather than smite you.
Boon effect:
At each stage of Ascension you reach, you will be able to choose a new Framework from among a list. The Rank of the Framework will be determined by the stage of Ascension as well as any excess growth that you achieve. Divine servants of the gods that are offered as Frameworks become yours alone and can be modified even without the deity's personal direction.

You are now able to create your own Frameworks, either from an existing Framework or from scratch, using Divine Potential. The gods will help you with this by providing instincts on Framework shaping. The Rank of created Frameworks is limited by the number of core Ascensions.

Current number of core Ascensions: 1
Maximum Rank allowed for created Frameworks: Rank E – Bronze

The title "Tiny Dungeon" has transformed into "Transcendent Tiny Dungeon - Divine."

Title granted: Transcendent Tiny Dungeon - Divine
As the tiniest dungeon in existence, you have been granted this title. As the tiniest divinity in existence, this title has been upgraded to Divine Rank instead of the Core being given a separate title.
Title effects:
Aether costs to claim territory are significantly reduced. Territory claimed by the dungeon may be transformed into a divine domain by spending Divine Potential. Uses of Authority within a divine domain cost no Aether.

Divine domains may be named by the Core with a further cost of Divine Potential depending on the size of the domain. Name effects are determined by the meaning of the name given. The High Council will provide guidance on this.
Aether costs to summon creatures from Frameworks you obtain that are larger than "tiny" are reduced by 90%. Frameworks of creatures you obtain will be reconstructed automatically to fit a 1/24 ratio. Exceptions have been made (see below). Names may now be given to creatures with a cost of Divine Potential. Depending on the Rank of the creature and the meaning of the name, the cost may change. Exceptions: Any creature whose size is tiny and below is exempt from this title. Plants, fungi, and other such growing things are exempt as long as they are created from a seed or base form. Aether may be used to accelerate growth as normal. Tiny Frameworks that Ascend through combat or Aetheric saturation are exempt from the 1/24 ratio of automatic size reconstruction. The new unlocked Framework will not be exempt if summoned separately.

Valterra looked at the notifications, stunned. So he was like the High Council now? And they had adopted him? Valterra felt a flood of warmth overtake him at the idea. It touched a part of him that he didn't know was empty and filled him with a desire to achieve more than he already had. From his memories, he had a hazy idea of what adoption was. It was a long, drawn-out process by which a child became the responsibility of another who entered into the process willingly.

That individual or pair of individuals would choose to take care of, nurture, and see to the growth of the child. That the High Council had chosen to adopt him spoke to his soul and reassured him that everything would be all right and that they would watch over him. He felt... comforted. Even as that feeling spread inside him, he felt the pinging of yet more notifications, and he honed in on them eagerly.

Your "Mouse Guard" is ready to Ascend!

Please choose from among the following stages:
Mouse Soldier (Unique, Rank E - Bronze)
A path for mice that have dedicated themselves to the way of war and discipline. These mice are loyal and steadfast, elevated from simple guard mice to fearsome combatants. Wielding all manner of weaponry, these mice are heads and tails above their former occupation.

Mouse Scout (Unique, Rank E - Bronze)
Eschewing war and conflict, this mouse seeks to range far and wide. With an Ascension that provides a larger-than-normal Aether core but reduced overall capabilities, the Mouse Scout is able to leave the dungeon's territory for short periods of time both to explore and to bring back useful Frameworks for their dungeon's perusal.

Mouse Guard Veteran (Unique, Rank D - Iron)
Giving up all future potential, this mouse has chosen the path of the guard. Strong, durable, and persistent, it is in its awareness of its surroundings that the Mouse Guard Veteran shines. Able to sense fluctuations in Aether, this mouse is almost never surprised and is able to respond to any threat a young dungeon might face.

Ah, so his new Mouse Guards were already at the point where they could reach the next stage. That was good news and something that pleased him greatly, despite the loss of one of the mice. One of the mice in particular caught his eye as he went ahead and chose the Mouse Soldier option for the first three.

Your "Mouse Guard" is ready to Ascend!

Please choose from among the following stages:
Mouse Squire (Unique, Rank E - Bronze)
Rather than follow in the paw steps of its kinbeast, this mouse gives up the direct path of the Mouse Soldier to gain glory by serving its kin instead. The life of a Mouse Squire is one of service and learning. Serving as a shield bearer and armorer for its master, the Mouse

Squire is proficient with all the weapons its master wields, if in a lesser way. This is so that it might stand beside its master side by side on the day of battle without flinching, guarding its master's blind spots.

Another unique Framework meant that it was the first of its kind and only available to his dungeon in particular. He knew the mouse that unlocked the Framework. The little guy was the first of the mice to be born and had become attached to the older mouse. It was the mouse who took care of the needle many times, cleaning it with moss. It seemed his devotion had paid off, and the Core looked forward to seeing the results.

That line of thinking interested the Core because it could mean that there was some way to influence future Ascensions. He would have to think about it more later. Valterra selected the Ascension, turning to the next notification, and his metaphorical eyes went wide.

Chapter 24

Rewards Continued

Valterra looked at the screen in his soul before turning his attention to the wider dungeon to confirm the information. His third-floor guardian was also glowing with golden light. It seemed his endless devotion to his floor, coupled with participating in the war against the ants and this most recent invader, had been enough to push him over the edge. Valterra could feel the Aether buzzing in his servant's body and quickly went to work reading over the new options.

Your "Sylcyne Garter Snake" is ready to Ascend!

Please choose from among the following stages:
Emerald Adder (Rank D - Iron)
Giving up its constricting coils, this snake has chosen new weapons. With a powerful strike, this snake is capable of delivering deadly poison directly to its foe's body. With its mental affinity, it has the ability to channel Aether into its eyes, allowing it to freeze weak-willed prey for mere moments before striking.

Iron Scale Boa (Rank D - Iron)
Growing much larger and longer, this snake exchanges normal scales

for iron ones. Although treasured as a dungeon monster for this fact, it is also found in the wild around iron deposits rich in Aether. Preferring to constrict prey with its heavy body and consume it whole, this boa is a fearsome defender of its territory.

Ah, it would seem the Path was diverging completely. By doing so, it would be forcing him to choose between constriction and venom. It was a tough decision, and he wished there was a third option where he could take both Paths. That was a bit childish of him, but that was what he was, and he couldn't really escape his nature.

Then again, there was someone he could ask, so he slipped into his snake's mind and received his answer. He found frustration. During the fight with the invader, the snake chafed at being unable to end the fight himself. He played an integral part and knew it, yet he found himself wanting something more. He wanted to strike quickly and finish fights before they could start.

Valterra wondered at this new side of his guardian that he hadn't seen before. It seemed his serpent was more self-aware than he had thought. He chose the Emerald Adder and felt his serpent's satisfaction as it curled up inside the third floor to Ascend. Valterra shifted the earth and grass to hide his guardian better, not wishing him to be attacked while on the road to becoming stronger.

Finally, Valterra turned to his Mouse Soldier. His first and most loyal creature. He eagerly began looking through the notification.

Your "Mouse Soldier" is ready to Ascend!

Please choose from among the following stages:
Mouse-At-Arms (Unique, Rank D - Iron)
Adept with all manner of weaponry, the Mouse-At-Arms is a formidable fighter and elite soldier. Another step along the path to greatness, this mouse focuses on martial prowess beyond anything else. Armed further with bodily enhancement that stems from an upgraded Aether core, the Mouse-At-Arms is a threat to all that

would oppose its lord.

Mouse Captain (Unique, Rank D - Iron)
The next step on the road to leadership, this mouse chooses to be an example to all mouse-kin. Adept with the sword, the mouse treads a path few will walk but all the more noble for it. To lead is to display courage in the face of opposition and to serve steadfastly. By the sweat of brow and whisker, the Mouse Captain will see its lord's will done.

Mouse Berserker (Unique, Rank C - Steel)
Giving up all future potential, this mouse has chosen the path of everlasting war, wrath, and ruin. Able to enter a battle rage at any moment, this mouse is a powerhouse fighter, willing and able to shrug off the worst of hits and deal them back two-fold. Wielding fearsome claws and growing armor-like fur, this mouse is a walking, squeaking terror on the battlefield.

Even though he knew which one he would choose, Valterra carefully examined each option with childish excitement. The Mouse-At-Arms would be so useful. From the sense he got from it, the mouse would become totally at home on a battlefield, able to take orders and obey them, and even be capable of minor tactics. Rather than throwing themselves at an enemy, they would work together with other mice to take down larger foes, using their impressive weapon skills to do so.

The last one was the total opposite. They took "throwing themselves at an enemy" to be their own personal code of honor. Instead of relying on crafted weapons, they reverted to savagery and natural weapons. It was similar to the Mouse Guard Veteran with its emphasis on giving up future potential. Valterra wondered if the last option was available because of the way his Mouse Soldier was filled with anger during his fight with the invader or whether it was always an option.

There was really only one choice for his Mouse Soldier when all was said and done. His first guardian was a leader and warrior, not a purely martial elite or a berserking mad mouse. Neither of the other two Framework options fit him quite as well as Mouse Captain. Valterra chose and watched the golden light settle into the mouse's fur. Once again, he would need to create more guardians, but he already knew what he wanted to do.

If his new Mouse Captain was going to have fellow mice to lead, then there would need to be more mice. While the Mouse Scouts would help out, they were not exactly an army. No, Valterra would need others to take up the mantle while his guardian slept. Luckily, he already had the Frameworks he needed. Now, he just needed to implement them. Turning his attention to his dungeon, he gathered the Aether he would need.

The five remaining Mouse Scouts were on a self-imposed mission to discover the whereabouts of the ant Queen that had been invading their lord's territory. For a day or two, they had been searching the outside lands, frequently returning to their lord's outskirts in order to replenish their Aether cores. While they could remain outside of their lord's domain for an extended period, it was uncomfortable, and they wanted to make sure they had the Aether needed to fight if it came down to it.

That time was now. The five mice were perched on a tiny grassy bump that barely provided elevation but was enough for their purposes. One of their number had found the colony and had called for the others. They watched as ants crawled out of the entrance in ones and twos, the massive pillar of wood they were departing from creating the appearance of a daunting citadel. Still, the mice were determined, and their Aether was diminishing steadily so it was either now or later, after returning to their lord's domain to recover.

The mice were unwilling to leave it alone for that long. After all, they didn't know how long they had until the ant Queen replenished her forces. As one, the mice began moving, spreading out and creeping through the grass that led up to the colony. They made their way slowly, making sure not to rustle the grass or give themselves away.

That being said, it didn't take long for the ants to notice them. Whether it was the reverberations of their steps or some other sense, the ants guarding the colony stiffened in alarm, and then violence broke out. The mice broke cover and charged, moving swiftly to take advantage before the ants either retreated or gathered into dangerous numbers.

Clenched in the mice's paws were spears of wood—little more than tiny sharpened stakes, really. They had seen the needle of the mouse, and though it had taken time to find the twigs they needed, they had all eventually found some wood. Their sharp front teeth had let them gnaw a sharp point, and now their impromptu weapons were put to devastating use.

Wood pierced chitin as the mice fell on the guards, making quick work of them. To their credit, the ants didn't lie down and die. By the time the mice finished with their brutal work, they each sported minor gashes and bruises. They were undeterred, the Aether of the fallen already helping to refill their cores, and they made their way over the entrance that led deeper into the colony.

One mouse took the lead, a sharpened stick leading the way as the scouts proceeded on their mission. From there, it went relatively quickly. They got lost for a time in tunnels that were obviously built to hold more members than they had seen. Some tunnels were still rather small, showing signs of renovation. That helped the mice find the right paths as they delved deeper into the larger tunnels.

They fought a few more ants, and though the fights were slightly more challenging due to the enclosed space, it wasn't anything they couldn't handle. It wasn't long after that that they found the Queen. She was in a long chamber toward the back with a small horde of ants between her and the intruders. They clicked their mandibles in what was meant to be a threatening display, and while it was mildly disconcerting, the overall feeling was one of desperation.

The Queen simply stared at the intruders with something like resignation. None of the mice balked at the display. They simply waded into battle, looking forward to being done with their mission. While their

stage of Ascension wasn't directly geared for battle, they were still of higher Rank than their opponents. With that and the fact that ant monsters were naturally weaker than their Rank would normally suggest due to their reliance on numbers, the mice had no trouble decimating the loyal guards of the Queen.

They put them down efficiently, though the numbers did hurt them in the beginning as they took multiple bites from the swarm of defenders. By the time the scuffle ended, the mice were standing over the corpse of the Queen, bloody but victorious. The Queen had attempted to fight but wasn't very effective at it and fell quickly after the last of her guards.

As the Aether of the fallen filled their cores and saturated their bodies, the mice quickly left. They could sense something building within them and wanted to be back within their lord's territory before it fully occurred. They had to leave the ant corpses, which was a shame, but they needed the protection that would come from their lord.

They made it just as the pressure became unbearable. As soon as they passed the threshold, their fur burst with golden light. Aether flooded into their cores, and they felt their lord's presence as he homed in on their location. Then there was nothing but oblivion as they fell into the Ascension process.

Chapter 25

Ascensions & Expansions

Well, that was certainly something. Valterra was about to summon new creatures when he received a prompt from the System. It seemed like his Mouse Scouts had returned from somewhere with the power of Ascension bubbling beneath their fur. As soon as they passed into his domain, the System reacted by giving him a prompt. And boy, were the options exciting.

Your "Mouse Scout" is ready to Ascend!

Please choose from among the following stages:
Mouse Ranger (Unique, Rank D - Iron)
With a further condensed Aether core, this mouse has determined that the outside world beyond its lord's territory is a threat that cannot be waited upon. Adept at wilderness survival with enhanced instincts and physique, the Mouse Ranger can survive hostile environments long enough to bring information back to their dungeon lord.

Mouse Sneak (Unique, Rank D - Iron)
Mice are rarely seen if they don't want to be, and the Mouse Sneak

takes this to the next level with the beginnings of a Darkness Affinity and a penchant for sneaking up on prey. From blinding enemies to wrapping themselves in shadow, the Mouse Sneak has everything it needs to surprise and confound the recipients of their dungeon core's wrath.

Mouse Whisperblade (Unique, Rank C - Steel)
Giving up all future potential, this mouse has chosen the path of the perfect assassin. No one sees the Whisperblade unless it wants to be seen. Armed with the ability to make weapons from its enhanced Darkness Affinity, this mouse is never unarmed, and any enemy that makes that mistake will find a quick death.

Valterra couldn't stop himself from giggling at the options. What had they been doing to be offered such great options, the final one in particular? He glanced through their minds and received some hazy images and thoughts. Huh. Apparently, they had gone and dealt with the ants that had been invading him. Well, that certainly deserved a reward, and he was in a position to make that happen.

Unlike with his guardian, he wasn't as apprehensive about choosing an option that gave up future potential, but he was also leary about separating the crew of mice. While he could do what was best for his dungeon and get each option, he didn't want to abuse his creatures like that. It was perhaps childish, but he could at least take his creatures' feelings into account. With that thought, he hovered through their minds to gather any subconscious desires to help him make his decision.

What he found surprised him. They all wanted different things. While they had remained together thus far, out of a sense of kinship, their bonds were weak. It wasn't at all like he was expecting, especially compared to the relationship his mouse guardian displayed with his kin. Perhaps that was because they were born as children and he had partially raised them?

Valterra didn't know, but their individual desires actually gave him the leeway he had been afraid to use. He crafted a hole in the ground and moved the mice there before choosing. Three of the mice, the ones with the strongest bonds, would become Mouse Rangers. One would become a Mouse Sneak, having chafed against failure to slip in unnoticed. The final mouse would become a Mouse Whisperblade.

While Valterra was uncomfortable choosing something that limited future growth, the mouse herself couldn't care less. Her mind was fixated on the fact that if the Queen ant had died first and died fast, the ants would have lost cohesion and unity, allowing the mice to kill them without taking as many wounds. She was a beast that desired further strength regardless of the cost. Valterra was a little unnerved, if he was being perfectly honest, but he respected her subconscious desires and selected the option.

As they were wrapped up in golden light, the Dungeon Core moved on, content to let his mice Ascend. They would awaken in time, though he was interested to see how long it would be before his Whisperblade woke up. He had found that the time it took to Ascend to the next stage took longer based on which Rank was being reached. He pushed aside that consideration before moving on to his next project.

The first thing Valterra did was summon around fifty mice, twenty of which were *house mice* and the others an even spread of Mouse Guards, Mouse Scouts, and Mouse Soldiers. He figured that would be a good test base, and the mice didn't take much Aether to create or maintain. He summoned them in rows and then held them there with his will. It was hard, but the mice seemed to acknowledge his presence after a while and turned their attention to him. Projecting his thoughts to the arrayed mice, he gave them their orders.

Loyal Dungeon Mice! You have been created with a purpose. You are to grow and Ascend so that you might take your place in my dungeon as its defenders. He then directed them to the turf war and released them, watching as they scurried to do his bidding. He chuckled internally. He had never given a speech like that before and found he kind of liked it. His goal was to continually seed the territory outside his third floor with mice.

Lots of mice. And perhaps some other creatures.

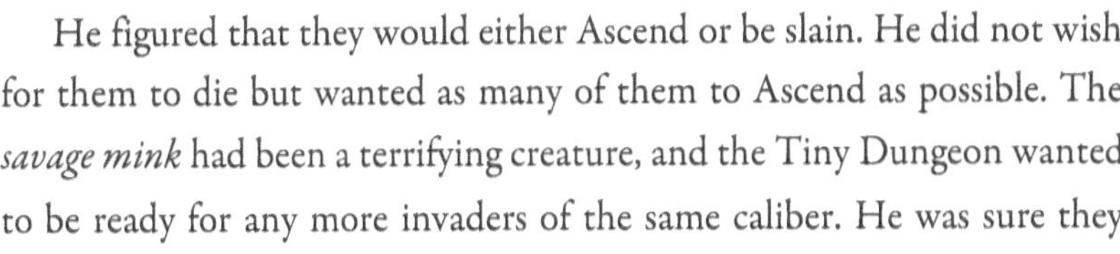

He figured that they would either Ascend or be slain. He did not wish for them to die but wanted as many of them to Ascend as possible. The *savage mink* had been a terrifying creature, and the Tiny Dungeon wanted to be ready for any more invaders of the same caliber. He was sure they would come.

With that done, he turned to his dungeon. Sinking his senses into his dungeon body, he tried to get a feel for just how large his spaces actually were. His first floor was twenty inches by forty inches and also contained his core and Aether funnel. His second floor had started as a little half-circle pocket barely ten inches in diameter set roughly two feet up the inner wall, with a little tunnel through the wood that led down to an entrance set at the bottom. Feeling the boundaries of the second floor, Valterra was surprised to find the floor had expanded by at least twenty inches upward and horizontally across the wall.

Tunnels had been carved into the wood, creating miniature highways that the Empowered Danians could use to get from one place to another. Interspersed between these highways were five floors that descended until the entrance. Each floor had columns that held it up and workers who continued to dig and expand. The original alcove where he had placed the Queen was still in use and contained each of the different stages of the Danian life cycle. There were eggs, pupae, and larvae as well as a few hatchlings that had just begun adult life.

The Danians fascinated him as he watched them industriously move about but also left him feeling a little bewildered. They had floors just like him but were almost done with five and were moving on to a sixth, just above the alcove. Valterra didn't know how to feel as he watched the Danians build a more cohesive dungeon than he had. Did he feel... impressed? Proud?

He figured it was both. After all, the Danians were the first actual manipulation he had done on a Framework, and with an additional stage, they were formidably energetic. He would have to come up with a suitable reward for them. Maybe he should try and do what the Spirit of the Natural Order had done for this latest stage of Ascension.

Yeah, that could work. Instead of relying on the gods, he would craft his own Path of Ascension for them. Excited, Valterra turned away. He wouldn't be able to do it yet since the Rank of the Frameworks he could create only went as high as Rank E, but that would change once he Ascended.

That led Valterra to his next task. He wanted to make additional floors. Each floor had brought him closer to his own Ascension, and he figured he just needed to make more. To do that, though, he needed space. Lots of space.

He could decide to make small floors. His third floor was only a half-circle twenty-five inches in diameter if measured from the entrance to his dungeon, which was tiny compared to the 200-foot labyrinth of the fourth floor. He found that he didn't care much for the idea. He wanted to create impressive areas with ecosystems like his fourth floor.

Valterra recognized that the fourth was unique since he had created it primarily for his only Rank C Framework, which had been massive. His next rooms would not need to be that big, but he was also blessed in the sense that he did not need to build something new when he could just claim something already built.

Using the vast amounts of Aether from the "ritual room," as his memories called it, Valterra began happily claiming the entirety of the cabin. He started with the area directly outside the ritual room before moving into the "living room" and then into the "kitchen" from there.

In the middle of claiming the "kitchen," he stumbled onto a patch of white cottony growths on a particularly damp section of the floor and wall. In fact, he claimed it so quickly that he had partially moved on before the system brought it up, startling him.

New Framework acquired!

Mold (Mundane)

The bottom of the barrel of fungi, mold grows naturally in the wild but is also found growing in structures and buildings. Considered an infestation, it is normally eradicated swiftly to prevent health problems. When disturbed, mold releases spores, which, if inhaled, can cause respiratory problems. If care is used when disposing of it, then the risk of infection drops to almost zero. All in all, this microorganism is rarely, if ever, a threat to most creatures and is content to consume dead matter to further its spread.

As the first dungeon to use such a microorganism as a dungeon environment, you will be able to create and modify its Path of Ascension freely.

Warning! May have unforeseen consequences.

Valterra hummed in satisfaction. He had no idea what he could do with the fungi, but he figured he would apply his mouse approach combined with his grass approach. It felt fitting, considering it wasn't quite like a plant but clearly wasn't an animal.

He finished claiming the kitchen before turning to his new Framework. He figured a little experimenting couldn't hurt and decided to spice it up a bit. Diving into the Framework, he quickly found that they were decomposers of dead matter, turning the decomposed material into food for itself. This was especially interesting to Valterra since it reminded him of himself and how he turned dead creatures into Frameworks and Aether. Now that he had claimed the mold, he could feel how it ate at the dead, damp wood, slowly but surely turning it into fuel. That gave Valterra an idea.

He dove into the Framework, eager to begin playing again, especially after his close brush with death. Like a child, he moved on, shoving aside the trauma and anger at Trik'Weri in favor of his new toy. In the back of his mind, though, the trauma lingered, and a subconscious part of his mind held onto the rage that had begun to simmer.

He poked at the Framework for mold, shifting it this way and that. He knew he couldn't change it a lot without sacrificing on the altar of change, but he did have an idea. First, he changed the structure of the mold to give it the ability to decompose more efficiently before also changing how it decomposed.

Instead of simply eating dead things and turning them into food, it would eat the dead things and whatever Aether remained inside before turning it into a pseudo-aetheric substance. It then would go through its normal process of fueling itself, and the leftovers would be further converted into an Aether-like dew. Valterra figured the dew would attract prey that would then disturb the mold, causing its spores to spread. He increased the mold's capability for infection and then released his hold on the Framework.

A new stage on the Path of Ascension has been synthesized from an existing Framework! The Framework "Mold" may now be automatically Ascended into the following Framework:
Aether-Dew Mold (Rank F - Copper)
A fungus with new tricks. Synthesized from mundane mold, this fungus now boasts a trap made from the remnant Aether in dead material. Drawing prey in with this Aether-dew, it sprays its target with spores that cause infection. If the prey dies, the spores begin decomposing the body and the cycle begins again.

Valterra hummed again, pleased with his new creation. It certainly wasn't the most powerful thing in his dungeon, but it would do as the backdrop for a floor at least. He spread it, only to find a problem. His new Framework worked fine, but it was decomposer, not a plant that could live with just Aether. He supposed he could change it again, but he worried it would become a whole new species at that point.

He glanced around his dungeon. There were very few dead things in his territory since his Aether kept most things alive. Then again, the wood that was used in the making of the cabin was already dead when he claimed it, and it didn't seem like it was coming back to life. He wondered if it would work and swiftly began spreading his new mold into various places in the kitchen to see what worked.

He found that the mold liked wet wood best in out-of-the-way places that didn't see much sunlight. He spread his mold into the places he found and left it at that. He would come back and try to figure out more places later.

From there, Valterra moved on to claiming territory. He claimed the "porch" next and the "West Wing" before moving up and claiming the roofs of both buildings. Pushing himself to go further, he expanded to include the shadowed sections under the "porch" and the foundations of the cabin. It took him another day to claim everything, which he was pleased with. It had taken him far longer to claim the basement, and he could already feel his enhanced boon and title making their presence known.

He would have to sit down and go through the upgrades in more detail, but for now, he was content to create his newest floor. It was at that moment that he felt a pinch. All the new territory he had claimed was drawing even more Aether out of his core to fuel his domain. Valterra knew instinctively that he would have to either craft a larger column or move to a larger room where the storm would be able to flow easier and thus lessen the amount he had to spend.

In fact, looking deeper into his instincts, he realized that while those instincts had succeeded in pushing him to his first Ascension, they hadn't been so concerned with the proper flows of Aether. Valterra felt how, in comparison to his third and first floors, his second and fourth floors didn't receive nearly as much Aether as they should. His fourth floor especially should be receiving a much higher ratio, considering its size and the size of the creatures in it. Valterra realized that he would need to change how he was going about building his floors and was glad he had a ton of room to experiment.

Chapter 26

Of Spiders & Rats

The Wolf Spider hid, watching his prey move closer. He was in the territory outside the third floor along with an unforeseen ally. A mouse, a creation of the Great Web-Spinner, had seemingly taken a liking to him. She wasn't big but was still larger than he was, and he found her company to be helpful when capturing prey. He'd had very little success in that department before she showed up.

When he was first sent out to hunt by the Great Web-Spinner, he had quickly found himself to be low on the predator list. He had been wounded multiple times in the process of trying to hunt and had fled to hide and heal. Now, though, he had an ally and hoped it was a sign that things were looking up.

Leaping out of cover, he charged, waving his mandibles menacingly. The prey, a beetle, turned and ran, unfolding gossamer wings to carry it away to safety. It would have escaped too like all the other beetles the Wolf Spider had tried to hunt. This time, though, he had an ally. With a squeak, the mouse leaped out from her hiding place and crashed into the beetle.

Using her paws, she grasped the beetle's wings and tore at them. Deprived of its ability to fly, the beetle tried to fight back with its small mandibles but failed to do much before the spider entered the battle. With

 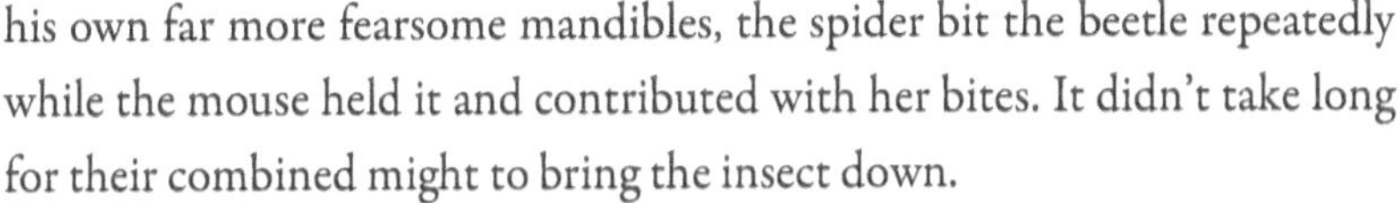

his own far more fearsome mandibles, the spider bit the beetle repeatedly while the mouse held it and contributed with her bites. It didn't take long for their combined might to bring the insect down.

Triumphant, the spider hopped up and down before freezing as the post-battle Aether flooded into him. Turning, he saw the mouse also pause before turning to the beetle. This was the second one they had managed to kill together. Last time, he had eaten the whole thing before realizing he was supposed to let the Great Web-Spinner know he had killed something.

This time, he wouldn't forget. Focusing on the thread that bound him, he sent news of his success and felt the thread reverberate in response. He watched as the beetle dissolved and felt satisfaction resonate down the thread. The mouse turned to him, and he found the same fire burning in her eyes. They turned and moved away to begin hunting once more.

It had been some time since the tall one had last come to administer his magic. In that time, their home had been flooded by the dark waters, and even now, those waters gave the other rats pause. Not He-Who-Chitters-In-The-Dark. He had been one of the first to notice when The-One-Who-Was-Not-There had taken over the stone room. Even now, his presence could be felt in the walls and water.

He-Who-Chitters-In-The-Dark had been the first to take advantage of the distraction caused by the flooding of the room to shove Broken Fang through the bars of their shared cage to plummet into the water. He-Who-Chitters finally had the whole cage to himself. Broken Fang wouldn't have lasted long in the next series of challenges anyway. Too thin, on account of He-Who-Chitters having muscled him out of eating what food they were given.

Broken Fang had swam around for hours trying to climb the wet walls. Then that creature had come up from the depths. The other rats had squeaked in terror and tried escaping their cages. Not He-Who-Chitters-

In-The-Dark. He had watched in fascination as the creature swallowed Broken Fang whole before disappearing into the murky water.

And then the ledges appeared, and everything changed. The light had changed everything. It must have been formed by The-One-Who-Was-Not-There because it reeked of Aether and power. It had exploded, and He-Who-Chitters-In-The-Dark had been struck by one of the crystals. A large chunk had sliced deep into his hide and burned him where he could not reach.

The pain had been agonizing, and he had fled to the lower ledges, knowing his kin would sense weakness. He had barely made it and slipped into the murky water to ease his burning side. It had helped somewhat, but as he pulled himself out and huddled near the edge of the half-moon ledge, he shuddered as more pain wracked his body.

Unbeknownst to He-Who-Chitters-In-The-Dark, the rat was undergoing a metamorphosis. As his body shuddered, eerie green-blue light inched its way across his veins. Beginning at his wound and pulsing through his body and Aether core, it gradually made it to his left eye where it sparked, sizzling the flesh away. Squeaking in pain, the rat clutched at his head as pain flooded his genetically enhanced brain. The eye popped and sizzled with power as He-Who-Chitters-In-The-Dark suffered with muffled squeaks.

Shuffling nearby awakened the rat to danger, and he staggered sideways even as another rat attempted to bite him, thinking him weak. Not He-Who-Chitters-In-The-Dark. Even as the hostile rat lunged towards him, He-Who-Chitters let go of his head and swiped with his paw, trying to funnel the pain away from himself. Like a wave, green-blue fire exploded from his paw and slammed into the hostile rat, who was flung away with a sizzle and a pained squeak.

Immediately, the pain in his head subsided, and He-Who-Chitters looked up to find his opponent slumped to the ground, steam rising from the corpse. Staggering over to it, he looked around, finding other rats that had crawled down to the last ledge. He bared his teeth, his new eye flaring, and they backed away.

He had eaten well that day and every day since as he clawed his way to the top ledges. He had gathered the others, the ones like him. The-Mad-Touched-Ones, the other rats called them. He-Who-Chitters-In-The-Dark cared little. His little brain was already flooded with ideas of how to get more of the crystal stuff. If a little piece had given him such power, what could he do with more?

That was the basis behind his current plan. He had rallied the other Mad-Touched to join him in bullying the other rats. It had worked too for a little while. They had claimed the top ledges and had sniffed out deposits of the Spark-rock before getting their kin to begin digging it out. He-Who-Chitters stood overlooking the new mine, his veins crackling with power as he watched his fellow rats working. The current issue was with Bone Crusher. She was a giant rat that the tall one had favored. She was smart and large and did not like the new regime on the ledges. If that was everything, then He-Who-Chitters wouldn't have cared.

No, what he cared about was the way she went about communicating her displeasure. She was quiet around the Mad-Touched and moved about claiming allegiances in the dark. He could respect that to a certain extent, but he would let nothing stand in the way of obtaining more Spark-rock. For now, everything was fine. The work continued, and he could focus on the little pieces of Spark-rock that had been removed. Soon he would have the power he sought. He watched as Bone Crusher moved around, her fur gleaming in the light of the Spark-rock, and he narrowed his beady eyes as his brain contemplated a new idea. Perhaps Bone Crusher could be brought into an alliance of sorts.

New Framework acquired!

Iridescent Ground Beetle (Mundane)
Content to live their lives on the ground, these beetles also have

beautiful gossamer wings that they use to escape from danger. For danger they cannot escape, they rely on their shiny carapace for protection. This insect is dangerous to very little but is a voracious consumer of plant life, fungi, and any insect or arachnid smaller than it is.

As the first dungeon to use such a creature as a dungeon monster, you will be able to create and modify its Path of Ascension freely.

Warning! May have unforeseen consequences.

Chapter 27

Further Expansion

Valterra barely gave a thought to his spider's successful hunt and the subsequent Framework, though he did think to send a hint of satisfaction to the creature so that it would continue the good work. The number of Frameworks he had at his disposal was rising, but it wouldn't do him much good if he didn't fix his floors.

He dove deeper into his *dungeon sense*, getting a feel for his newly grown body. He had taken the whole cabin and made it his, but there were too many sensations that clamored for his attention. Similar to when he had claimed the basement, he knew that things were slipping through the cracks, but he couldn't focus on it all directly due to the overwhelming amount of Aether that was continually being drained from his core.

Valterra could feel the building and its construction. It was built solid and immovable, anchored into the earth through its foundations. Pinpoint sensations of carved sigils were also present, and each one burned pleasantly in the background.

He could feel them take in his Aether and do... something, but he wasn't sure what. His instincts weren't screaming at him, so he left them alone. They had been created by Calamvor, so Valterra figured they would be safe enough for him to keep and would perhaps prove to be beneficial.

He figured he would start with the outside and make his way in, and by doing so, he would make a fortress for himself and his creatures. He expanded the boundaries of the third floor to include everything under the porch around the entirety of the building. His experiment with the rats had shown him that creatures could remain within his floors and not be claimed, so he figured it would be all right.

Ironically, despite the pain they had brought him, it was his fragmented memories of Calamvor's life that gave him his next idea instead of his instincts. Calamvor had delved into dungeons before, and each one had guardians that oversaw a floor. Some of those guardians weren't stuck guarding the entrance deeper in and instead roamed about to deal with any delvers as they saw fit. Valterra figured his newly Ascended snake guardian would prefer to do that rather than remain stationary.

Using his Aether, Valterra dug new holes into the walls of the cabin to provide new entrances to his dungeon. He knew it was probably a silly idea, but he also thought it would work extremely well. For normal dungeons, he knew from Calamvor's memories that it was often a giant hole in the ground that led ever deeper.

Valterra, on the other hand, had a whole building, and if invaders didn't know where his core was, then they would have to choose a hole and stick with it. Valterra chose to hide within a dungeon edifice with a labyrinth of choices between himself and any who might come to claim or destroy him.

Using another idea from Calamvor, he created little fortresses in a half-circle around the holes. He then populated those fortresses with different ranks of mice while he populated the outside with snakes, spiders, mantises, efts, slugs, and his new beetles. He gave them the same orders: fight and Ascend by whatever means necessary to protect the dungeon.

With that major project done, he turned inward. He still had plenty of Aether left, but the drain was increasing, so his main goal was to create more "mouths." In a normal dungeon, he figured they would grow deeper rather than up or to the side, digging down and down and down.

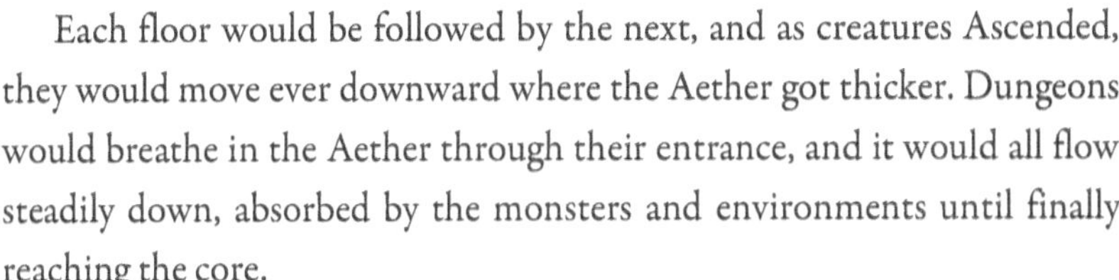

Each floor would be followed by the next, and as creatures Ascended, they would move ever downward where the Aether got thicker. Dungeons would breathe in the Aether through their entrance, and it would all flow steadily down, absorbed by the monsters and environments until finally reaching the core.

As he was right now, Valterra was only getting Aether through one entrance, and it almost immediately collided with his core since it was still on the first floor. He had the body of a bigger dungeon without all of the floors in direct succession.

Using his new entrances, he tried directing his "breathing" to include them. It was hard since his instincts really didn't like the idea, but eventually, he felt an almost audible click, and Aether began being drawn through each entrance at the same time.

It flooded into his dungeon and he heard a phantom chime that filled him with excitement. It seemed that his ingenuity had brought him closer to his own Ascension even though he hadn't even started on his fifth floor.

Continuing on his remodeling streak, he shifted the boundaries of his first floor to include all of the open space between the inner and outer walls as well as all the fortresses crewed by mice. He created additional caverns similar to his first at each corner intersection of the building and populated them with mice as well.

He then turned to his second floor and expanded it to include all the wood of the inside walls from the foundation to the ceiling. He then planted three new colonies of Empowered Danians, setting them at least two or three walls away from one another so that they could grow in peace before encountering invaders or the other Danians. He knew the separate colonies would most likely fight if they ever came into contact, and although he didn't want his creatures to die, he was resigned to the fact that his core needed to be protected.

Finally, he directed his attention to his Aether and watched how it moved through his territory. With his new way of breathing, he could feel the difference in how the second floor received Aether. However, his fourth floor was still lacking.

In each of his corner caverns, he drilled a large tunnel that led down to the fourth floor. Shifting his Aether further, he directed it down the tunnels and through the entirety of the fourth floor before directing the excess up the basement stairs where it spilled into what had been the kitchen.

Not quite done yet, he shifted material around and built a massive spire of rock right in the middle of what was once the living room, since it was central to the rest of his dungeon. He continued controlling the rock until it formed a massive column reaching the ceiling. With that done, he repeated the creation of his Aether funnel but magnified its effect while creating internal caverns crafted inside the column to hold the pools of Aether that would inevitably drip lower.

He then repeated the feat in the basement and formed another column that went all the way until it hit the limit of his body. The successive caverns in the column gained in size until the base cavern was around two feet in diameter. It was there that he fashioned a final small pedestal within the final pool.

Now all he needed to do was move his core to the column, after which he would have a ready-made funnel and be prepared to safely craft his new floors. He would be ready for anything or anyone seeking to claim his core.

It felt strange and uncomfortable, but he successfully moved his core to its new home. He directed the excess Aether in the kitchen to make its way to the top of the funnel, where it once again formed an Aether storm before being absorbed into the funnel. The storm was massive, and he quickly cycled it so that even more Aether was sent raging through his halls. Only after that was done did he turn and check the storm of notifications bouncing around his core.

Multiple entrances created!

The Core has created multiple entrances that have direct access to it. Aether absorption has been diversified to include every entrance.

Progress to Core Ascension: 60%

Chapter 28

Interlude: The Council of Five

Cormac Torgir watched the rest of the Council of Five deliberate, disgusted with their weakness. There was a dungeon, a solution to all of their problems, sitting a mere week's travel from the Mother Tree, yet they continued to deliberate.

Slamming his fist down on the table, the *leprechaun* rose to his feet and raised his voice. "What are ye blatherin' on and on for, eh?! How long has it been since the tall folk locked us out of their dungeons? Over a century; that's how long! Why are we still deliberatin'? Let's set up a strike force and claim it!"

Horace, the *fairy* he had interrupted, turned and scowled at him. "So you would have us send in a force without scouting first? For all we know, this is a trap set by the archmage who lives in that cabin. He has hunted us before. Successfully, I might add." The fairy shook his head. "I do not wish to sacrifice our kin on speculation, even if my son was certain it was indeed a dungeon."

Two other heads nodded at this. One of them was Olga, one of the *daoine* or "Good Folk," as they called themselves, which the leprechaun thought was rather presumptuous of them. She was at the 3rd Stage of

Ascension for a *light elven* and one of the more powerful ones, hence her position on the council. Cormac still found her to be insufferable.

The other was Maric the *asrai* from where he lounged in his little pool of water. He was also a 3rd Stage Ascension, a far cry from the *undine* 1st stage.

They were both inconsequential. Olga rarely wanted conflict, and Maric was a slothful coward. If it couldn't be reached by water then he couldn't be bothered.

Cormac focused his gaze on the one who hadn't nodded, Dialgar of the *slua sidhe*. As the commander of the Fairy Host and one of the only fairies at Mother Tree with a 4th Stage Ascension, he was the highest Ascended being out of all of them and commanded the military arm of their dwindling community.

As if feeling his eyes on him, Dialgar spoke, "Do not look to me for support in this, Cormac. I will not pull my elites from their duties for a shot in the dark. I will not risk losing the Mother Tree to some monster because I sent half of them off to confront an archmage in his home."

His dark red eyes turned to Cormac, and the leprechaun felt the Rank of the fairy bear down on him before diminishing. "I do, however, agree that some scouting should be done. If there is a threat to the Mother Tree present in this situation, then we should be made aware of it."

Cormac sat down and stewed as a vote was called to send out scouts. When called upon to vote, he stood again. "If you all insist on being weak, then fine, you have my vote. But this is a mistake. We cannot fuel even the most basic of Ascensions among our kin."

"The Mother Tree is growing too old to sustain our population; you all know what that means. When she no longer produces the amount of Aether Dust we need, then we will all starve! All that will be left of us will be our stage 1 kin. Think of that before you dismiss me out of hand next time."

With his final words said, he departed, stalking down the tunnels that made up the inside of the Mother Tree. Behind him, he heard the others begin to discuss the scouting operation, and he scoffed. *Blitherin' fools, the lot of them.* They could scout all they wanted.

When Cormac became *Keeper of the Core,* they would have to listen to him then. He licked his lips, fantasizing about all the Aether that a dungeon could put out. Not to mention the creatures it contained; they wouldn't dare mock him with such an army at his disposal.

The leprechaun dove into the caverns that made up the inside of the Mother Tree. He would have to seek out some worthy delvers to join him. They would be easy enough to bribe. They couldn't be stage 3 like himself, but perhaps a large number of stage 2s would be enough. After all, he didn't want them to get any ideas of betrayal.

He had a few trinkets saved away, and the lure of fresh Aether would entice even the most recalcitrant of them to join him. There were plenty of malcontents who desired the ability to delve once more. They would obey him, or they would get nothing. Cormac smiled wickedly. Oh yes, the Council of Five would rue the day they didn't listen to him.

"So what do you think?" Horace asked the others cautiously, eyeing the tunnel through which Cormac had stormed off.

"He will most certainly go after the core of the dungeon," Olga declared. "He has always desired more power, even when we had plenty to go around."

"He was right, though," Maric drawled sleepily. "Mother Tree isn't getting any younger. We have held on due to the Fairy Host's strength, but we are fading." His sleepy eyes held sorrow. "Without a change, we will perish as Cormac said."

"We have agreed to scout out the situation. Let us continue to do so," declared Dialgar. "Cormac will set out with a crew. They will inevitably be weaker than he is and will provide an adequate test of the dungeon's capability. If there's something in the dungeon that can pose a threat to him, then we will have been right to be cautious. If he succeeds, we will need

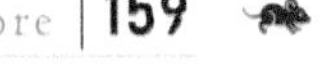

people on hand to resist him and claim the core for the Mother Tree. Either way, one of us will need to take on this task, and I cannot do it. I am needed here in case the Pack Matron comes sniffing around again."

"I'll do it," Horace said, determined. "My son knows the way, and I still have a few contacts here from my adventuring days. I'm sure they'll be thrilled at the chance to delve and will understand the threat posed by Cormac controlling a dungeon core."

After looking around the table and receiving affirming nods, Horace stood. "Then I'll be off. I want to be ready to move once Cormac has begun to move out."

Dialgar nodded. "That would be wise, my friend. May the Mother Tree guide your journey." Horace nodded and departed, moving quickly toward his quarters. His old battle-ax had hung on his mantel for far too long. It would be good to have it in his hands once again.

Chapter 29

Planning & Finishing the Fifth Floor

60%

Valterra stared at the screen in his core in shock. Just making additional entrances into his dungeon and learning how to absorb Aether from them at the same time had given him a jump of 15% toward Ascension. If the pattern with his floors continued, then he would reach his next Ascension by floor six. That was without any other unexpected upgrades that he achieved along the way.

He knew it was just a matter of time before his newly enlarged third floor gave him Frameworks. He would have to be present, of course, but he figured he would be able to do that soon; after planning out his fifth floor, that is.

He didn't know exactly what he wanted yet, but he had figured something out while working on his other floors: he wanted them all to connect in some way. It wasn't just that he wanted his Aether circulation to be better so that it would hit all his floors, he also wanted them to work together so that invaders would have little idea of just how many floors he actually had. Combined with his multiple entrances, Valterra was certain

that this would prove to be devastating to anyone who might wish him harm.

He turned to what had once been the kitchen. Gradually, an image took shape in his mind, but he needed something first. He went looking and immediately found what he was looking for, claiming what he needed.

New Framework acquired!

Wind-Blown Moss (Mundane)
A plentiful moss that forms a dense cushion upon rocks, soil, and logs.
Using wind to disperse itself far and wide, this moss can be found
anywhere it can grow effectively.

It hadn't taken very long for Valterra to find where the newly Ascended Mouse Squire had acquired the moss he had used to clean his first floor guardian's needle. Valterra's interest deepened when he didn't get the option to freely modify it. He then determined that the moss wasn't a new Framework and had been used by other dungeons. He quickly realized it wasn't that farfetched. Most dungeons probably had a simple cave as their first floor, with moss and other plants as the basic environment.

It didn't matter as much now. If he truly wanted to modify the Framework, he could use his Divine Potential. For now, though, it would suffice for what he wanted it to do. Directing the Aether that was coming into the kitchen from the rest of his dungeon, he created stone out of it by activating his Authority. Using the stone, he created ledges and cemented them to the interior wooden walls. Then, going once more to his borrowed memories, he built "bridges" out of stone to connect the various slabs that sat on top of the "cabinetry." Tall folk had weird names for everything, it seemed. He then shortened the steps leading down to the basement so that smaller creatures could climb up and down.

Next, he spread his moss everywhere he could, using Aether to make sure it would grow properly. While he was at it, he spread his Aether-dew mold as well, creating little, wet, out-of-the-way areas where it could thrive.

In between the cabinets, he fashioned large five-foot pillars that he anchored to the floor. Going below to the ceiling of the fourth floor, he was reinforcing it when he had an idea. Chuckling to himself mischievously, he began creating what his memories called a "trapdoor." Apparently, other dungeons had them.

They would seemingly look just like any other bit of floor until someone triggered the trap, and then the person who triggered it would find the floor suddenly falling away beneath them. Valterra figured it would be the perfect way to make sure invaders couldn't avoid his fourth floor once they realized it was all aquatic.

Having finished all of that, Valterra still felt as though something was missing, even as he sealed the top half of the big kitchen from the bottom, creating a rock ceiling that was supported by his five-foot pillars. He now had a large cavern, though still much smaller than the tall folk might find comfortable, which was all to the good as far as Valterra was concerned.

What was he missing?

He knew he still needed creatures, but that wasn't all of it. The large entrance into the living room hadn't been sealed off yet, but it wasn't that. He had shut it temporarily, making sure to leave holes so that his Aether circulation wouldn't be ruined again. The last thing he wanted was for Aether to pool up on the fifth floor without reaching his core.

As he was finishing up, he realized what he needed. He needed conflict. He only had one major predator in mind, and it wouldn't be enough for the kind of ecosystem he wanted to build, one based on the struggle to Ascend. Contemplating this, he looked through his various creatures. He wanted something that would fit the wooden cave aesthetic he was going for and yet also smart enough to trigger his traps for him.

When the solution finally dawned on him, he mentally berated himself. He already had the solution and had, in fact, summoned some for his first and third floors already. He went to the bottom of the basement stairs and began forming an impressive citadel right on the edge of the waters.

And then he populated it.

With Mouse Soldiers and Scouts.

He really had no excuse as to why he hadn't thought to include them within his fifth floor, other than the fact that he already had those creatures throughout his dungeon in suitable numbers. In the fifth floor, the Aether content was greater. Furthermore, the environment and the ensuing conflicts would help these mice evolve quicker into what he wanted them to be.

Now he just had to make their competition.

He started by summoning some *savage minks* and releasing them onto the floor. As a higher Rank creature, they would be the apex predator of the floor and thus push the surrounding creatures further up the Path of Ascension. They immediately began competing for the choicest spots of moss, so he figured they would be fine until he finished with the rest of the floor.

Moving quickly, Valterra went to his Deeplight Belchers and dove into the Framework, looking for some way he could use them. They were integral to the fourth floor, and he wondered if there was some way he could manipulate the Framework so that they could be a part of his fifth floor as well.

He ended up settling on making a variant. It wasn't even that hard. He rid them of their paddles and shrunk them a little to make them around eighteen inches long and nine inches high. They retained their inner lighting and ability to spew superheated, highly nutritious liquid.

He also sharpened their front pair of limbs to make them fearsome weapons in their own right and kept their need to lay eggs in water. He wanted them to head down to the water of the fourth floor to lay their eggs, where they would then have to fight the mice and their cousins before they could. As he released the Framework, he was pleased to see a variant separate from the original, only to frown as the line went down rather than sideways or up.

A new stage on the Path of Ascension has been synthesized from an

existing Framework! The Framework "Deeplight Belcher" now has a preceding Framework:
Deeplight Stalker (Unique, Rank E - Bronze)
The preceding Framework to the Deeplight Belcher, these insectoids have been fashioned to live on land yet remain tied to the underwater layers of their higher Rank cousins. Unlike their underwater cousins, this insect is even more dangerous after it has spewed its caustic load, although they sacrifice control to affect a larger area. Having done so, it makes use of its dimmed interior to pounce on prey once they have been blinded or scalded by the liquid.

Huh. I created a lesser stage? I didn't even know I could do that, Valterra thought to himself. He felt a presence descend and heard a voice he identified as Qual'Dorn.

"Hmm, yes you did. It is most likely because you didn't add anything new, other than making their front legs extra sharp. You mostly just took things away, which, coincidentally, means that its Aether core went through diminishment. Ascension is all about growth, so if you wanted something extra powerful, you would have had to add things to what you already have. I can't say much else, but I figured you might want some answers."

Yeah, that helps a lot! Thanks, Uncle Dorn! Valterra said cheerfully as he went back to work, unaware of the effect he had on the divinity in question.

"Huh. Valterra just called me Uncle Dorn." The other high spirits looked at Qual'Dorn in confusion.

"He... what?" Tal'Irieth asked.

"He called me his Uncle?"

"Well, we did kind of adopt him," Krat'Imos stated calmly. "It figures he would take it literally. You all keep forgetting he is like a kid."

"I kind of like it," Qual'Dorn said with a smile.

"Of course, you would," Trik'Weri said with a smirk.

"What is that supposed to mean?!"

Hmm. Adding things increases the Rank of the Framework; removing things lowers it. Valterra pondered Qual'Dorn's words even as he continued the creation of his fifth floor. He set his *stalkers* loose and watched as they hunted and were hunted by his *minks.*

He now had three creatures that populated his little wooden cave system but still wanted more diversity. He continued to think about it as he created more overhangs and tiny alcoves within the wood before layering the outside with stone.

I need some small things, he realized. He looked at the different Frameworks he had for small things and frowned mentally. *I have a ton of small things*, he thought in frustration, *but none of them seem quite right.*

Then again, he did have his new mold and moss. Every other creature had been used up except for his *bumblebees* and he didn't think they would be happy on the fifth. Also, his instincts really didn't like that for some reason. When he thought hard, he gradually came to understand what they might be warning him of.

His mind went back to his first meeting with the High Council and Tal'Irieth's warning about monsters. Then, Trik'Weri had given him a rundown of Aether cores and their effects on the Path of Ascension and Frameworks in general. Suffice to say, his instincts were telling him that the amount of Aether flowing into his fifth floor would, at best, kill any mundane creature he summoned. The worst thing that could happen would be if the pain twisted them into a monster.

Valterra shuddered. *No, thank you,* he said to himself. *Pretty sure we are going to make mistakes, but let's not make that one. I think we can just let this floor be for now. Besides, it's not like I can't add things later, right?* Satisfied with his internal argument, Valterra confirmed the floor before drifting off into thought. There were more floors to come, and he needed to determine how he was going to fill them.

Fifth floor created!

The Core has created his fifth floor with an active and diverse ecosystem that combines prey, predator, and environment with Aether.

Progress to Core Ascension: 80%

Chapter 30

Discovering Options

Valterra knew he was close to Ascension. Only one more floor and he would be ready to Ascend again. Through his dungeon body, he could sense that most of his problems would be fixed if he just gave it time. His dungeon, now that he had fixed the horrendous Aether flow, was beginning to work properly. Aether flowed in and met his creatures, who used it and various invaders to grow.

His fourth floor was looking healthier, with the grasses growing taller and more vibrant now that they had more Aether to draw from. His Deeplight Belchers seemed happier and were a lot more numerous than when he had first seeded them. His Great Tidal Whale was doing her best to cull their numbers, but it seemed like a losing fight. The Deeplight Belchers were expanding rapidly throughout the floor, and while that was a good thing, the Core also didn't want them to think they owned it.

Valterra decided to think and act at the same time. Even as he pondered what to do for his sixth floor, he went about summoning more whales. It still took a ton of Aether to do, but he also wasn't summoning complete adults. They were more like juveniles, halfway into adulthood. He notified the original even as the new whales slipped into the water.

As she raced to meet them, she seemed rather excited. Looking into the Framework, Valterra winced a little. Of course, she would be happy. Great Tidal Whales, for all of their massive size and impressive powers, were also part of a pod. They swam together, ate together, and hunted together. His lone matriarch had been without a pod for a while now.

Satisfied that he had fixed that little issue with his fourth floor, he moved around checking on his previous work. Each floor was working fine. There could be a bit more variety for all of his floors except the third, but he supposed that would come with time. At this point, he figured he could get away with a few experiments. He wasn't fully set on what he wanted in his sixth floor, but he had some ideas.

His first three floors acted like concentric rings that drew invaders in. His fourth floor was a death trap in case anyone decided to try and dig their way to him. The fifth floor was a war zone between three different creatures and protected the east side of the house. His Aether funnel stretched from the ceiling of the living room to the floor and descended straight down through the fourth. The West Wing began where the living room ended and contained the ritual room, the furnace room, and the bedroom. The furnace room felt particularly odd to his senses, so he made a mental note to check it out after his Ascension.

Each of these rooms could be utilized as floors; some could even be made into two if he so desired by separating the bottom from the top as he had with the kitchen and his fifth floor. Right now, the dungeon was balanced, and he needed that in order for the Aether to continue to flow to his column so that it could reach his core. Any floors he placed in the West Wing would throw that balance into chaos.

I could redo everything again, I suppose? he thought idly to himself. He shook off that thought as soon as he had it.

The main issue was that he lacked the Framework and the creative energy to create those extra floors anyway. Then redo the Aether flow on top of that? Forget it. For all that he wanted to play and create, Valterra hadn't really seen much of the world. He could see a little bit more of it now that the whole house was a part of him. He could see the clearing and the surrounding trees, but that didn't really give him an idea of what to create. So he settled on what he could do.

He still had some Divine Potential left. He knew that he could name creatures and he certainly wanted to. His Mouse Captain came to mind as deserving of one. He knew that he could create a divine domain that would give him the ability to shape the space in any way he wanted without using Aether to do so. To be honest, though, that wasn't a major consideration at the moment.

Sighing to himself, he turned to the space he had set up above the fifth floor. For now, this would be his sixth floor, but it needed its own kind of ecosystem if it was going to be enough to push him to the next stage.

Valterra reached for his new powers and froze as his Divine Potential activated. Reality shifted, and his mind expanded to include concepts he had never heard before. Using his power to create his mouse guardian's artifacts paled in comparison to the raw data flooding his core at the thought of making a new Framework.

Alien ideas mixed with other thoughts and concepts beyond his understanding. The composition of a Spark Matrix and the right way to connect it with a nascent spirit provided by the Maker. How to form an Aether core and connect it to the Aether conduits that ran throughout a magical creature's body.

In a panic, Valterra disconnected from the stream of divinity. As he recovered, he felt his System light up. Checking the screen, he was surprised to find a message from Krat'Imos.

Hey there, little one. If using your Divine Potential to create creatures is too much for you at the moment, I figured I would install a little help in the form of a new kind of system. I call it the Framework Helpdesk.

The name needs some work, but it should be ready for you to use. I look forward to seeing what you can create.

— Krat'Imos

Valterra sent a grateful feeling upward and began looking for the new system. He found it as a new icon within the system, just above where his Frameworks rested within his soul. He gingerly permitted it to open and was relieved when all it did was open a new series of messages.

Welcome to the Framework Helpdesk!

Please choose from among the following basic templates:

Animal:
A living organism that feeds on organic matter typically has specialized sense organs and a nervous system, which allows it to respond rapidly to stimuli.

Plant:
A living organism of the kind exemplified by trees, shrubs, herbs, grasses, ferns, and mosses, typically growing in a permanent site, absorbing water and inorganic substances through its roots, and synthesizing nutrients in its leaves by photosynthesis using the green pigment chlorophyll.

Fungus:
Any of a group of spore-producing organisms feeding on organic matter, including molds, yeast, mushrooms, and toadstools.

Valterra didn't hesitate to choose animal. He needed different creatures for his new floor, and he didn't think plants or fungi would provide the best template. Once selected, animal expanded to include more options.

Please choose from among the following:

Vertebrates:
An animal of a large group distinguished by the possession of a
backbone or spinal column, including mammals, birds, reptiles,
amphibians, and fishes.

Invertebrates:
An animal lacking a backbone, such as an arthropod, mollusk,
annelid, coelenterate, etc. The invertebrates constitute an artificial
division of the animal kingdom, comprising 95 percent of animal
species and about thirty different phyla.

Valterra didn't read the options as much as he felt them. The vertebrates contained creatures as small as his house mice to creatures as big as the Great Tidal Whale. He only got vague hints of what it entailed, but he gathered that they would be what he wanted.

The invertebrates also contained creatures that could fly, especially the arthropods, which he gathered were where the majority of his current creatures came from in the form of various bugs. He knew he would return, if only to customize the Framework for his Danians. For now, though, he chose vertebrates.

Please choose from among the following:

Mammal:
A warm-blooded vertebrate animal of a class distinguished by the
possession of hair or fur, the secretion of milk by females for the
nourishment of the young, and (typically) the birth of live young.

Bird:
A warm-blooded egg-laying vertebrate distinguished by the
possession of feathers, wings, and a beak and (typically) by being able
to fly.

Reptile:
A vertebrate animal of a class that includes snakes, lizards, crocodiles,

turtles, and tortoises. They are distinguished by having dry, scaly skin and typically laying soft-shelled eggs on land.

Amphibian:
A cold-blooded vertebrate animal of a class that comprises frogs, toads, newts, and salamanders. They are distinguished by having an aquatic gill-breathing larval stage, followed (typically) by a terrestrial lung-breathing adult stage.

Fish:
A limbless, cold-blooded vertebrate animal with gills and fins living wholly in water.

Additional notes by Krat'Imos:
"Be aware that these are base templates and do not have a Rank attached to them. The Ranking system exists to provide dungeons with an idea of how much Aether is present in a creature at its current stage on the Path of Ascension. To create your own Framework, you must utilize the base templates and then add Aether to it.
"This is usually a highly chaotic process, and it is at this stage that your Divine Potential comes into play in the form of this Helpdesk. You pick and choose what you want, and it will tell you the resulting Ranking and what it will cost in Divine Potential to create. If you accept, the system will do the rest. Be creative. I look forward to seeing what kind of unique creatures you bring to life."

There was a lot to take in. The insane amount of diversity hinted at in just these five options made him glad he had chosen it instead of the invertebrates. He would touch the other 95% of animals when he had Ascended further. The note at the bottom filled the Core with a measure of relief. He was excited to use his new powers, but if he was being honest with himself, the incident with the monsters had scared him worse than he liked to admit.

Now, though, he had a way to use it safely, and he felt some part of himself itch to get started. He also wanted to prove to himself and to the

gods that he could make a worthy creature for his sixth floor. He wanted to wow Krat'Imos with how he used the new system he had been given and show that the time spent on him wasn't a waste.

Valterra turned back to the Helpdesk and began going through the different types of vertebrate animals. He immediately dismissed fish because, although there were examples of flying fish listed within, they couldn't live without water for very long. Amphibians had the same problem, although he took note of both of them for later. They might help him flesh out his fourth floor with more options.

He settled on mammals, birds, and reptiles because they had the most flight examples between them. Birds interested him, especially the hunting birds known as raptors. They were fierce and fast with wickedly sharp beaks and talons. If he wanted a flying creature, the raptors would be a good choice.

Despite their advantages, however, Valterra was drawn to the mammals and their one species of flying creatures. Bats. They fascinated him, and it helped that they looked like large fuzzy mice. They weren't, of course. They were a totally separate species, but the similarity was there, and Valterra had a preference for mice. On the other hand, they were far less fierce than the raptors. They didn't have beaks or talons that could rip and tear flesh.

They were still impressive, though. They didn't rely on a hollow bone structure like birds and didn't have feathers. Their wings were more like oversized hands with membranes stretched between the fingers, and Valterra found that fact hilarious. They were omnivores and ate a wide variety of small creatures, and they ate a lot. The rate at which their bodies went through food was insane. The fact remained that they weren't the terrifying aerial hunters that he wanted for his sixth floor.

Valterra mentally shrugged. He would just have to experiment. It wasn't like he hadn't done similar things before. He dipped into the reptiles briefly to see if they had anything he could add and largely liked what he saw. Many of them were carnivores and had various ways of devouring prey. None quite caught his fancy as much as the bats did, but maybe he could use some aspects of them in his new creature. He especially appreciated their use of scales and shells as protection.

The Core began by choosing the basic bat template. In his mind, an image of a bat formed like an in-depth drawing. Veins, muscles, ligaments, tendons, and cartilage could all be seen within the model. He took his time looking at the original model before he got to work. One thing he noticed that was missing was Aether conduits. For whatever reason, the template didn't have them present.

Huh, I wonder why that is. Valterra then looked back at the note that Krat'Imos had left for him and things became clear. *Oh, if it doesn't have a Rank then it wouldn't really need Aether conduits since it has no Aether to begin with. I wonder if they gain them over time as they're infused with Aether or if it is a result of the Ascension process.*

He turned to look at his boon to confirm that the max Rank he could create was Rank E. *Hmm, so I guess I'm in charge of how the creature will develop its conduits. I suppose it would depend on what I want it to be able to do.*

Having reasoned through this development, he looked at other creatures that had caught his eye to add them to his bat template. He started with the reptiles since they had a wide variety of interesting features. First, he chose to replace the bat's legs with scaled limbs that ended in clawed feet. He wasn't sure which lizard it was from, but he thought it looked pretty good. The addition made his creation lean too far forward, so the Core added a long flexible tail to help it maintain balance. To finish off the wings, he gave them a single sharp talon where the primary joint was. He figured the creature would use it to hang off of things and latch on to prey.

Next, he toughened the skin and fur of the main body using a mammal called the *honey badger* and combined it with the scales of a reptile called a *crocodile*. The badger provided a tough skin that was still able to stretch easily, and the crocodile added a length of rigid studs along the spine of the creature. The scales reminded Valterra of the armor plates he had seen in his borrowed memories. He figured it would make it easier for the creature to flex when flying while also protecting it if it got into a fight.

He strengthened the wings and expanded them to the maximum distance he could make them while remaining within the domain of his title. Compared to the body of the creature, the wings were massive, but they would need to be to carry its new weight. For the final touch, he changed the head to be a rough mix of a bear and a wolf. He also lengthened the neck to make it twist and bite where it needed to. However, the neck wasn't too long because it had to remain fairly stocky so that the muscles that powered its bite weren't affected.

Finished, he carefully looked over the creature he had made and felt excitement bubble up from within him. Now this was a true monster. With its scales and bristly fur, it made for quite the sight. He accepted the system prompt and watched as the system moved things around internally so that the resulting Framework would work properly.

Valterra was grateful for the assistance. Maybe if he was as large and old as a normal divine dungeon would be at his stage, he would have the ability to do it all himself. Unfortunately, he wasn't at that level yet. He knew he was unique—the gods had said so—but that didn't mean he was as powerful.

He shook those thoughts away and looked at the new prompt that rolled across his screen, showing him the results of his experimentation.

Congratulations! You have crafted your very first dungeon monster via the Framework Helpdesk!

Would you like to name your creation?
Yes / No

Valterra couldn't smile but if he could, he would have been beaming. *Yes please!*

Chapter 31

Naming a Monster

Valterra immediately chose the "Yes" option. He didn't want his new creature to be an unknown, and he wanted to name it something that would strike fear into the hearts of any delvers that eventually made it to his humble abode.

The system then prompted him to make a decision, but he was ready with an answer. He had a name already picked out, one which he thought was rather good. *Flying wolfbear!* He declared excitedly, only to jump when a presence descended rapidly. As the voice started speaking, he realized with a start that it was Maph'Ira who had come this time.

"No, no, no, my dear little one. I cannot allow such a travesty!" The horror in her voice made Valterra shrink a little.

Is it really that bad? he asked sadly. He felt the goddess's tone change as she backtracked hastily.

"No, no, it wasn't terrible at all," she said, and Valterra narrowed his metaphorical eyes at where he imagined her presence to be.

You said it was a travesty, he accused, and he heard her sigh.

"It wasn't the name that was the travesty per se," she said. "It's just that your first created monster should have some pizzazz to it."

Valterra pondered her response before asking, *What's pizzazz?* His question seemed to encourage her because she responded with excitement.

"Pizzazz is possibly the greatest invention of mortal kind! If something has pizzazz, it means that it's got a life of its own and it's full of vitality and glamour! I can't imagine a more beautiful thing!"

Valterra absorbed the goddess's description calmly. *So... why is that important?* He could feel the goddess deflate slightly before rallying.

"If your creature names have pizzazz, then when delvers come to brave your dungeon, they will treat it with the proper respect and caution. There are rituals and abilities they can use to reveal the names of your creatures and some of their strengths and weaknesses, so if you name it right, they will be much more respectful and less dismissive."

Valterra accepted this explanation without comment. He could tell she was serious, and he appreciated the fact that she cared enough to try to help. *Okay then, what should I name it instead?*

He could almost see her rub her hands together gleefully. "One of the best ways to add pizzazz is to use the Old Tongue. It adds depth to a name that otherwise wouldn't be there. Your name is based on that language, too, as a matter of fact."

So it will seem older than it is? Valterra asked.

"Yes, exactly!" Maph'ira praised. "Delvers will leave with the names of your unique creatures, and scholars will ponder their meaning. It will encourage delvers to be more cautious when entering your dungeon. The more unique creatures you have, the less they will be able to plan ahead, and the more time you will have to grow. It will make you safer."

Valterra finally gave up and surrendered to the fact that his creation would not be called a flying wolfbear. *What should I call it, then? I don't know the Old Tongue at all.*

Maph'Ira just laughed. "That's why I'm here, silly. All of the high spirits know the Old Tongue." She paused for a moment before continuing, "Perhaps we can include a primer on the Old Tongue with your next

Ascension. I'll talk to Krat'Imos about it." She seemed to shake herself before continuing.

"Anyway, here's what I'm thinking. There was an old monster ages ago that looked remarkably similar to your creation. Of course, it was massive and far uglier than what you have created. It was also a natural, unique Ascension and therefore couldn't breed in order to pass on its peculiar traits. Despite all of that, it was a fearsome predator and the people of the past took to calling it the wyvre. In current common, that would translate to swooping death. It was never killed, to my knowledge. Died of old age."

Valterra liked that fact. He liked that a lot. An ancient monster that had never been killed, seemingly resurrected en masse within his dungeon, albeit on a much smaller scale.

As if reading his mind, which he suspected was highly possible, Maph'Ira spoke up. "While we're on the topic of naming, one of the things you can do when creating a creature is to denote whether it is the adult form or not. By denoting it as young, you are telling the system, and through it your Divine Potential, that you want it to have room to grow."

Oh, oh! Like my newts! Valterra interjected excitedly.

"Yes, dear, exactly like them. Most creatures in the wild don't follow that pattern. They usually Ascend to a higher Rank and their offspring match it as long as they mate equally among their species. Dungeons can do things differently, and having a Divine Spark is a massive boon to the process. The only exceptions to this rule in the wild are things like your Sylcyne Mountain Efts who transform their very nature multiple times."

"This will cost more Potential at the start," she warned, "but it will enable you to build upon the Framework more easily later on. Because of your boon, you're perfectly situated for creating juvenile creatures that can grow beyond the limits of your title as they Ascend. This will allow you to control just how big your creatures become rather than letting the system do it for you."

The Core appreciated the advice. He knew that without targeted Ascensions, his creatures could become much larger than he was capable of

containing within his floors. He could expand, of course, and he knew that his lower floors would have larger spaces, but he liked being small and he liked his title. It was just... who he was. His dungeon, and therefore his creatures, would reflect that reality. That might change as he got older, but for now, this was enough.

So, Valterra said slowly, *I should call it a young wyvre?*

Maph'Ira confirmed it for him but spoke up to further explain. "The system may use the term juvenile, but it means the same thing."

Valterra put the name in the system, and sure enough, the creature was labeled a juvenile wyvre.

Unique creature "Juvenile Wyvre" base template created!

Analyzing... Base template cost... Divine Potential cost confirmed!

"Juvenile Wyvre" currently costs 20 Divine Potential to create.

Would you like to infuse the base template with Aether?
Note: If you do not choose to infuse the base template, then the Framework "Juvenile Wyvre" will have no Rank assigned and will have to Ascend normally.

I would like to infuse the template, please, Valterra projected to the Helpdesk. As soon as he did so, he felt the new system respond with the equivalent of a mental question mark. The system wished to know what attributes he wanted to impart. Valterra figured he would go as high as he could while still remaining in Rank E territory, and he figured the system would tell him when he reached that point.

Smarter, stronger, faster, heal quickly, have power over elemental affinities, and manipulation of Aether itself, Valterra declared, and he watched as the system responded.

Attributes chosen:

Enhanced intelligence, enhanced physicality, enhanced vitality, elemental affinity, Aether manipulation.

Analyzing... Resulting Framework Rank... Rank B - Silver
Recalibrating... Attributes synthesized... Rank E – Bronze

Attribute given: Aether Blood (Low)
This creature's blood has been modified to contain Aether itself, albeit in a small quantity. It has no need for Aether conduits or an Aether core as its heart and blood take over their function. The Aether in the blood provides a minor healing effect on the creature while strengthening musculature, increasing bone density, and generally providing an increase in raw physicality. By harnessing the Aether in its blood, this creature gains a small affinity for the various basic elements and is able to sense Aether flows in the air.
Applying Aether Blood (Low) to "Juvenile Wyvre"... Complete!

Creating Framework...

Juvenile Wyvre (Unique, Rank E - Bronze)
A unique creation of the Dungeon Valterra and carrying the legacy of the first wyvre, this amalgamation of various creatures has become a true creature in its own right. Its blood has been transformed into a pseudo-Aetheric substance, giving it minor control over the basic elements and even the flow of Aether itself. Furthermore, its heart now acts as a pseudo-core. Roosting like a bat and living in small colonies, these hunters have been created to be apex aerial predators. Still juvenile, these creatures have plenty of room to grow and have been given every means to do so.

This Framework costs 250 Divine Potential. Potential left after creation... 294 units.

Would you like to create this Framework?
Yes / No

Valterra looked upon his creation with awe. It was perfect. Not the true terror that he had set out to make, but the Potential was overwhelming as shown in its cost. Two hundred and fifty Divine Potential was almost half of what he had left after igniting his Divine Spark. It was probably the best Bronze Rank Framework he could make with what he had, but it also meant that he wouldn't be able to create the Iron Rank stage of Ascension for his Danians. If the highest price he could get for a Bronze was 250, then it made sense for the higher ranks to cost even more.

The Core mentally shrugged. This was what he had decided to do in order to complete his sixth floor and Ascend. He mentally selected the *Yes* option and felt power flow out of his core to shape his creation. He felt Maph'Ira give him a smile of approval and then begin to depart. He sent her a feeling of gratitude and then became completely focused on his new creation.

Once the Framework was fully formed, he wasted no time in summoning the first one. He summoned a male first, forming him out of Aether. His body was long and sinuous, and his wings flexed wide and powerful. He looked like a wonderfully terrifying monster. Valterra sent a feeling of pride at his new creation and watched as it preened at the attention. He summoned a whole colony after watching the lone one fly around for a while and let them do their thing.

Then he went about finishing up his sixth floor. He made a few more ledges and roosts for the *Wyvres* and created a door leading into the living room. He set it in the largest roost where Aether could flow to his central column and delvers could eventually travel deeper.

He then went ahead with an idea he'd had for some time. He formed little islands and carved the Aether holding runes from the ritual room onto their sides. Then, he took hold of his Authority over the element of air and infused it into the Aether currently pouring into the runes. As the islands gradually rose off the ground, Valterra cackled happily. He created multiple islands with a different number of runes on each one, which seemed to control how high they could rise. This fact delighted the Core to no end.

The Juvenile Wyvres seemed to love them as well, darting back and forth among the various floating islands. Valterra seeded them with moss and let them hang over the edge until they reached the next islands in line. In this way, he connected each island with moss bridges. Then on the islands at the top, he created little craters and divots that led to the edge. He then repeated the runes of holding but infused them with water and watched as water bubbled forth to fill the craters and then trickle to the edge, where they fell in tiny waterfalls that helped to hydrate the moss and make them trickier to climb by delvers.

He finished things off by creating openings in much of the ceiling leading to the fifth floor, which would allow both delvers and other creatures to climb higher. He couldn't wait for his creatures to grow and Ascend. They would make their way deeper into the dungeon and would have to confront the Wyvres to travel further, even as the Wyvres grew themselves. He confirmed the boundaries of the floor and felt it lock into place deep in his soul.

What followed was a sensation of deep exhaustion as Valterra felt himself breathe deeply, sending a flood of Aether to slam into his column where it was condensed down until it eventually reached his core. He felt himself sink into a different kind of state but wasn't alarmed as he continued to be semi-aware. He saw his gem begin to shine, converting the raw Aether into something else as golden light exploded forth.

Sixth floor created!

The Core has created his sixth floor with active rune structures, integrated with the environment, and an apex predator. All parameters for the Core's second Ascension have been met. Prepare to begin the climb.

Progress to Core Ascension: 100%

Preparing to Ascend!

Chapter 32

Ascending

Within the house of Archmage Calamvor, the tiniest dungeon core in existence was going through his second Ascension. Golden light bubbled forth from Valterra's inner depths, almost physical in the way that it formed layers upon layers of gleaming blue-green crystal. The inner workings of the jewel that made up his core shifted back and forth, the space inside growing larger.

The Spark Matrix of the young core grew but stuttered to a halt as the tiny sigils etched into the jewel became strained. No longer able to support the Spark Matrix that had begun to grow, the sigils failed one by one. The Ascension ceased as Valterra died. Or he would have, if he did not already possess a Divine Spark. And divinity, no matter its size, was extremely hard to kill.

In a subconscious bid to save himself, Valterra's Spark drew on his reserves of Divine Potential to fuel his own Ascension. The sigils that had been carved with great care by the archmage dissipated completely before being replaced by something else. The place where the sigils had been were smoothed over as the interior of the gemstone changed under the power of Aether and Potential.

In its place formed a complex array of crystalline structures, each interlocking with the other. The latticework slowly grew in complexity and size until the Core rested complete upon his pedestal, a gleaming jewel without a trace of his prior artificiality. Valterra's Spark Matrix, in his altered state of consciousness, integrated completely into its new home. The latticework lit up, and the light of Ascension shone once more as the Core continued on his path of growth.

None of Valterra's creatures noticed the infinitesimally small time it took for Valterra to recover, but there were sighs of relief from the divinities clustered around the scene as they scried the young core. Krat'Imos in particular sighed loudly. "That was certainly something. Looks like we missed another dangerous loophole in the System. Should've known those sigils would fail. In fact, I'm surprised they didn't fail when his Spark ignited divinity."

Tal'Irieth nodded quietly while Trik'Weri spoke up. "It probably has to do with the fact that although he became divine, his Spark didn't grow in size but quality." His comment was greeted by nods from his other deities. The tranquility of the moment was shattered as another divinity burst onto the scene.

"What did I miss?!" Ata'Laya exclaimed as she gave Qual'Dorn a quick kiss on the cheek, their opposite domains sparking slightly from the contact.

Qual'Dorn smiled fondly as he gave his wife a peck back. "You missed a lot, actually. We might have had to step in again to save Valterra, which is exactly what he doesn't need at this point in time. Our priests are already starting to notice our attention, and I would hate for Valterra to feel the weight that our clergy can bring to bear on him—especially at this point in his growth."

Ata'Laya groaned in response. "Tell me about it. All my priests want me to do for them is 'Destroy this!' and 'Destroy that!' Not to mention all the revolutionaries praying that I help them overthrow their governments."

Qual'Dorn scoffed lightly, but then his face took on a flirty look. "Well, my dear, perhaps you should let loose a little. I haven't seen you go off in a little while. And we haven't sparred in ages. Maybe one or two revolutions would shake things up."

Ata'Laya ignored the good-natured groans of the other divinities as she got close to her husband's chest and began playing with his beard. "Hmm, that does sound nice. Then maybe you can catch bad little me and..." Whatever she was about to say was interrupted by a cough from Tal'Irieth who looked at her pointedly. Grinning, she leaned up and whispered loudly into Qual'Dorn's ear, "Later..." Qual'Dorn just chuckled and gave her a roguish wink. The deities ignored the two and went back to watching over their young charge.

The following days drifted by as Valterra went through Ascension. The first few days had been a deep sleep with very little interaction on his part. But slowly, he became more aware. It was an interesting thing as he didn't think this had happened the last time he Ascended. Then again, he hadn't been fully sapient at the time.

His thoughts weren't a conscious thing either; they were more like threads that he aimlessly followed to their conclusion. Those threads led to other threads, and so his thoughts continued. More than that, though, he was more in tune with his dungeon than he had been in a long time.

Rather than being and feeling like a singular entity with many moving parts, he now felt like those many different pieces. It was like his consciousness had fractured into many points of semi-coherent awareness. He saw bits and pieces from his creatures' perspectives and their various struggles.

Despite the conflict, the feeling he got back was of completeness. His dungeon, now that he had fixed the horrendous Aether flow, was now working properly. Aether flowed in and met his creatures, who used it and various invaders to grow. They, in turn, Ascended into various new forms.

Your "Mouse Soldier" is ready to Ascend! x2
Your "Mouse Guard" is ready to Ascend! x3
Your "Constricting Green Snake" is ready to Ascend! x2
Your "Sylcyne Mountain Eft" is ready to Ascend!
Your "Hunting Pack-Mantis" is ready to Ascend!
Your "Iridescent Ground Beetle" is ready to Ascend! X3
Your "Mouse Scout" is ready to Ascend!
Your "Sylcyne Slug" is ready to Ascend! X3
Your "House Mouse" is ready to Ascend! x5
Your "Wolf Spider" is ready to Ascend!

And so on and so forth.

Unlike when he was fully conscious, it was so much easier to choose a stage of Ascension while in this "sleep." His different points of awareness gave him clues here and there as to which Ascensions his creatures wished for. A dim part of his mind recognized that he chose things he might not have while awake, but that part was still tired even after all these days of rest.

Not all his creatures made it. Some invaders were stronger than others and were able to catch and feast on his creatures. In his fugue state, Valterra knew only contentment. His dungeon was a crucible that forged his creatures into stronger versions of themselves. He had known some would die in this pursuit even when he had been conscious.

So he watched as his creatures struggled, Ascended, and moved deeper. With his awareness splintered so widely within his dungeon, it made it so much simpler to be present when they hunted invaders as well. Then, he simply dissolved the invader and soothed the creature with some Aether before drifting on, his awareness ebbing and flowing with his breath.

New Frameworks acquired!
Kindling Brushtail (Rank F - Copper)
A type of squirrel found in the north, this creature has reached a stage of Ascension adapted to frigid temperatures, utilizing its Aether reserves to more perfectly regulate its temperature and surroundings.

Often characterized by its habit of lighting small fires to keep itself warm, the Kindling Bushtail is active all winter. Its powers grant it a decent defense against most predators as a nasty burn accompanies most attempts to make it a meal.

Coppertip Mole (Rank E - Bronze)
Found around copper mineral deposits, this mole has evolved to dig through such material. Consummate burrowers, these moles live by feeding on the magical grubs and other creatures drawn to magical ore. Like their more humble counterpart, they are unable to see, but unlike them, they can manipulate Aether to give themselves a form of tremor sense.

At the beginning of each breath, he was on the third floor. He witnessed the waking of his third-floor guardian and the absolute terror he inspired on every living thing on the floor. He was impressive with beautiful green scales and gleaming golden eyes. He saw the moment his guardian hypnotized a mouse and struck with lightning speed. It wasn't even a contest, and he felt his guardian's satisfaction.

He watched the struggle on the third for a time before being drawn inexorably into the first and second floors. Then, he flowed into the fourth floor before drifting into the fifth. This occurred at every single one of his entrances before they met up at the fifth floor, continued on up through the sixth, and reached his column, which was condensed down until it finally seeped into his core.

It was in these moments that he was most aware, and it was in one of these moments a week into his sleep that he felt his Mouse Captain stir. His kin beasts had already awoken and had been standing guard, the Mouse Squire in particular.

Valterra dimly noted that twelve days had passed since his loyal first-floor guardian had gone to sleep. He must have spent around six days reshaping his dungeon and creating the fifth and sixth floors. His track of time must have been dreadful since it had taken only a couple of days from his perspective.

The Mouse Captain stirred and shook himself before glancing around. He started by looking at the pedestal before rising quickly and looking every which way, growing more and more panicked.

He's looking for me, Valterra realized as he was drawn away towards his core. In that almost awareness, he crafted a message for his loyal guardian. It wasn't much of a message. More like an image with an "I am here" sign attached and a vague sense of direction.

Valterra struggled to hold on to the message through his fragmented awareness, and when he got to his Mouse Captain, he released it with a sigh. *Hopefully, that made sense.* Valterra thought sleepily as he once more fell into a deep slumber, his mind tired from the strain of the message and his continuing Ascension.

Throughout the dungeon, creatures looked up as *the call* resounded through it. Hazy images of a core on a pedestal were imprinted on their minds with a vague sense of direction. They fought all the harder to Ascend. They had seen their creator, and even the barest hint of the divinity present in his aura called to their most primal instincts.

His ear flicked upright as he heard *the call.* Unlike the other creatures, he knew that it was addressed to him. His master had let him know where he was and had seen fit to give him a challenge. The Mouse Captain would answer. He rose and looked around at his kin.

They stood straight and tall, and he was pleased to note that the creator had seen fit to grant them the same Ascension as had been given to him—except for one. Following the nudge in the back of his Ascended mind, his gaze zeroed in on the odd one out.

In that mouse's gaze, he saw something that mirrored his own heart toward his creator. Loyalty and devotion. It both pleased and frightened him. He understood by that one glance that he was now responsible for this mouse in a way that only his creator might understand. His whiskers quivered at the thought.

Placing a paw upon his squire's shoulder, he gave him a nod before turning to the others. He communicated via his deep bass squeaking. "*Deeper we are called. Deeper we go.*"

The other mice looked up at him in wonder at his ability to talk and nodded vigorously. Hefting his new battle blade, the Mouse Captain returned the nod before leading the way. He left his nest behind along with his old treasures. He had a bigger prize waiting for him below. At the head of his small company, he began his first dungeon delve.

Ascensions complete!
"Mouse Guard" has Ascended into the Framework "Mouse Soldier."
"Mouse Guard" has Ascended into the Framework "Mouse Squire."

New Framework acquired!

Mouse Squire (Unique, Rank E - Bronze)
Rather than follow in the paw steps of its kin beast, this mouse gives up the direct path of the Mouse Soldier to gain glory by serving its kin instead. The life of a Mouse Squire is one of service and learning. Serving as a shield bearer and armorer for its master, the Mouse Squire is proficient with all the weapons its master wields, if in a lesser way. This is so that it might stand beside its master side by side on the day of battle without flinching, guarding its master's blind spots.
"Sylcyne Garter Snake" has Ascended into the Framework "Emerald Adder."

New Framework acquired!

Emerald Adder (Rank D - Iron)
Giving up its constricting coils, this snake has chosen new weapons. With a powerful strike, this snake is capable of delivering deadly poison directly to its foe's body. With its mental affinity, it has the ability to channel Aether into its eyes, allowing it to freeze weak-willed prey for mere moments before striking.
Ascension complete!

"Mouse Soldier" has Ascended into the Framework "Mouse Captain."

New Framework acquired!

Mouse Captain (Unique, Rank D - Iron)
The next step on the road to leadership, this mouse chooses to be an example to all mouse-kin. Adept with the sword, the mouse treads a path few will walk but is all the more noble for it. To lead is to display courage in the face of opposition and to serve steadfastly. By the sweat of brow and whisker, the Mouse Captain will see its lord's will done.

Chapter 33

Danger Comes

"Move faster, you lollygagging excuses for Fair Folk! We're almost there!" Cormac heard his second-in-command roar. The person in question was a large *boggart* named Killian. By the aura he gave off, he was only a little ways from his third stage, hence the reason he had joined this little expedition. Cormac was glad for his help, though he would watch Killian like a hawk anyway. It felt good to have another earth-aligned in charge underneath him, even if boggarts did tend to absorb water essence as well.

There were others in his band he would have to watch out for. Most were barely sapient first stage fodder. They had a pretty even group of *gnomes, sylphs, salamanders,* and even a smattering of *undines.* However, those weren't who he was watching.

His primary focus was on the three *lesser drakes* accompanying them. They were brothers and young enough into their second stage that he didn't need to worry about them too much. However, drakes, even lesser ones, had dragon blood running through their veins. There were enough legends about salamanders who had Ascended to true dragonhood that he couldn't afford to turn a blind eye.

His other source of concern was the pair of *pixies* that had come along. They were a stage down from true *fairies,* but they concerned him nonetheless. He hadn't wanted to take them in case they were spies for Horace or the council, but he also didn't want them telling on him if they were rejected. So he brought them along and kept a close eye on them. It would be hard to keep the rabble in line once they got to the dungeon, but that was fine by him. He just needed enough bodies to get him in the door and a good group to delve deeper. He already had them picked out too.

Killian was one of them. Boggarts had a regeneration gland in their bodies that activated when they were hurt badly. They could even regenerate limbs, although that was only if it hadn't been used yet. The gland, accompanied by a boggart's larger size, made him an excellent frontline choice.

Besides Killian, Cormac had chosen two others. One was Fiona, a *brownie* and Cormac's fiancée. She was pretty enough, he admitted to himself. Their engagement had been a political and financial arrangement orchestrated by her father a long time ago. Cormac's only stipulation had been that she would need to match his stage of Ascension. That had been before the tall folk had locked them out of the dungeons. Her fire to Ascend and delve was perhaps even stronger than his, since an unmarried woman, even an engaged one, was seen as an unenviable position.

He snorted in derision at the thought. Fiona was a brilliant craftsman, even hampered as she was by her lack of leprechaun magic. She even had her own shop. He'd even found over the years that his initial dismissal of her had only emboldened her to new heights. He had to admit that her list of achievements was impressive, and in the deepest parts of his subconscious, he knew he desired her company. His pride kept him from any public or even private displays of his growing desire, but she had been the first person he had told about his plan, and her immediate acceptance had warmed him like a forge's bellows.

Shaking away those distracting thoughts, he turned his attention to the last member of their band as he stepped out of a shadow ahead of him.

Ascended from a *dark elven* into a *scáth*, Eoghan was Cormac's secret weapon. He had promised the elusive Fair Folk that he would guarantee his next Ascension in exchange for his help. Scáth were notoriously difficult to pin down due to their darkness affinity, and Cormac would need that flexibility to take out larger threats on his way to the core.

"So?" Cormac asked. "How close are we?"

Eoghan answered his question by pointing, and as Cormac followed the scáth's finger, he saw the trees begin to thin ahead of them. He smiled and rubbed his thick hands together. "Let's go, Fair Folk!" He called over his shoulder. "We've got a dungeon to delve!" As the cheers of the others washed over him, Cormac led the way forward. It was time to conquer a dungeon.

The Mouse Captain grunted as his blade deflected another blow from the large mantis creature. It was larger than the one he had fought so long ago, with black and green chitin providing a pretty decent defense. It wouldn't stop the mouse's blade from penetrating, but it did largely prevent his slaps and deflections from doing serious injury. It had decent battle instincts, he grudgingly admitted as its wickedly bladed front limbs flashed out again from another direction.

He continued to fight off the large bug's advances, monitoring the wider battle as his younger kin fought off the larger bug's smaller evolutions. The pack of insects was slowly overwhelming his group. Despite being of higher Ascension, his mice lacked the one thing that would make the most of their skills—weapons.

That was the Mouse Captain's primary objective, and they had been on their way when the bugs had attacked. It had been a lack of observation on his part, the mouse knew. He had failed to recognize that the first floor had expanded to include all of the space between the inner and outer walls. So much had changed while he slept, and his lord had been busy. The Mouse Captain took a deep breath even as he leaped over another strike, using his tail to unbalance his opponent. Aether-rich air flooded his lungs. Something had changed, because the Aether was purer and cleaner than it had been before.

It was also moving. There was a current now, and despite his desire to delve deeper, the guardian knew he needed to outfit his kin. His blade carved gleaming lines in the air as he fought back the bug, steadily wearing it down with each deflection and swing. Flicking his tail toward a leg, the mouse waited for his chance. The moment the large creature darted to slice off the offending extra limb, he bulled forward in a charge. Caught off guard, the insect attempted to retreat but found itself trapped against the outer wall.

With a quick movement, the mouse headbutted the creature and watched as it shrank away. He placed his blade at its neck and cracked his tail. He didn't know why he did it, but it felt good and it did its job of getting the bug's attention as well as that of its lesser kin. They chittered at him, enraged, but a click from the larger creature made them pause. The two beasts looked at each other, and the Mouse Captain spoke slowly.

"We fight? You die. We go? You stay. Live. Yes?" It had taken him a while and much practice, but his Ascension had slowly trickled knowledge of communication into his brain and he used every opportunity to practice. This exchange would serve two purposes. Either the bug agreed and they went on their way, or the mouse would get a nice bit of Aether. He did not really want the Aether. He was the first, and he knew his lord's heart. He did not wish for meaningless death among his creatures. As the first guardian, the Mouse Captain felt duty-bound to uphold that unspoken law. The bug would be a mighty defense against any intruders, and the mouse refused to take that away from his lord.

Slowly, the bug retracted its deadly limbs and clicked in cautious approval. It would stay and live. The mouse, likewise, slowly retracted his blade and stepped back, walking backward until he was amongst his kin. The lesser insects clearly wanted to strike but were held back by the greater insect's will. Nodding to his opponent, the mouse gathered his kin and set off.

He heard the insects communicate to each other by clicks and chirps, but they did not follow. He checked his kin and found they sported minor wounds that would heal with enough time. He nodded in satisfaction and then motioned them to follow him. He knew where he needed to go.

They wandered the inner road between the walls until they arrived at a small hole. They didn't meet any opposition. A few spiders had scurried up the inner wall, but they were lesser Ascensions and knew to stay away. Upon reaching the hole, he found it to be much smaller than he remembered. Snorting to himself in amusement, the mouse looked down at his muscular Aether-enhanced body and snorted again. Of course, it would be smaller.

With a gesture, his squire came over and received his blade with reverence. That would still take some getting used to. Turning to the hole, he gripped its edges with his mighty paws and flexed. The wood splintered with a loud crack and gave way as he widened the hole. His kin dutifully carried the bits of wood away as the large mouse ripped pieces off the inner wall. Grabbing his blade from the squire, he carved the jagged edges off before squeezing through the newly widened hole.

A familiar sight greeted his eyes. It was dark in the cabinet, but it didn't last long as the Mouse Captain held up a paw, a flame coalescing into existence and brightening up the room. He almost shuddered at the feeling of using his lord's authority. It felt spiritual, in a way that he would never be able to explain even if his Ascension had granted him the knowledge. Shaking off the euphoria, the mouse looked around and honed in on his target.

A large, bulky basket lay close to the huge door that separated the room from the larger edifice. The mouse moved to it and climbed inside, his kin following. Inside the basket were various clothes, and he kept his flame well away from them. On an instinctual level, he knew they would burn, and he did not wish to have to flee from the ensuing flames. His animal instincts shied away from the idea in fear. Glancing at the flame he carried, he wondered whether he would be able to stop the fire with his lord's power. He shrugged. He wasn't going to test it now.

Turning, he grunted, motioning toward a large box. "There," he squeaked gruffly. His kin beasts moved to the box and worked together to remove the lid. The gleam of metal met their astonished gazes. Inside the box were various needles of different sizes, some small and some larger than his original broken needle. The large mouse squeaked in pleasure. Laying his blade down, he moved over to the box and reached inside, choosing a larger needle. He ran his paw over it and felt the Aether within warm his hand.

Enchanted. Just like he had remembered, only he now had a word for the warm feeling. He put it back and motioned to his kin to pick out needles. They took to the task with eagerness, experimenting with various sizes until they had what felt right. When they were finished, he nodded and led the way back out of the basket, picking up his blade on the way out. Going to the door, he attempted to push it open, only to be stopped. He strained harder only to have his efforts be for naught. He slashed at the wood in frustration, only to have his blade meet rock on the other side.

He pawed at his muzzle, cleaning his whiskers as he thought. Using his blade, he slowly carved away the offending wood and was left with a wall of stone. Placing his paw against the stone, he tapped into his lord's authority and began shifting it. He cancelled the fire to use both hands, and the task became more manageable. Gradually, light spilled into the cabinet as a hole formed in the rock.

Almost immediately, Aether—massive quantities of it— flooded into the space. From the richness, the mouse knew they had breached a higher floor. He looked around and took in the huge cave system. Higher up, he could barely see floating rocks connected by long green plants and the shadowy movements of flying beasts. They would have to be careful, but now the mouse knew that they were getting closer to the master. He moved to the other side of the cabinet and closed the other hole by forming a rock

wall. He didn't know why he did, but his instincts told him the path to the new floor shouldn't come from the first.

Returning, he finished making a hole large enough to squeeze through. His smaller kin would be fine. As he exited, he froze at the sound of battle that reached him. Turning to peer deeper, he noticed multiple small forms fighting something larger. Acting again on instinct, he formed a flame and launched it at the larger form. The flame splashed against the creature, and it hissed in displeasure. The light from the fiery flare revealed the monstrously big insect for what it was, but it also revealed the smaller scurrying forms.

Mice. Or more specifically, Mouse Soldiers. The mice in question squeaked in greeting, but the Mouse Captain could see they were in dire straits. They were like his kin behind him had been only a short time ago, in that they had no blades to bear into battle. They valiantly faced a foe with nothing but their empty paws and teeth. The Mouse Captain refused to let them face such a monstrosity alone. Turning to his kin behind him, he motioned at one of them and said, "Collect needles. Then follow." Turning to the rest, he motioned with his blade outstretched. "You follow now. We go!" With those words, he let out his signature bass squeak of challenge and tore across the space separating him from the battle, blade raised high.

Chapter 34

The Raid Begins

Warmeister Geckodo looked out over the clearing to the immense cabin that lay at the center. Over the days since they had arrived, he had seen no sign of the great mage that was said to have been living within. Finally, his kin had overcome their fear and were ready to begin. Cautiously, he led a group of his finest warriors out from the treeline.

Just as he and his warriors were about to step out, he caught sight of movement and froze. Turning, he saw a group of fairykind leave the safety of the forest's edge and begin moving confidently toward the cabin. Hissing quietly, he had his warriors retreat slightly back into the shadows. He watched, livid, as the Fair Folk strolled across the clearing like they owned the very ground they walked on. Geckodo felt his fangs sharpen, and he strived to calm down. It would not do to lose control here.

The fairykind had moved faster than he had expected. They usually took longer to decide on a course of action. At most, the Warmeister figured they would send scouts, but scouts did not worry him. The stage three that led the current assault, though, certainly did. The little figure was arrogant in the way it strode across the green grass leading to the cabin. *As the strong can*, Geckodo thought to himself sourly. He and his kin had long lost the ability to vocalize

normally. He watched, silently seething, as the little people ducked under the outer wooden section before disappearing from sight.

Geckodo hissed in displeasure but contained himself after. His eyes narrowed in thought. Perhaps this was for the best. It was a small group that had come, and only one was a stage three. Many of the Fair Folk were only stage one. As weak as the Fallen had become, they could still defeat those. And Geckodo now knew what they were after—a dungeon.

A young one evidently, and the great mage inside must have either left or died. The Warmeister thought that last one was a bit farfetched, but the human had been old even by tall folk standards. The dungeon might have found some way of dealing with him. Maybe in his sleep.

It didn't matter. What did matter was that his scouts had already identified multiple entrances leading into the dungeon. The Fallen would not fail this time. He waited a few minutes more to make sure the Fair Folk had fully engaged before he mentally goaded his warriors forward. They circled to the opposite side of the building and ducked under the porch there. As Geckodo felt the increased Aether in the atmosphere, he smiled, his fangs glinting white in the shadow cast by the porch. He breathed deeply and caught his warriors doing the same. Here was Aether aplenty and perhaps a solution.

As he breathed in, the Warmeister stiffened in shock. It was barely there, but the Warmeister had never forgotten the smell and taste of divinity. It didn't matter that it was barely noticeable. It didn't matter that it was a dungeon. All at once, the Warmeister's plans changed. He glanced around to make sure his warriors suspected nothing. They did not. He snorted in derision. They had fallen further than he had, after all. It didn't surprise him that they could no longer acknowledge divinity.

Not Warmeister Geckodo, though. He remembered. Remembered the feeling of his Authority being stripped away. Remembered the loss of Potential. He remembered *falling*. This dungeon. He would test it. But perhaps... Perhaps the Fallen had found a new master. All he had to do was pay for an audience. And if he had to pay in blood... so be it.

Cormac breathed deeply as he ripped his claymore out of the mouse he had planted it in. The Aether present in the air revitalized him as nothing else had in a long time. He felt like he was finally living again. A tiny mote of Aether seeped into him from the mouse, but it was barely worth mentioning. He didn't care. After living so long without the satisfaction of a monster kill, he wouldn't say no to any opportunity to deal some mayhem.

The cohesiveness of his group could have been better. As soon as they entered the dungeon's territory, they had encountered chaos—different creatures battling it out all over the place. At first, it had been hard to notice which creatures were normal critters and which were dungeon creations, but as they delved further under the porch, they had come across more and more opposition. The range of creatures was decently impressive, but many barely had any Aether present in them. It was clear from the range that the dungeon had been utilizing any creatures it could get its hands on.

Cormac smiled with glee. It didn't matter at the moment whether or not the dungeon revealed stronger creatures as they delved deeper. All that mattered was the feeling of proper delving once again. He flexed, feeling his muscles drink in the Aether as he breathed it in. The smile never left his face as he charged at another target. He brought his claymore across in a blindingly quick maneuver and separated the mantis's forelimbs at the joint. From there, it took him a single movement more to cleave the insect in two.

Taking a moment, he turned and observed his group. A handful of the stage ones had disappeared in the chaos, most likely confused about the proper way to delve a dungeon. He didn't care much. He still had a tight rein on most of them, and they were moving quickly enough toward the fortress in the distance. That was where the Aether drained deeper.

The Aether content did cause a slight twinge of anxiety within him. The amount of Aether flowing deeper was less than he would have imagined. The floor he was on spread out to either side of him further than he could see, wrapping around the building. He grimaced. He supposed it could be possible that multiple entrances had been made, but as to why the dungeon would do that, Cormac had no answers.

He shrugged. It didn't really matter either way. When he had conquered the dungeon, he could get it to change whichever way he wanted it to. He smiled a little wider at the glee on Fiona's face as she battered another insect to the ground before hardening his expression. The conquest hadn't happened yet. He turned his gaze upon the fortress and marveled at its construction. It was obvious that the dungeon had made it. It looked like a fully functional miniature fortress like the ones he had seen in the lands of the tall folk. It was picture-perfect, which was why he was convinced it was a dungeon creation, since he couldn't imagine the dungeon having any sapient servants.

At the rate they were plowing through monsters, they should reach it soon. Cormac felt a grin overtake his face. The dungeon obviously hadn't built the fortress with earth affinities in mind. He would break straight through those walls with ease. He pushed forward even as the others did, racing to delve even deeper.

A *salamander,* lost from the main group, had happened upon a mouse. She had fought it, of course, and found it a tougher foe than she had originally believed. Still, she had managed and was now feasting on the roasted meat of the mouse, enriched as it was with Aether. Even as she ate, she kept her eyes on a swivel, aware that she was in a dungeon with its many dangers. As her eyes shifted back and forth, they caught a glimmer of something. It was like a deep liquid that just had to be stared at. The salamander forgot her meal and went closer to investigate.

The deep pools drew her closer, and she even found that the liquid hissed like a hot spring, only that the sound was even more soothing. Only as the pools drew closer did she see the vertical slit within denoting them as eyes. Even as she regained awareness, it was too late. All she felt was a soothing kind of pain as the liquid pools, that some part of her recognized as a reptilian pair of eyes, consumed her whole.

Chapter 35

Guardians At Work

A chittering roar sounded overhead, and the Mouse Captain ducked, feeling the whoosh of the large insect's tarsus as it passed over his head. He brought his mighty blade to bear and scored another deep gash into the creature's front section where the torso would be. He dove to the side to avoid its lunging mandibles and redirected another of its leg strikes.

During the fight, it had become quite apparent to him that the creature he was fighting, for all of its size and strength, did not possess the power of his own Ascension. He was more deeply connected to his lord's Aether and was therefore more capable. Combined with the might of his lord's gifts, his stage of Ascension made him a truly fearsome combatant. He processed this without pride, for he could feel a tension in the air that hadn't been there when he had started this fight.

Something was happening elsewhere in the dungeon and there was no longer time to waste. Summoning his connection to his lord's Authority, he set his sword ablaze. The creature hissed in both outrage and fear, backing away. The Mouse Captain would not let it retreat. Motioning to

his kin, mice poured onto the creature, gripping its legs tightly and holding on with all their might. Before the insect could do something about the new weights upon its legs, the mouse guardian lunged forward, his fiery blade leading. He slashed deep into the bug's torso section, causing the ensuing wounds to pop and sizzle as the fire met its ichor.

With a bellow, the creature snapped its mandibles down at him, only to have one of them shorn off with a single movement. Without ceasing his motions, the mouse plunged his sword deeper into the wounds he had dealt in order to deal one more grievous wound. Then he retreated and watched as the insect hissed and groaned before slumping to the ground, defeated and dying. Flicking his blade clean of ichor, the large mouse let go of the fire but continued to watch until he was sure the bug was dead.

He shivered as the creature released its Aether. Some flowed to him, but most flowed to the many mice that had been fighting before he arrived. Those mice looked at him with something like awe, and he shifted uncomfortably. His primary kin gathered with his squire, who approached and received his blade out of habit before cleaning it with some moss. The mouse guardian nodded to the other Mouse Guards around, then groomed his whiskers thoughtfully.

He was interrupted as he heard a voice reverberating through the dungeon. The voice of his lord. *Intruders have come. Defend the dungeon.* The mouse guardian stiffened and watched as the rest did as well. He turned to look at where the stairs curved down to where he imagined the fourth floor would be and knew it would be right under them. As he continued to think, a new thought appeared in his head. A last message from his lord, who continued to slumber.

He moved quickly to a section of the floor not far away and felt around. Finding a groove, he pushed with his paw and watched in wonder as the bottom fell out with a creak. Looking down, he saw the dark waters of the fourth and understood what his lord wanted of him. He turned and motioned to the mice gathered nearby. They looked up at him with grave expressions on their muzzles. They had received the same message he had.

"I teach you." He spoke softly, his deep voice echoing slightly in the cave-like area. "I teach you, then I go," he said, pointing upward. The mice understood. The five that had joined him would go with him, but the rest would stay here to defend the dungeon. He would teach them how.

The third floor guardian watched as the group of invaders pillaged the fortress of the mice. His instincts screamed at him to attack, but he knew that it would be folly. The little hairy one had split the very rock of the fortress walls asunder with a simple gesture. That was a kind of power that the serpent associated with his master, hence his hesitation in directly attacking.

This did not mean he was idle. Few of the invaders that split off from the main group lasted long inside the serpent's domain. One by one, he lured them in and struck with his new powerful muscles. He had to admit that the invaders were extremely tasty and the Aether they gave off was miles above his normal prey. He had already exceeded days of normal hunting with only a few invader kills. During his hunts, he had also shifted some of his master's Ascending creatures out of harm's way, hiding them in the grass and patrolling regularly.

Luckily, the invaders seemed entirely focused on proceeding deeper into his master's dungeon. The serpent hissed in displeasure at his inability to do more. His tongue flicked out, bringing scents to his sensory organs. His brain processed the information and combined it with what his eyes could see. He paused in his patrol as a new smell entered his awareness. It came from around the corner of his territory. His eyes did an impression of a squint as he realized the ramifications.

More invaders. He flicked his tongue out again and took in the position of the invaders pillaging the fortress, watching as they continued deeper. He could do no more unless he wished to follow them inside. Despite his desire to defend his master, he knew that once he entered, his length, green scales, and powerful muscles would only be a detriment in the close tunnels.

His striking power would be diminished, and he would no longer be capable of his new ambush tactics.

He hissed again and turned to follow this new scent. He would deal as much devastation to the enemy as he could before he was no longer able. He would follow deeper later and bide his time in order to strike when they least expected it.

The Queen watched as her council gathered. Once more, her master had gone to slumber, and right as he did, intruders had invaded. They were different from the normal animals that attacked, too, and she allowed herself a short feeling of pride that she had foreseen this threat. She had prepared her colony as best she could for this day, and now her nobles gathered to give her updates.

One stepped forward and clicked his mandibles, asking permission to speak. She waved one of her limbs, and he spoke in their language, one consisting of clicks, chirps, buzzing, and pheromones.

"The invaders have arrived, my Queen, and they are dangerous. They have already breached the fortifications of the mice and are now pouring into the first floor. Some of our people have begun to engage and managed a few kills but are now pulling back. Some of the creatures spit flame, and some hurl rocks through the air as if with their mind. Others use powerful tools to break through our people's carapace. The workers are doing their best to stall while the nobles attempt to make use of their distractions. The most positive outcome we have witnessed is that the fire does not catch. Our master's domain is not so easily set aflame."

Having fully stated his report, the Noble clicked his mandibles one more time to show that he was done before backing away into the circle of other nobles. The Queen spent a little time thinking over his words to show her appreciation for them. "This is good news," she said calmly. "We must learn all we can of these invaders. Draw them in and make them overconfident. We have built our colony to be as confusing as possible for outsiders. Let us use it. I must rely on you all to assist in this endeavor." She watched as the assembled Noble's clicked their mandibles in the affirmative. She was pleased as the pheromones in the air contained nothing but confidence and determination. "Go forth! For Core and colony!"

"For Core and colony!" The assembled nobles cried as they turned and began charging down toward the entrance to the nest. The Queen sat back on her wooden platform and felt the Aether around her. The colony was close to their second Ascension since becoming Danians. She could feel it. She could feel the rising Aether levels, perfectly displaced between every single Empowered Danian within her colony. She did not know the exact parameters, but as Queen, she could feel the full weight of her colony's Aetheric accumulation. These invaders would prove to her master that the Danians were a force to be reckoned with within the dungeon—if they survived.

The Warmeister of the Fallen looked on as his warriors destroyed the fortress full of mice. As they stood around two feet tall and weighed almost fifty pounds, it did not surprise him in the least to watch them succeed in slaughtering the mice. What did surprise him was the tenacity of the dungeon monsters. They had managed to hold off his warriors for a time and even kill one with rushing tactics while the rest were busy tearing down the walls to get better access.

Even now, the remaining tried valiantly to defend a hole in the building that was obviously one of the other entrances into the dungeon interior. The Aether in the air was palpable, and he almost licked his lips at the thought of the increasing nature as it flooded into the hole in front of him like waves on the shore. He turned to speak to his scouts, to tell them that they were almost in, when he froze. His scouts were still where he had left them, spread out across the floor so that they could keep an eye on the wider area in case of major threats.

Only, it seemed as though the threat had found them first, because his scouts were frozen stiff in a rictus of death. One was leaning against a post of the porch like he had fallen asleep, while the other was on the ground, his eyes wide open and face a caricature of agony. The Warmeister backed away toward the dungeon entrance and panned his eyes over the area. A hint of movement caught his eye, but all he found was a normal dungeon monster, one of the beetles, scuttling away into the grass.

The grass. The Warmeister continued to back up and gave a mental command for his warriors to begin shifting. They would hate the loss of endurance, of course, but they needed to be small enough to enter the main dungeon. It would also make his job later easier. He continued to pan his gaze over the grass and was rewarded by a flickering tongue. It still took him a moment or two to find the creature. Brilliant green scales and deep golden eyes stared back at him from within the shadowed grass. He felt a probe on his mind and dismissed it, though to his surprise, he struggled to do so.

He backed away with a bow toward the magnificent defender and sensed its confusion as it watched his subservience. He could sense its anger at their intrusion and winced at the amount that was directed at him. It couldn't be helped. The dungeon needed to know his people were capable, needed to feel the power they had at their disposal despite being *Fallen*. Geckodo could do little else but follow his plan to the letter. He would see a future for his people no matter what.

With his warriors shifted and inside, the Warmeister did the same, shrinking rapidly and cloaking himself in his alternate hide. Colors brightened, and his sense of smell increased. He darted inside the hole and found his warriors gathered, barring a few. He sent a mental command, and one of his warriors pointed at another floor's entrance set in the wall. A few of his warriors had decided to have their own excursion.

He hissed in displeasure but dismissed the fools from his mind. The dungeon was not a place to go off on an adventure. He would miss those warriors by the time his mission came to fruition, but perhaps this was for the best. He spoke-thought another command, and the group headed deeper at a pace far faster than their first form would have been able to. They raced through the space between the walls until they reached a corner.

It was here that the Warmeister stopped. The scent of Aether was strongest here. The way deeper was close by. Even as he had the thought, enraged squeaks echoed from the foundation beneath their feet. Mice poured out of a hole nearby and engage his warriors. The Warmeister let out a bray-hiss and charged into the fray. It was time to show his warriors why he was the Warmeister.

Chapter 36

Waking Up

Valterra knew pain. He continued to Ascend, helpless as his creatures were slaughtered by the dozens. His points of awareness kept him locked in on his creatures as they were killed. He experienced their destruction even as he was forced to abandon them to their deaths as he breathed Aether in and out. Their occasional victories seemed to pale in comparison to the wanton death the invaders seemed bent on dealing.

Every breath brought to him awareness of the destruction being caused by these new beings. What was worse was that he couldn't get a full idea of what the invaders looked like. In his fugue state, his awareness largely extended to just his creatures and their well-being. It didn't quite allow him to look through their eyes. He caught flashes only—a bit of a face here and there or a smell in other circumstances. What was even more concerning was how his Aether reacted to the invaders. Like the animals that had been his main source of conflict, these beings somehow interfered with his ability to sense his own Aether, but on a scale that dwarfed the previous interference.

They absorbed copious amounts of it. It was so noticeable that even asleep, Valterra could feel the drain. It was like his awareness ceased to exist when it came to them. He breathed in, and any invader in the way absorbed a portion while some absorbed a simply massive amount. It was hard to even maintain what awareness he had as his thoughts and senses flowed with the Aether. No Aether, nothing to see.

In the early moments of the invasion, he had managed to send out a message to his creatures that there were invaders. He had even sent a personalized message to his Mouse Captain, now that the guardian was on the fifth floor. That, though, had taken just about all he had left, and he had fallen into a deep sleep for a time. His slumber had not stopped the pain. He felt the pinprick of every dungeon creature slain and the feeling of their Aether being ripped from their bodies. Only a small amount made it back to his core.

That had no bearing on his Ascension, of course. An Ascension that was finally ending.

Valterra woke slowly, riding the last waves of Aether from a larger-than-normal breath. The golden light surrounding his core winked out as he came to full awareness. He yawned, or at least that was his impression. The result was a massive intake of Aether as it ripped through his halls and floors. Every creature within responded in some way. The invaders responded by gasping at the sudden influx, with some even passing out from the strain. The dungeon creatures, on the other hand, rejoiced as they felt their master return.

Valterra hummed to himself and felt his crystal respond in ways it hadn't before. It actually vibrated with his humming and transmitted it to the surrounding air. He homed in on his core despite the threat of the invaders. They would be dealt with in due time, but the changes to his core required his attention. The first thing he noticed was its size. It was much larger than it was before, although he was sure he was still far smaller than any other dungeon core. The second thing he noticed was the lack of runes and sigils. Instead of Calamvor's careful minute inscriptions, there was an incredibly complex latticework.

Valterra hummed again and watched as the latticework lit up from within before vibrating outward. He summoned fire, air, water, and earth, and watched how each element caused the latticework to light up in different ways. He manipulated the core room, watching his core the whole time. It fascinated him to no end. He felt... organic... alive, in ways he had never known before. It was as if he had been a toddler and had finally grown into his own body.

He scoffed at that thought and watched with a thrill as even that expression was captured by his enhanced Core. *Of course, I feel that way. I was a toddler.* He watched as his thoughts flickered in his core and "smiled" to himself. This was going to take some getting used to. But first, there were invaders to deal with and Ascension rewards to go through. First, a status report. Then he would see what his Ascension had given him. Hopefully, there would be an answer to his current predicament.

He breathed deeply and felt the dungeon respond. As his awareness rode the wave of Aether, he took in the changes that had taken place. His body, the dungeon, and its creatures were doing their best to halt the invaders' advance, but it didn't seem to be going well.

They had breached the third and first floors, leaving a path of destruction in their wake. Some had invaded the second floor in different places, but he wasn't able to stick around to see more than fleeting flashes of combat. The Danians seemed to be holding well, although the first colony he had set in place was doing better than the other one being attacked.

He was pleased to see that several creatures were either currently going through Ascension and had been hidden away, or they had already Ascended and had moved deeper. One of the more fascinating examples was a specimen currently running around the first floor between the walls. To his surprise, the system brought up its information without him needing to go looking. *Well, this is convenient!*

Pack-Leader Mantis (Rank E - Bronze)
Evolved from the Hunting Pack-Mantis, this insect has Ascended to lead the pack. Its instincts are primitive but effective in guiding its

lesser brethren to better hunting grounds. Larger and fiercer than its prior form, this bug is a natural killer and lethal to those who run afoul of it and its pack.

Oh, now that is nice. Valterra thought as he looked upon the fierce-looking insect. It was currently waiting in ambush with its pack, and Valterra left it there and went to observe the invaders. He was not prepared for the sudden surge of anger that overcame him at the sight of them. His anger boiled over as he saw one of them skewer a mouse without a care in the world.

His Aether roiled in his anger, and he manifested fire to crush them, water to drown them, wind to choke them, and earth to bury them. It didn't happen. Instead, he found himself helpless to stop the carnage as his Aether refused to obey him. As soon as it manifested, it flickered and died. It was like there was a bubble around the invaders that refused all attempts at control. So he was forced to rage silently as they slaughtered his creatures. His feeling of helplessness was total.

At least it was until he saw one of the invaders buried under a tide of mice before the others could get to him. Slowly, he understood. He breathed again and watched intently as the Aether washed over the beings, with most of it entering them instead. He was reminded of the vague notions he'd experienced while Ascending and brought them to the forefront of his mind. They were different from the basic animals that had attacked before. The difference was so startling that Valterra wondered how he could have ever mistaken Calamvor's memory of delving with the lowly creatures that had tried to make a living in his territory.

There was something that protected them while delving. If Valterra had to guess, it was this amorphous quality that prevented him from absorbing their Framework too. *Probably that Authority thing that Trik'Weri spoke of,* Valterra thought bitterly. *How dare they keep me from my retribution! Just die!*

His exclamation fell on deaf ears, at least as far as the invaders were concerned. His own dungeon creatures were a different matter and seemed to fling themselves on the enemy with renewed vigor. Valterra grimaced as he realized that his salvation would be upon the backs of his creatures and their savagery. He had known that dungeon cores created their monsters for a reason. He had always known, but in a dim, far-away sense.

He had been told by the high spirits to keep creating floors and was pushed to do so by his own desire for Ascension. The dimmest reason of all was for the exact situation he found himself in now. Oh, he had dealt with invading creatures before, but nothing of this caliber. He mostly created new creatures and sought evolution because he thought them interesting and he wanted to play.

Foolish, Valterra thought as he looked back on his prior childish ways. He supposed it wasn't all bad, but there were definitely some changes he was going to make as soon as he was able to. For that to happen, though, he needed to survive his delvers, and for that to happen, he needed to calm down and observe them in action. So that was what he did.

There were two separate groups, which he found odd. They were so different as to appear like entirely separate instances, as if both groups had stumbled upon the dungeon from completely different sides. One group was composed of tiny people, at least from what he could see. The leader was a small, hairy individual with a large sword Valterra's memories denoted as a claymore, although a very small one. It was wonderfully crafted, as were all of the invaders' weapons in this group. It was easy to denote the leader since he moved with grace and strength that were totally at odds with his tiny form.

The others in his group varied in appearance, from many fair-skinned individuals to other more elemental creatures. They all retained the same basic structure, but it was clear that four basic types prevailed with many having hints of one of the four basic elements present on their bodies or constantly in use. There were tiny rock men and women, fair-skinned wispy creatures that flitted from place to place, people with webbed feet and gills, and what looked like four-legged lizards without scales that breathed fire or were hot to the touch. At first, he thought the last type were just beasts, but he saw one shift into a flame-like caricature of a person before shifting back.

The second group was much more raggedy but also more savage. They behaved more like beasts than people, which was an opinion encouraged by their appearance. Dark scraggly fur, muzzled heads with jaws full of teeth, a propensity to switch between loping on all fours or standing upright on two, and a willingness to engage in bloodshed that Valterra hadn't seen even in his most violent creatures. These little guys loved it. They were fast too. *Not too durable, though,* Valterra thought as one of them was dog-piled by mice, their little teeth finding purchase in the creature's hide and ripping small chunks out of it.

They were long, lithe, and reminded Valterra of the Savage Mink that he had claimed so long ago, if far smaller. They were also far more intelligent as they coordinated with each other and communicated in some unspoken way. One, in particular, seemed to command, with sharp glances and motions that couldn't be misunderstood. It was larger, stronger, and faster than any of the others, and the rest obeyed its motions without much hesitation even in the throes of their blood lust.

Both groups would make their way to the fourth floor soon, and Valterra flitted down there to tell them to be ready. He watched the pod of whales acknowledge his warning with a flap of their tails on the water before diving deeper to hide among the grasses. The Deeplight Belchers could not hide as their shells gleamed with inner light, but then again, maybe that was for the best. The invaders did not know that these were not his highest-Ranked creatures, and they would pay for the ignorance.

Leaving it be, he finally turned to see what his rewards for Ascending would be. Last time, he had gotten his whale, and while he didn't expect anything on that level again, he hoped it would be useful for his current predicament.

Chapter 37

Cormac Finds a Whale

Cormac looked around him at his gathered group. They had breached the cavern of the mice with decent ease and were now resting after the giant wave of Aether had struck them some time back. Many of the stage ones had passed out from the strain, and despite his hurry to get to the core, Cormac wasn't going to sacrifice the majority of his group to see it done.

The wave, though, had bothered him. He had seen how the dungeon creatures had reacted to it, and their subsequent rush had almost broken through their lines to get to the weakened stage ones. It could only mean one thing, and it was simultaneously good and aggravating. Good, because it meant that he and his group had arrived while the dungeon was going through a metamorphosis—an Ascension, the priests would call it. That meant that his group had faced less organized defense when breaking through the first few layers of the dungeon. That would no longer be the case now.

It was aggravating because if he had arrived even a day or two earlier, he could have pushed through to the core without significant organized resistance. Now he would be facing an awake core with new abilities, perhaps even tailor-made for his group's presence. It was no secret that dungeons grew in power periodically, and after every metamorphosis, new creatures would show up and new environments would be given. Cormac shuddered to think of what would happen if the core gained some creature evolved to hunt Fair Folk exclusively. He knew they were out there and had even fought a few when he had been young and stupid.

His thoughts were interrupted as Fiona approached and laid her hand on his arm. For all that their delve had been suddenly complicated, Cormac couldn't deny that he had gotten closer to his betrothed in ways that wouldn't have been possible back at the Mother Tree. There was something about fighting side by side that drew people together, and he wouldn't trade his newfound closeness with Fiona for anything in the world.

"The last few are beginning to wake up," she said softly, unwilling to wake some of the stage twos that had decided to take a nap while others stood guard. He nodded and took up her hand in his. He was a gruff, proud man and knew it, but that didn't mean he was unknowledgeable or unromantic. She smiled at his attempt at forwardness and traded his hand holding for enfolding their arms together before resting her head on his shoulder. They stood that way for a time before she spoke again.

"I'm close, I think."

Cormac looked down at her and grinned widely. He made no secret that her approaching stage three made him happy, for it meant that they could finally marry. He couldn't explain his happiness, even to himself, because he could've lowered the stipulation and married her earlier. He had no one to blame but himself for the long betrothal. Part of it was his council duties and his desire to save the Mother Tree. But if he was honest with himself, it was because he had been scared of the commitment.

The betrothal had been made a long time ago, and although he had done his duty and met with Fiona many times, there was no spark to light his forge. There was certainly a spark now, and he couldn't rightly claim when it had been lit. Now that the bellows were pumping, he found very little reasoning within himself as to why he should stop them. He was committed now.

"Wonderful," he said gruffly, pressing his lips to her hair. "Let me know when it clicks." She nodded and they lapsed back into silence, a silence only broken by the waking of the group around them.

Climbing stages was always an interesting process. There was very little choice in the matter. There were certain things you could do to affect the outcomes, but for the most part, whatever process occurred was largely up to chance. Certain routes had been mapped out, of course. It was largely confirmed that the main Paths were set in stone. By accomplishing certain things or learning certain skills, you were more or less guaranteed to get the stage of your choice. There were exceptions, but for the most part, it had to do with skill, accomplishment, and temperament. Fiona, with her long list of accomplishments and skills, was almost guaranteed to become a leprechaun like him.

Reluctantly, he released her arm and separated. She frowned at him but let go as well when he motioned with his head toward the mobilizing group. "We've got to keep moving," he said with a slightly regretful smile. Fiona gave him one back and moved to collect her gear. He watched her go admiringly for a moment before moving on to check on things.

He made his way over to Killian, who stood looking out over the next floor. From what they could see, it was a massive, flooded expanse taking up what would have been the basement of the house they were in. Aether-luminescent grasses swayed in some kind of current below while massive glowing forms moved underneath the water. The light did a pretty good job of masking the forms of whatever moved under the water, but Cormac shuddered anyway. He hated deep water. He spoke once he had stopped next to the towering boggart.

"Well, what do you think?"

The boggart looked down at him and out once more before answering, "The water affinity is high, for one, but that could just be the nature of the floor." He pointed below to where the grass swayed. "There's some kind of current which doesn't bode well for swimming unless you're an undine or one of its higher stages." He shrugged. "I could do all right, I think, but something else worries me." When Cormac motioned for him to continue, Killian spoke again hesitantly. "It feels dangerous. Moreso than the floors we've come through. I don't want to enter that water, and I don't think we should. It would take longer, but I think we should build earth bridges along the walls until we reach the stairs."

Cormac thought it over for some time, waiting for the rest of the group to finish gathering. The cavern was a pretty safe spot with only one entrance leading in and one leading deeper. They could ostensibly forge ahead and leave guards at the entrance so that dungeon creatures couldn't come up behind them.

While he was thinking over the situation, he heard a childlike sigh of "Finally!" from behind him and watched as an undine leaped past him toward the water. He tried reaching to grab the stage one back but missed and could do nothing but stare as the little Fair Folk slipped into the water with barely a ripple. He sighed in frustration and turned to order the others to keep back when he noticed movement below.

Turning to look at the water, he could see the silhouette of the undine below cavorting around, pleased at being in water once more. What the undine couldn't see, and what Cormac could, was the massive shadow homing in on its position. He motioned quickly to Killian to remain silent but also motioned for the others to stay back. He watched with growing apprehension as the still unaware undine swam gleefully around. What worried Cormac the most was that he hadn't seen the creature until it was so close. The undine was already dead; it just didn't know it yet.

However, this wasn't Cormac's first time delving, and his reflexes kicked in as he summoned an earthen spear via his Authority. He manipulated its rotation, causing it to spin rapidly before launching it as powerfully as possible at the creature. The missile pierced the thing's skin, and for a moment, he thought he saw it flinch in pain.

However, his apprehension turned into true fear as the creature disregarded his attack entirely to focus on its prey. The massive form opened an equally large maw rimmed with baleen and slowly trapped the

undine between it. The poor Fair Folk only had time for one terrified scream before the top jaw slammed shut, locking its unfortunate victim away forever. "It's a bloody whale," Killian whispered next to the leprechaun with something akin to terrified awe. "By the Mother Tree, how does the dungeon have a bloody whale?!"

"A tiny whale," Cormac spoke but with no less fear. As a creature of the earth, his worst fear was deep, dark water, followed closely by heights. "I think we need a ritual. We need to know what this thing is." Even as he said it, he watched as the long head turned and saw the creature's eye looking at him. The rage contained in the one lidless orb shook him, but not enough to divert him from his course. "Regardless, Killian, I think your plan is our best bet if we can manage it. Have the shapers begin forming the bridge. I'll join them once the ritual is complete."

Chapter 38

The High Spirits Look On

"So, how's he doing?" Trik'Weri asked as he made his way over to Ile'Fen. The High Spirit of Conflict looked over to him from where he stood hovering over the pool where they scried the mortal world. The other high spirits were out and about performing their miracles and dealing with the supernatural threats that occasionally cropped up. This also served to distract their priests and various religions from noticing their attention. Ile'Fen ironically had much less to worry about on that front as most of his *marshals* and religions were all crusading or in one war or another. Most wouldn't notice his lack of attention since he could answer prayers from anywhere within the god-scape.

"He is doing fine, although there have been complications. His Danians have been pushed back on both fronts, and one of the colonies is struggling to pull through. The Fallen seem to be adept at killing them, but perhaps it's that particular colony's lack of experience showing itself. The first colony's Queen has shown immense foresight in the design of their home." Here, the high spirit's voice became tinged with excitement, and Trik'Weri had to hide an eye roll. There was nothing Ile'Fen liked better than commenting on tactics.

"There are traps and dead ends, and those, combined with the Danians' love for attacking from above, have silenced quite a few attackers. Most of the *fae* have abandoned conquering the second floor and have instead rejoined the main group, who are about to attempt to cross the fourth floor. Others have decided to explore other ways to get deeper."

"Oh?" Trik'Weri said, a question lacing his tone. "Some have broken away from the main pack?"

"Aye, brother, they have," Ile'Fen confirmed. "Three dragon-kin and a couple salamanders. They seem to have had enough of little Cormac. An interesting persona there, wouldn't you say, brother?"

Trik'Weri nodded and answered his brother's insinuation. "Yes, brother, I have my eye on him. Have for a while, actually. We shall see if our young nephew can humble him to the point where he sees sense."

Ile'Fen turned and looked at his fellow high spirit searchingly. "Hmm, I'm not sure that Valterra will be willing to let him walk free, even if you do manage to claim him as a disciple. Not to mention that he may make it to Valterra's core." Having said that, his face grew cloudy. "Have we decided what we will do if the fae manage to reach his core and try to claim him? Do we let them? I, for one, am unwilling to let such a thing happen."

Trik'Weri held up a hand to calm his brother. "Do not be so hasty, Fen. Valterra has his Ascension upgrades to help him and quite a bit of Divine Potential from these invaders of his. Depending on how he goes about defending himself, there's a high chance that the delvers never see the inside of his Aether funnel, much less his core. As for whether Valterra will let the fae go, well... let's just say I'll have to convince him of it."

He ignored Ile'Fen's look of disbelief and moved to observe the dungeon himself. The deal he had made with Valterra was not something he had discussed among his fellow brothers and sisters, largely due to the fact that once it came to light, he expected to be grilled mercilessly by them for exposing the young core to danger. He shrugged mentally. He would deal with it when the time came.

With that line of thinking reaching its conclusion, he turned to a new line of thought. The Fallen were certainly an interesting development. He had known there was a remnant within the Sylcyne Forest, of course, but he had dismissed them in the same way that all the other higher beings had. They barely clung to their sapience and had been in danger of descending further for decades. Their society had obviously deteriorated after the breaking of their Authority and the silencing of their parasite gods.

He watched them thoughtfully as a few Fallen raided the Danian colony on the far side of the house, away from the fae. Their leading group had already delved lower and were seeking a way across the waters of the fourth floor, but Trik'Weri ignored them for now. He focused on the ones above, observing their shifted forms critically, watching how they slavered and drooled, throwing themselves into combat with very little concern for their own safety.

The Fallen in his sights were barely more than animals. They communicated through psionic waves, which, while impressive, only revealed the depths of their stagnation. Mind magic and magic of the blood had been their forte for ages, and to see it reduced to a state of mere communication was almost enough for Trik'Weri to pity them. But then he remembered their attempt at blasphemy and promptly went back feeling disgust for the vile little creatures.

He watched as they tore through the Danian defenses like wet paper despite heavy losses. They wouldn't succeed in conquering the entire floor, of course, but the colony they were targeting might well be entirely destroyed by the time they got done. He moved on from them to watch the three fae brothers moving down a section of the in-between. That is, the section of space that existed between the inner and outer walls.

I suppose that would be the first floor? Trik'Weri wondered to himself. He clicked his tongue in disapproval. The first thing his nephew should do after this invasion was over was clean up his floors into something more manageable. Then again, perhaps this unmanageability would be what saved young Valterra from being conquered. The high spirit shrugged and

summoned his throne to continue watching in comfort. The young drakes were getting awfully close to one of Valterra's Ascended bugs, and he looked forward to seeing what would happen.

Chapter 39

Ascension Rewards

Welcome back, Valterra Unok'Davaas!

The following has happened since you started your Ascension…

Valterra looked on as notifications began streaming into his consciousness from the System. Much of it was information on his dungeon—things that had happened while he was asleep. He would return to those later when he had the time. He knew from his hazy memories that much of it most likely had something to do with his creatures and their Ascensions. While he was excited to see what they were, he had bigger things to worry about.

After a while, he found the Frameworks that he had claimed while Ascending.

New Frameworks acquired!

Kindling Brushtail (Rank F - Copper)
A type of squirrel found in the north, this creature has reached a stage of Ascension adapted to frigid temperatures, utilizing its Aether reserves to more perfectly regulate its temperature and surroundings. Often characterized by its habit of lighting small fires to keep itself

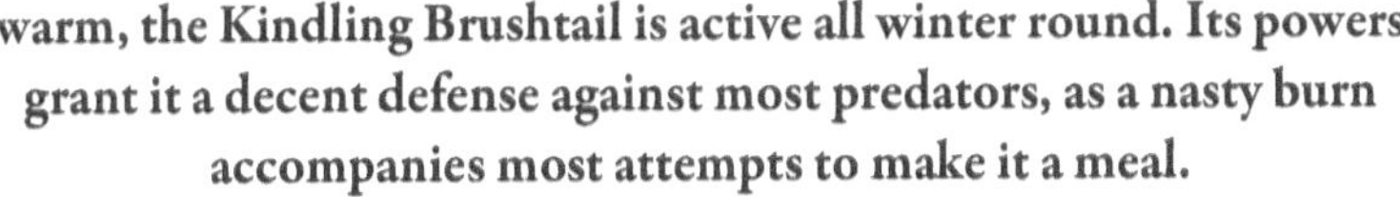

warm, the Kindling Brushtail is active all winter round. Its powers grant it a decent defense against most predators, as a nasty burn accompanies most attempts to make it a meal.

Coppertip Mole (Rank E - Bronze)
Found around copper mineral deposits, this mole has evolved to dig through such material. Consummate burrowers, these moles live by feeding on the magical grubs and other creatures drawn to magical ore. Like their humbler counterpart, they are unable to see. Unlike them, however, coppertip moles can manipulate Aether to give themselves a form of tremor sense.

Interesting, he thought as he looked the two over. He had desired a little more variety for his fifth floor, and the moles would probably fit the bill nicely. The squirrel would be useful as well, but it also tickled the young core's mind. Maybe there was something there for the future. Shaking off those thoughts, Valterra turned to the rest of his notifications.

As he scrolled down the list, he found multiple warnings of delvers in the immediate vicinity, which would have been nice to know before they started slaughtering his creatures. He shrugged mentally, his core flickering in response. There was nothing he could do about it. After the delvers arrived, there were a couple of notifications that caught his attention.

You have attempted to absorb multiple sapient creatures!
Searching for Access... Access Denied!

Reasons given:
1) Under the protection of a guardian deity or
2) Error...

No Framework will be created at this time...

Searching for Aether reserves and Divine Potential... Found!

Absorbing... Absorbed!

Total calculated units of absorbed Potential… 237
Total Potential: 237

That can't be right. Valterra thought. *I had over 250 units remaining after I created my Wyvres.* He went back to his logs and found nothing, just a whole host of errors. *Where did these come from? Did the High Council mess something up again?*

"Now that's just unfair," Krat'Imos said as he watched through the pool. He had just arrived from guiding his priests when he heard Valterra's comment.

"Actually, I think it's fair. We were the source of a lot of his System-related problems." Trik'Weri offered up from where he was cleaning one of his knives.

Valterra sighed and let it go. He had no idea where his Potential had gone, and there was no use wondering. He did wonder, however, at the second reason given for not being able to absorb delvers. He looked back through his logs and discovered that the error was associated with the second group of invaders. He made a mental note to check on them and was surprised when the system responded with an answering note. He smiled through his core and thanked Krat'Imos for his genius.

As for the missing Potential, he would just have to get more from the invaders currently in his dungeon. To that end, he turned back to his notifications and brought up his most recent ones.

Congratulations! You have Ascended! The gods look favorably upon this and have offered the following Frameworks as a reward.

Please choose one of the following:

Juvenile Mastodon (Rank D - Iron)

A large herbivore that roams the northern plains of Algerthrond, this creature is still in its youth. Unlike other species of elephantids, this specimen has woolly fur, which allows it to keep warm even in the frigid environment of the north. Having just begun to grow tusks, it is nonetheless a large and powerful animal with the potential to become even more deadly with time.

Fomorian Stalker (Divine, Rank D - Iron)

Recreated in the image of a Fallen race by the High Spirit of Chaos and Revolution, Ata'Laya, this creature is but a monstrous shadow of its former nature. Used by Ata'Laya to sow chaos and often able to be summoned by her high priests, these creatures are adept at finding and disrupting Aetheric workings and beings.

Sorial Skyhawk (Rank D - Iron)

Found high in the sky, these birds of prey are the only migrating species of raptor in the world. With their affinity for wind, they are able to traverse vast swaths of land by gliding on air currents. Fierce predators, these large birds are capable of diving great distances, striking quickly and decisively.

Arctic Bull Shark (Rank D - Iron)

Roaming the frigid coastlines of the north, Arctic Bull Sharks have Ascended to a stage that can withstand their extremely cold environment. Along with this trait, they can also survive in freshwater with special glands that allow them to keep a store of salt within their bodies. This has been made more efficient with their slight affinity for water, which allows them to "carry" saltwater with them as they swim. Fierce and deadly, these underwater hunters devour anything they can successfully hunt.

Valterra hummed thoughtfully as he considered the options before him. Each of them was interesting, but his eyes kept being drawn to the Fomorian Stalker. Ata'Laya was one of the high spirits, but he hadn't really interacted with her much. The fact that the offer had the label of divine was intriguing. Based on the description, it was a creature created to support her priests, specifically her high priests. He didn't know if that meant that the creatures were more powerful, but the fact that it was chosen to represent an aspect of a high spirit was something he couldn't ignore.

That didn't mean he chose it right away. He analyzed the other options for a time but continued to come back to the Fomorian. All the creatures would be reduced in size since they were larger than the parameters of what his title governed. With that in mind, many of them would be around two to five inches, either long or high, which wasn't much variation.

The mammoth would be nice because as a juvenile, he knew it had the potential to grow, and what glimpses he got of it revealed an already massive creature with low-hanging tusks and a long nose called a trunk. The shark was also large, being around seven to twelve feet long. It had a face full of teeth and a body covered in muscles. However, it wouldn't do for his dungeon, at least not yet. His sunken basement was freshwater, not saltwater, and the sharks wouldn't do well there. He didn't know if it was possible for him to manipulate the Framework once he had it, so picking it would be a mistake.

The hawk was intriguing yet humorous. It was a massive migratory bird that used air currents to travel long distances. While that might be useful eventually, Valterra had no use for the bird, especially once it was shrunk. It was large with an eight-foot wingspan, which would be four inches wide once his title got done remaking it. While it would be hilarious to watch delvers be struck by tiny dive-bombing hawks, he would have to wait for such a sight. He needed a creature that had a little something extra.

You have chosen the Framework "Fomorian Stalker"

New Framework acquired!

Title "Transcendent Tiny Dungeon - Divine" has gone into effect. When summoned by Valterra Unok'Davaas, the Framework "Fomorian Stalker" will be affected in the following ways.

Effect: Each Fomorian Stalker costs 90% less Aether to summon but is reduced in maximum size by a factor of 1/24th. The maximum size, therefore, is now reduced to 2.5 inches tall from five feet.
Due to the boon "Child of the Gods," the Fomorian Stalker may be modified freely and cannot be taken away.

Valterra looked at the final line and smiled, his core lighting up. He would summon the first one to get a good look at it and its abilities, but having the ability to modify it was exciting. With his choice made and new creatures to experiment with, Valterra turned his gaze to his dungeon. He had new tools now, and he was eager to drive these invaders from his halls.

Chapter 40

The Fae, the Whale, and the Rat

Rising from the remains of the ritual circle, Cormac went over what they had learned. That creature was labeled as a Great Tidal Whale and was Rank 4 on the dungeon scale, which meant that this dungeon was more dangerous than he had thought. What interested him even more was that the ritual depicted it as a massive creature almost as long as the Mother Tree was tall. But here in this dungeon, it was at most five to six feet long.

Cormac couldn't wrap his head around it. For it to be that small, it would have had to shrink a good deal, and the kind of power that could do that was outside his understanding. For the first time, he pondered the wisdom of delving deeper. He was no coward, but he was the only stage 3 here. His teammates were closing in on *climbing* to the next stage to join him but there was a danger inherent with climbing stages within a dungeon. He did not have the means to protect them adequately if they all underwent the climb simultaneously—not against Rank 4s. Of course, this might be the only creature of such power that the dungeon had.

Did he want to gamble on that outcome? Gamble the lives of his team and his betrothed? Even as he had those thoughts, others pushed their way to the forefront of his mind. The power that would be at his disposal with such a dungeon would be truly great indeed. If he claimed this dungeon, he could actually succeed in his goal of saving the Mother Tree. He could return a hero, having shaped a dungeon that could provide for his people what they needed to climb higher. Their race... Their race might even grow enough to Ascend completely. If enough Aether was brought back to the Mother Tree... it might be possible.

He turned and headed over to where Killian was directing the bridge building. "How are we doing?" he asked, looking over and down to the edge of the water. "I don't see the creature anymore." Despite his words being a statement, there was a hint of a question in his tone.

"The building is going fine. The dungeon stone is hard to manipulate, but it's possible with enough people, and we certainly have that. As for the creature, it slinked away after it saw that we weren't going to try to swim for it. What is it anyway? I saw you finished the ritual."

"It's called a Great Tidal Whale. Rank 4." He heard Killian whistle next to him in appreciation with just a hint of fear.

"I'm glad I chose the high road then," Killian muttered.

"So am I, my friend. So am I," Cormac said as he turned to look out over the inky blackness. A few of his salamander kin had lit small fires using the heavier Aether as a fuel source, but the lights didn't penetrate very far into the gloom. They could already see the far side, and what he saw wasn't encouraging. It just kept going, and he could see how the basement went further down until it was completely submerged underwater. That was a lot of space to hide in.

Perhaps it was a sixth sense that guided him at that moment, but he turned to Killian and said, "Make sure our team is ready for anything. I don't trust that creature to remain idle. I'm not sure what it can do, but I don't want to be surprised. We need to be ready to move at a moment's notice." Killian nodded as he moved off. Cormac was determined. He would conquer this dungeon for his race, no matter what it took to do so.

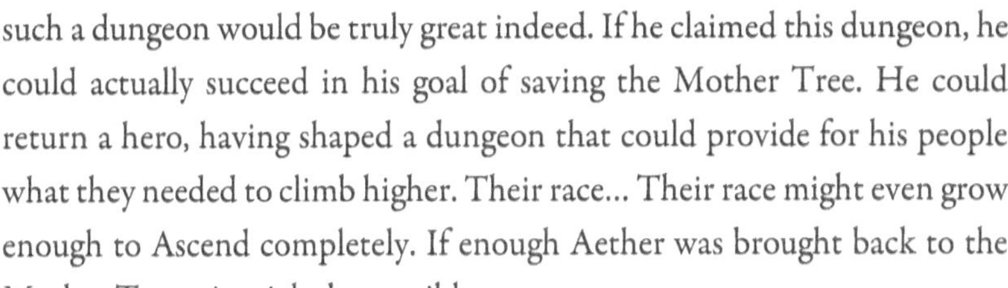

The matriarch hummed a song in satisfaction of another successful rat hunt. She had gotten adept at using her affinity to flood the low rock shelf the Maker had put there for their use. When caught off guard, the rats would be washed into deeper waters where she and her pod could feed. As she was breathing deeply for the return journey, she heard a song echoing through her sunken hall. It was from one of her "sons," and he was telling a tale of pain and victory. The invaders had come and had wounded her son, but not before he had eaten one of them. He claimed they were delicious but were now above his reach, on high shelves of rock where he could not reach.

She called back to him, telling him to join her, the message also calling to any other member of the pod to do the same. *Gather in the lowest section,* she sent via her song. *We will wash them off their perch.* Jubilation echoed through the waterways as her fellow podmates joined her in swimming deeper. Soon they were all gathered, and she communicated her plan. They marshaled their affinities together and swam. Swiftly and gathering their Aether together, they meshed their multiple affinities into one song, and the water responded.

Something in the motion sang to their deepest being, beyond their lived experiences. Images of giant waves and rough seas appeared unbidden in their minds, and they clung to the image as it coalesced out of their fury. It did not matter that they had been summoned to an underwater labyrinth far from their place of origin. Right now, the tide sang to them, and when they sang back, the tide answered their call. The invaders would taste the fury of a tiny ocean unleashed.

He-Who-Chitters-In-The-Dark looked out over his kingdom and smiled a snaggle-toothed grin. His eyes sparked in satisfaction as he watched his rats move rock and stone to dig deeper into the dungeon. They had learned much in the time since The-One-Who-Was-Not-There had set them free upon the ledges. They had learned to dive for the glowing grasses to make bedding and to light their way, for the grass continued to glow after being ripped from the bottom of the water. They had learned to lure the giant insects onto the lowest rock shelf in order to hunt them despite the constant dangers of the The-Ones-That-Lurk. The divers were compensated for the increased danger, and the clan was fed.

For that is what they were now... A clan. His plan to woo Bone Crusher had worked. She found his eyes entrancing when he wasn't in one of his mad fits. Those fits had been increasing in regularity. He saw things in the dark of his sleep. The-One-Who-Was-Not-There sent him images that were like thoughts and yet not. He saw images of creatures in the likeness of the tall two legs but smaller and knew that they sought to harm The-One-Who-Was-Not-There. The anger was often transmitted in the dream, and he would often wake to a beating by Bone Crusher for having nipped her in his sleep.

He always apologized profusely, and she seemed pleased by his offerings to her. Their mating had become official, with all the proper ceremonies involved. He had brought her an abundance of insect meat and a carapace that shone. He had even fastened it around her upper torso to protect her from harm, using crude wrappings of dried grass. She had loved it. Their nest was on the highest of ledges, and their litter was safe from harm, far away from the giant creatures that lurked in the depths. He smiled again at the thought of the litter. Eight pups were up there, resting after gorging on insect meat. It was tough to feed so many mouths, even for him, but it was nice to be the leader. And to have a mate that was physically superior to other rats.

He-Who-Chitters was not like her in that respect, but he had his own route to power. The mining of the spark crystals proceeded under his direction, but even beyond that, the tunnel that led to their freedom was proceeding apace. He directed the efforts flawlessly, for his mind knew where The-One-Who-Was-Not-There held court. He could feel it in the Aether coursing through him. He did not go straight there, of course. He needed to prove that he and his fellow rats were worth keeping around. What better way to do so than to take care of its infestation?

Yes, he would direct his people well. They were close... He could feel it. He moved deeper into the tunnel, his guards helping to shove other rats out of the way until the rest got the message. Summoning the other Mad-Touched in the tunnel, He-Who-Chitters led them in the chant. It didn't actually have words, but it did contain meaning. The meaning was simple but profound. Destroy. And the Aether in their minds and flesh responded. Green lightning sparked from their eyes and crackled down the length of their bodies. As one, they ended their chant and thrust outward. The lightning roared forth with all of their collected might and began chiseling through the rock at terrifying speed. With an explosion of dust and rock, light poured into the tunnel from the new opening ahead.

Many rats flinched away from the light as it burned their retinas from their long time in their subterranean home, but not He-Who-Chitters-In-The-Dark. He had a destiny, and nothing would stand in his way to claim it for himself, his mate, his pups, and the rest of his clan. Clan Spark would claim everything they could get their paws on.

Chapter 41

Deepwater Revenge

Valterra watched with glee as his pod of Great Tidal Whales began their journey toward the invaders. They were a ways off, but the invaders were almost three-quarters of the way across on their bridges. More and more of them were clustering on the bridge, ready for the final segments to be placed so that they could cross in safety.

He smirked. Their desire to delve deeper would be their downfall. With growing expectations, he watched the two forces converge, one static and one moving. It was the bearded one who noticed something first as the water was sucked away from the farthest wall, exposing the Aether Grass and the shiny backs of some of his insects. He was able to let out one warning shout before the pod arrived.

A massive wave slammed into the wall and geysered upward, causing a great number of the invaders to topple over into the water. From there, the fight became completely one-sided. The massive forms of his whales battled to consume as many as possible. Out of the twenty that fell into the water, one made it to shore, climbing the stairs at a rapid pace to escape the churning waters. Turning his eye upon the bridge, Valterra was frustrated to find that the bearded one had managed to save his team and another twenty-seven by encasing their legs in stone right before the wave hit. He continued watching as they started moving.

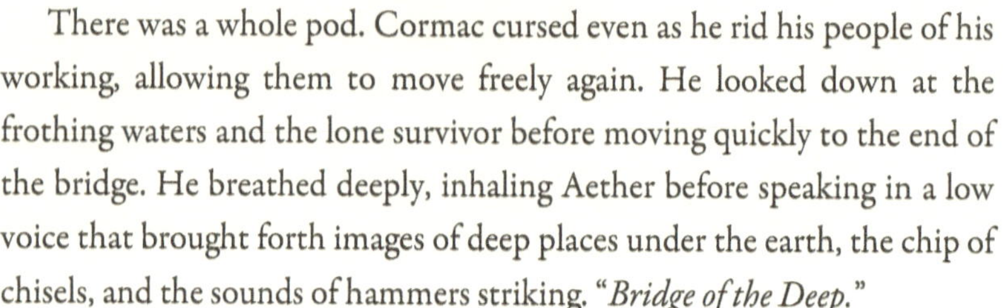

There was a whole pod. Cormac cursed even as he rid his people of his working, allowing them to move freely again. He looked down at the frothing waters and the lone survivor before moving quickly to the end of the bridge. He breathed deeply, inhaling Aether before speaking in a low voice that brought forth images of deep places under the earth, the chip of chisels, and the sounds of hammers striking. *"Bridge of the Deep."*

The rock of the dungeon exploded into motion under his hands, and he bore the strain as Aether was sucked out of him. He hadn't wanted to use his *Legacy Working* in this way, but he was left with no choice. He didn't know if the whales were able to repeat what they had done, but his team had to cross now before those monsters came up with another way to knock them into the water.

Under his hands and through his words, a bridge of black dungeon stone expanded outward, crossing the last section left before uniting with the basement stairs that twisted upward. "Move, people! Get across now while we still can! Once you're on the stairs, keep moving upward and away from the water." As he rose, he motioned to his team and they hurried across, occasionally casting glances down at the frothing water below that was now settling a little as the whales finished their feeding frenzy.

Cormac couldn't shake the feeling that they were watching his group escape and weren't pleased by the fact. He breathed easier once they reached the stairs leading upward, and he got his people moving. They needed to in order to keep their minds from dwelling on the catastrophe that had just taken place. He found what he needed just around the bend—a fortress teeming with mice. He didn't even have to say anything. As soon as the fortress came into sight, his people went berserk, their former fear being fueled into helpless rage against enemies their own size.

With a motion, he held his team back as the rest of the group rushed forward to do battle. A hand gesture was all that was needed to communicate that this was where they were splitting off. His group faded into the background and moved deeper into the floor even as their kin threw themselves into battle.

The three brothers walked side by side along the narrow section of stone that characterized the floor of the massive hall they were in. They knew it to be, in truth, the space between the inner wooden wall and the outer stone wall of the structure they were in. That did nothing to detract from the fact that once inside and walking along it, the whole aesthetic was almost like an unimaginably long hallway with a great, vaulted ceiling.

So far, their search for alternative ways deeper had ended in failure, but they were still optimistic. The occasional mouse attack helped to keep them sharp and gave them a little Aetheric boost from each death. As they continued down the hall, the eldest among them stopped and breathed in deeply.

"What is it Jaak?" Halaak asked. He was the youngest and prone to curiosity and bouts of maniacal flame.

Jaak breathed in again and turned to his brothers, a large toothy smile on his face. "I've got something. It's just a whiff, but I think there's an entrance to a higher floor nearby."

"Then let's get to it. I'm tired of walking around. I need to fight something," Siirnaak said, stretching his powerful limbs out. He made to move forward but froze when cries of pain and terror rang out from behind. The salamanders that had been following them scattered as a pack of large mantis monsters struck from the shadows. The ambush claimed quite a few lives as there were almost ten of the big bugs, including a truly massive specimen with a green and black carapace. It had killed three of the salamanders on its own and now turned to glare at the lesser drakes with fury burning in its multifaceted eyes.

The brothers only needed to look at each other once before grinning and entering combat.

Valterra looked on in anxiety as his Pack-Leader Mantis engaged the invaders in combat. He didn't want to lose his new creation, but he recognized that he could make more if he needed to. Once the creature Ascended for the first time, he had access to the higher stage. That didn't mean he wouldn't try and help out. Further down the wall and well outside the invaders' influence, he summoned three Fomorian Stalkers and commanded them to engage with the fiery invaders. It took a lot of Aether to do so but not nearly as much as summoning the pod of whales had. With an eerie shriek, they leaped forward to do his bidding.

To say they were interesting creatures would be an understatement. They ran lightly, their lithe wolfen forms quick and sure. They blended with the shadows and seemed to flicker between them without effort. They were also slightly humorous. He knew from the Framework that they were supposed to be around five feet tall, and if they still were, he had no doubt they would be terrifying. They still were, but there was only so much terror they could inspire when only two and a half inches tall.

He moved on. Hopefully, they would get there in time to save his mantis, but either way, he figured three rares would do the job. In the meantime, he headed back to the sixth floor. His Mouse Captain was still climbing, and Valterra figured that he would do some peace-making between his first guardian and his Wyvres. After all, they were his final line of defense at the moment. They had no time to be fighting amongst themselves.

The Warmeister stared across the black waters of the basement, stunned at the ferocity of the creatures there. He had seen the wave and how it smashed into the small folk. Even his usually fearless, bloodthirsty warriors seemed cowed by the display. He was glad now that he had stopped his warriors from trying to swim the distance. Even in their larger forms, they would have been hard pressed to make it before being attacked.

However, even as he stared across the waters, something subtle reverberated through the dungeon. He froze and heightened his senses as far as it could go. Three divine signatures had been summoned. They were faint and fading rapidly as they headed away, but it wasn't that fact that had the Warmeister frozen in shock. It was that he recognized the signature. *Those meddling gods!* He growled mentally. *So quick to move on as if we're already ended.*

Marshaling his will, he turned to his warriors and commanded them back up. He led the pack, tearing through the dungeon in the direction of the three signatures. He would show the gods and the dungeon that his people were not some template to be thrown around.

Chapter 42

Mouse & Mantis

The first guardian looked down from where he and his kin had climbed higher. There were six floating mountains, with each one being progressively larger than the last. Looking down from the edge of the third such island, the Mouse Captain witnessed the flashes of combat below as the fortress of his mice brethren came under assault. He stroked his whiskers, frustrated, as his kin fought and died below without him.

Those feelings did not keep him from his duty. He was to climb higher and provoke a final confrontation if needed. He would keep his lord safe. He turned to climb higher even as he felt his lord move. Reaching the moss ladder on the other side, the mouse paused to look below and witnessed large shadows moving forth to assist his kin. Savage Minks and Deeplight Stalkers dove into battle, and the tides turned. He smirked, running a paw through his whiskers. His kin would be fine.

He climbed, and his immediate kin followed. His squire was right behind him, followed by the others. Each one had proven capable on this journey deeper, and the guardian was proud to call them kin. Reaching the next floating island, the mouse pulled himself up and took stock of his surroundings. Moss coated the island except for a small trickle of water that ran off the edge.

His kin quickly followed him up, after which they spread out to either side. They had yet to encounter any of the creatures that guarded this floor, but the Mouse Captain was sure it was only a matter of time. They were halfway across the island when his hypothesis was proven correct. A series of roars split the air as three large forms dove toward them, wings tucked in to fall faster.

With a swing of his sword, the first guardian summoned his borrowed powers, calling forth stone pillars to rise around them. The creatures hissed in rage as they pulled up sharply, their long talons scraping the stone as they clutched at the pillars. They tried to grasp for their elusive prey, only to receive sharp jabs from the mice and their makeshift swords.

The Mouse Captain did not remain idle while he and his kin were attacked. He brought forth fire to scorch offending legs and to singe their snapping jaws. The creatures hissed and roared but eventually spread their wings and retreated, not willing to put up with the fire-wielding mouse. The Mouse Captain nodded in satisfaction and motioned for his kin to keep moving. They stopped at the trickle of water to refresh themselves and wash their wounds, using the abundant moss as bandages.

They continued their climb, and all the while, the Captain caught glances of a party of invaders further down. They, too, were climbing the islands and making their way higher. The mouse pulled a paw across his whiskers to clean them, thinking. They would make their stand soon, but they had time to prepare. Hopefully, he could convince these new creations of his master to help.

Blood. Heat. Pain. Ecstasy!

The Pack-Leader Mantis felt born again as he raced through the invaders that dared to trespass on its territory. He cared little for the flames that licked along his carapace. There was pain from the long gash hewn into his metathorax, but he ignored it all for the sake of carnage. His fellow mantises tried their best to keep up but got bogged down by the press of bodies. They were not as large or as agile but attempted to replicate his savagery with varying degrees of success.

A flare of light was warning enough for the big insect as he turned sharply, dodging another wave of flame from one of the more powerful invaders. They had been hunting him through the crowd of combatants ever since the battle started. Only after indulging himself did the large insect notice that his energy reserves were failing. He was tiring, and the three flaming hunters were still moderately fresh, having spent their time chasing after him as he slaughtered their allies.

One of the insect's lesser brethren screeched in pain as it was torched, and the Pack-Leader gnashed his mandibles in rage. He had gotten carried away like before with the large mouse. He rushed back into combat, only to jump away from a blast of flames that singed his forelegs. He watched as two of the invaders set about burning his pack to ash as the other kept him at bay with its flames.

The insect screeched in rage and attempted to charge but was met with flames. He leaped back and forth, attempting to save his pack but to no avail. Soon, there were only three members left, and as they burned, the large insect went insane. He charged forward, disregarding the flames that licked at him hungrily. He ignored the burns as they built up on his carapace. His eyes sizzled, and one popped before he broke through. The invader seemed surprised as it was grasped with both raptorial forelegs.

It gurgled its incredulity through blood-flecked lips as the Pack-Leader's mandibles plunged into its neck and drank. It was so good and the mantis was so far gone in his pain that he didn't even notice the twin roars of rage at first. However, he noticed the returning flames. He screeched and dropped his prize, bringing his forelimbs up to guard his face while simultaneously leaping away to gain ground.

He slumped there, smoke rising from his crisp body. He watched as the two figures kneeled next to his victim and checked it over. They screamed in rage then and the mantis warbled in glee. He had hurt them somehow. He could sense it in their tone. Somewhere inside, the mantis had hurt them. He tried to rise and found he couldn't. Spent and weak, he could only watch as the figures moved in.

Chapter 43

Fire & Fury

There wasn't a need for any words. The two lesser drakes turned their whole attention to the insect that had dared to kill their youngest brother. Rising from where he had been mourning their brother, Jaak opened his mouth and belched flame toward the creature. Siirnaak joined him, roaring in rage, his jaw shifting partially into its more animalistic form. The screech of the large insect was like music to their ears, but it wasn't enough.

Both brothers acted on instinct and shifted into their true forms, their bodies crackling into living flame before hardening into rigid scales carved from the fire. Frills of flame formed around their lizard-like jaws before a sail of flame ignited down their backs. There was no more playing as they leaped to rip the bug in half. Their rage blinded them to all other things as they tore into the insect savagely, only to stagger back as black tendrils reached out of the shadows to grab them. They fought their bonds, breathing fire in great curtains to burn them away. Even as they did so, more flickered forth to snag limbs.

In their panic, they lost sight of the insect, and when they looked again, they found it gone. In its place, they saw a sight that caused their flames to flicker in abject fear and terror.

The Fomorian Stalker soaked up the fear of the lesser drakes like it was the richest of vintages. The creature shuddered in ecstasy at the feeling, knowing that this was what he had been created for. He looked to where his siblings had already begun to engage and found his enjoyment mirrored in their snarling visages. He could feel his master's anger at these invaders, and the Fomorian Stalker was here to give his response.

He snarled in satisfaction and felt his fangs elongate in anticipation. He was utterly dwarfed by the larger drakes, but he didn't mind. He leaped forward and jumped, evading a fan of flame that gushed forth from the leftmost drake. Using a lasso of shadows, the Stalker encircled the drake's snout and pulled himself toward it. As it tried to recover, he kicked off a flat plane of shadow, slammed his foot, empowered by darkness, into the fairy creature, and sent it hurtling into the wall.

His brother and sister took on the other drake, his seniority of a few moments allowing him to punish the other. He took off, just as the drake shook itself as it emerged from the ruin of the wall. He slammed into it again, causing its midriff to concave and air to whoosh out of its lungs in a plume of smoke.

He cackled madly, giving his kind's screech of victory as he pummeled the invader into the ground and walls. It wasn't even a contest. Oh, he got scorched a couple of times, but each time he simply dug his fangs into the drake and let its Aether-rich blood heal his wounds. It ended abruptly as it always did in such a brawl. The drake got weaker, and the Stalker got stronger. It took only one mistake, but the Stalker was not one for mercy.

The drake snapped its head forward to take a bite out of him but was slow to retract it when it missed. The Stalker didn't hesitate as it slammed a spike of shadow straight through the invader's eye into its brain. Even then, the creature didn't immediately die, its remaining Aether reserves in its blood trying to heal it. It clawed at the spike, dealing more damage to itself in the process. Even as it succeeded in ripping out the spike, the Stalker simply expanded spikes from the end. He watched as the invader lobotomized itself, pulling its own brain out of its eye sockets.

The stalker smirked and turned to find that its siblings had succeeded in their kill as well, not that there had been any doubt. He greeted them with a screech of victory and they responded. He gave them a fanged, wolfen grin only to whirl when a similar roar to their own answered their screeches. Barreling toward them were figures much like them but wrong somehow. They moved similarly and had similar forms, but they did not hop from shadow to shadow like a Stalker. They were also too large, loping toward them at a height of around nine inches. The form in front was even larger and moved with a grace the others didn't have.

They smelled wrong, like a drink gone sour. The Aether around them twisted in odd ways, and the Stalker snarled at them as their master commanded them to engage. They were invaders, and they would meet their end here.

Geckodo howled as he saw his targets in the distance. They stood triumphant over some other invaders, and his blood seethed as he took in their arrogant stances. He would show the dungeon how a real **F*@#ErrorN** fought. He fought through the pain of the thoughts rushing through his head, thoughts long denied his kind. They were *Fallen*, and the god's blood no longer acknowledged them. Well, Geckodo would force it to.

There was no pausing and posturing where both sides sized each other up before engaging in combat. There was only a closing of the distance and a brutal clash. Geckodo felt his fangs and claws enlarge before he threw himself at the central figure. His warriors went after the other two, but he was unable to keep track of them. His opponent required all of his years of experience and savagery. They were a whirlwind of fur and blood as they flashed from place to place. The template would fade into shadow at times to disengage, but the Warmeister would simply follow the blood to where it would reappear before engaging again.

He kept on the smaller creature, his mouth ever braying for more blood. His claws left gashes and his fangs drank from its Aether-rich blood. It was strong, this template, but it was no Warmeister of the Blood. As far as he had Fallen, Geckodo felt more and more like his old self as he fought this fake illusion. The creature darted around, leaping off of shadows and empowering its strikes, but Geckodo shrugged off the worst of it, relying on his powers to heal him.

That changed, however, when the last of his warriors fell. He sensed it, like a shifting tide on the far north sea. One by one, they were defeated until he could sense the other two templates charging him. They were weakened from the battle, but not enough. He growled low in his throat and delved deeper into his instincts. They came quickly and attacked simultaneously, darting around him like wolves on a bear. He dodged what he couldn't block, but more and more strikes hit, his greater size now plaguing him. The fakes were flagging as well, but there were three of them, and their powers made them especially suited to the frenetic shifting pace of the battle.

Geckodo's flanks dripped with blood from numerous gashes in his hide, and his regeneration could no longer keep up with the frequency of his wounds. He panted even as he scored his own wounds on his opponents. The remainder of the fight was quick and brutal, ending with him gasping for air through lungs filling with blood. He staggered as one of the fakes pulled their claws from his chest. He went to one knee and struggled to breathe. This. This wasn't supposed to happen. Even kneeling, he towered above them. He looked down at the three templates and took in their sorry states. He had almost done it. He could have proven his people's worth to the dungeon and the gods both.

He continued to glare at the three as the central creature raised its claws once more. No. He was Warmeister of the Fallen. He could not fail. Not now. He let out a gurgling roar and swiped his claw out at them, forcing them away. He staggered upright and focused all his willpower on making his mangled vocal cords work.

"By... Blood... I... Am... Reborn!"

As the last notes of his roar faded, he could feel the shift inside as the old magic tried to ignite. It sparked, twisted Aether gushing forth in waves and radiating off his body. Even as it did so, something snapped. Geckodo howled in pain as his insides shattered and were remade. He watched as the magic latched onto his fallen warriors and stripped them of blood and bone. He watched as the tide of gore flooded into him, remaking him into something else. His mind strengthened even as it cracked under the strain of the magic. He grew in size and then his body condensed the extra mass into hard muscle. However, the pain never left him.

The false templates were not idle during this time. They continued to dart in and claw at his new form, but their strikes had a harder time breaking through. He cackled madly and lurched forward with a speed that shocked even him. It was more by luck than anything else that he was able to hit the creature, but when he did, it rocketed away from him and slammed into the wall of the dungeon with a crunch. He laughed again as more Aether filled his blood and body. His eyes crackled as he began the slaughter.

"Well, that's not good," Ile'Fen stated dryly, and Trik'Weri nodded in agreement beside him. Trik'Weri looked at the letters that were emblazoned next to the creature, lit in the same manner as the System they had built for the divine cores.

Shattered Avatar of the Fallen Shard - (Fallen, Unique, Rank B - Silver)

"Yes, not good indeed," Trik'Weri muttered. He sent out a call to his other brothers and sisters so they would be aware of the issue. "We may need to intervene after all. I did not expect there to be any surviving Fallen with the ability to do this."

"Neither did I, brother," Ile'Fen responded. "Regardless, there may be an opportunity here." At Trik'Weri's raised eyebrow, Ile'Fen continued, "Conflict breeds opportunity, and that soul is conflicted at its very heart. Valterra may gain something tremendous from the resolution of that conflict. We shall see." Having said his piece, he turned to gaze into the pool once more, and Trik'Weri followed suit, each of them lost in their own thoughts.

Chapter 44

A Sour Bargain

Valterra felt his core tighten almost painfully as he looked upon the invader who had just metamorphosed right in front of him, even as it laid waste to the other two Fomorian Stalkers. As he looked upon the creature, he analyzed what he was feeling and realized that for the first time in his sapient life, he felt true terror and fear. This wasn't the anxiety of invaders being in his dungeon—that he could deal with. This was far worse. His core tightened further before he forced it to relax. He tried observing the creature and realized that this time, he could see it through his system. What he saw, however, did not alleviate his terror.

Shattered Avatar of the Fallen Shard - (Fallen, Unique, Rank B - Silver)

He shuddered at the Rank and the power radiating off the invader's new form. That wasn't just a metaphorical shuddering either. His dungeon literally shook where it connected with the invader's aura. Aether went mad, bucking and twisting into loops and swirls that hurt to look at. Whatever it was doing to maintain its form was chipping away at Valterra's dungeon with malicious intent. He quickly looked away, trying to formulate some kind of response to this unexpected danger.

I'm not prepared for this, he thought. *How am I supposed to deal with a Silver Rank invader on top of all the others?* He flashed over to where his Mouse Captain was climbing up the sixth floor before diving down into the fifth to see how the battle was going. To his relief, other than the bearded one's group, the other invaders were being overwhelmed as their assault on the fortress of Mouse Soldiers was turned against once the other creatures of the fifth floor arrived.

His relief was quickly shattered as he felt one of his walls shatter. He darted back to see that the aura surrounding the Silver Rank invader had destabilized the walls enough that it could just blast its way through them. It wasn't going to go through the dungeon the normal way, it would seem. In a panic, Valterra racked his brain for some way to deal with this new threat but came up empty. That was until he noticed the rats. At least a hundred of the critters were flooding out of a new tunnel that had just opened up near his Aether funnel. He hadn't even felt them digging, but with everything that had been going on, that probably wasn't a strange thing.

Valterra panicked, and his panicking most likely saved his life. In his surprise at the new threat that he had thought was contained, he summoned his newest Framework to defend himself. And the Silver Rank invader went completely mad. It screeched out a horrible sound and began recklessly charging toward where the Fomorian Stalkers had been summoned. Valterra, seeing this, felt a measure of sanity return to him. He calmed, his thoughts no longer wild and chaotic. He looked at the rats and at the invader closing in and smiled. He made his Stalkers dart through the rats until they were on the other side.

For their part, the rats seemed confused, first at the summoning of the stalkers and then at their movement through them rather than attacking. That confusion shattered into fear as the invader crashed through the wall and into the room. After its transformation, the creature stood close to a foot and a half tall, but once it got into the room, it swelled obscenely. It grew to around three feet tall and brayed a harsh cackle-hiss that reverberated through the room. To Valterra's surprise, instead of running as he had expected, one of the rats moved forward and chittered loudly to the rats around him before squeaking something in a rhythmic manner.

Even more surprising was the appearance of other rats who did the same thing. Then the Aether went crazy. It blazed around the chanting rats and condensed itself down until, with a squeaky kind of roar, the rats unleashed a sort of spell. A green-blue beam of energy ripped from their outstretched paws and slammed into the invader with a crackle of searing heat. It flared further when it impacted the creature's aura but barely slowed down. With a screech of pain, the Fallen Shard staggered back under the onslaught even as it petered out. The rats involved in the spell staggered as the light ceased flickering around them. That didn't stop the rat at the forefront from squeaking loudly.

At his "command," the rat horde charged, leaping onto the creature ferociously. Valterra watched, fascinated, as the rats flung themselves at the twisted creature, biting and scratching relentlessly. His fascination quickly turned to fear once more as the creature retaliated by doing something with its aura. It flared out, flinging rats in all directions, the Aether lashing into them. It brayed out its rage and pain before turning on the rats and beginning its slaughter.

This wasn't how it was supposed to be. The invaders were supposed to fall, and Clan Spark was supposed to take their rightful place as part of the house. Instead, the one invader they had come across was stronger than the clan warriors and Mad-Ones combined. The rat squeaked orders wildly, trying to contain the chaos, but the slaughter continued unabated. The creature was huge with twisted muscles that somehow contained great strength. It regenerated as fast as the warriors cut and gnawed at it, its ugly wounds sealing over.

He-Who-Chitters-In-The-Dark would not be cowed, though. He continued to order his rats while looking for any weakness he could exploit. As another blast from the creature threw rats off of it, he saw something he hadn't expected to see. The damage from the spark lightning they had unleashed was healing slower than the other wounds. It was still there. Working quickly, the rat called his Mad-Ones to him and ordered them to bring the rest of the spark crystals. He had the other rats continue the fight while he prepared for the largest spark of lightning he had ever done. For the first time, he entertained the notion that he might fail but shook it away. Even if it took his own life, he would pave the way for his pups and his clan. Some of the rats might be afraid of death. Not He-Who-Chitters-In-The-Dark.

Valterra looked on as the Silver Rank invader continued to devastate the rats. He needed more creatures. He turned to the fifth and sixth floors, watching as his creatures continued to overwhelm the delvers there. He was trapped into only using higher Rank creatures due to the fact that the Aether density was so high in the room near his Aether funnel. He didn't want to summon his creatures only to have them turn into monsters. Regardless, he needed more forces.

Thinking quickly, he widened the area at the top of the sixth floor and commanded the majority of his Wyvres through. With their Aetheric blood, despite its lesser quality, he figured they would be fine in the higher Aetheric atmosphere. With bellowing roars and screeches, around a dozen of one of his largest creatures dove through the opening, swooping down to attack the Fallen Shard. They tore into the creature with their savage jaws, hanging onto its back with their wing talons and hind claws.

The Shard responded instantly, shaking itself violently to dislodge the Wyvres clinging to it before snatching a few from the air to throw them across the room. Valterra winced at his creatures' pained screams as they impacted the dungeon walls at speed. For all of that, though, his Wyvres were large creatures, and their jaws did damage even as the wounds were healed by the Shard's regeneration.

Something continued to bug him about the Shard. The way the creature's aura interfered with the dungeon's Aether and its single-mindedness toward pursuing the Fomorian Stalkers. Even now, it only sought to hunt down those creatures in particular. Why? He took up the Framework of the Stalkers in his mind's eye and compared the two. Only now did he see the resemblance between them. Despite the changes wrought on it by its transformation, the two creatures were remarkably similar. His core racing at the thought, he dove into his system messages to pull up the notification he got for trying to absorb the dead bodies of the fallen invaders.

Searching for access... Access denied!
Reasons given:
1) Under the protection of a guardian deity or
2) Error...

To test his growing suspicions, he tried absorbing some of the dead invaders from the battle in the walls.

You have attempted to absorb multiple sapient creatures!
Searching for access... Access denied!
Reason given:
1) Under the protection of a guardian deity

The small magical people are under the protection of a deity. He looked at the Silver Rank Shard again in realization. *The other ones aren't.* His core raced with ideas and speculations. *There must be another reason why I can't absorb them. Is it because they're sapient? Probably.* His core flickered as he thought through his assertions. *If I can't absorb the bodies... could I claim the living?*

"I told you he would get it," Ile'Fen stated calmly. Out of the high spirits gathered, he was the calmest. That didn't surprise his other brothers and sisters. As the High Spirit of Conflict, Ile'Fen knew his way around tense situations. The others were more anxious but still nodded along with Ile'Fen's statement.

"He won't have enough Divine Potential to claim it," Trik'Weri declared. "He will need some help, and as you know, we can't interfere without some kind of bargain. Such is the way of Divine Potential, after all."

"It's too late for any new bargains, Trik'Weri. Anything of this magnitude would have to have been set in stone already. You know this," Krat'Imos spoke as he looked into the Pool of Scrying. "Otherwise, the Divine Potential wouldn't transfer. The bond would need to be old and steady."

"Hmm..." The other gods noticed Trik'Weri's affirmative tone and looked to him. Noticing their stares, he couldn't help but smirk. "Oh yeah... about that."

As Valterra gathered his Aether and will, intending to claim the creature before him, he felt Trik'Weri descend. "Hey there, kid. You're going to need more than that to do what you're planning on doing."

What do you mean? I have a lot of Aether I haven't used yet. At Trik'Weri's silence, Valterra thought further and eventually got to the point he was trying to make.

I need Divine Potential, don't I?

"Yup!" Trik'Weri replied cheerfully. "And a lot of it. That's why I am here."

Valterra sighed as only a core could, by breathing a plume of Aether out of his crystalline heart. *Another bargain, Uncle? I still haven't repaid the last one.*

"Oh no, I'm not here to set up a new bargain but to receive payment for the last one. It just so happens that what I will ask of you will probably necessitate me giving something up in return."

Valterra felt something akin to what anxiety might be like as he responded to the god. *What payment are you asking for?*

"I want you to spare a select few of the invaders. Specifically, Cormac Torgir and his party."

Valterra felt the bargain like a blow upon his Divine Spark. But Trik'Weri was also right in the manner that the payment asked was high. He instinctively knew which invaders he was talking about. The leader of the invaders and his party. The ones who had slaughtered their way through his dungeon with the intent of claiming his core and enslaving him.

How dare you?! Valterra seethed. *You would ask me to give up the ones who would chain me, the ones who have killed their way through my host to see me brought low?!*

"Yes," Trik'Weri stated calmly, and Valterra could feel the weight of those words as they settled over him. They weren't something he could refuse.

Fine! he spat mentally. *How am I to do that?!*

Trik'Weri, as serious as Valterra had ever heard him speak, explained the plan even as the party in question neared the area of conflict.

Chapter 45

The End of Conflict Part 1

It had been a long, grueling climb upward for Cormac and his party. Even as they physically exerted themselves to climb the wet moss ladders, their souls and spirits took a beating from the cries of pain and death echoing from their people below. Cormac still held to his path of claiming the dungeon core, but even he was beginning to wonder if it would all be worth it in the end.

No. Cormac's jaw clenched as he shook away those thoughts. *This will save Mother Tree. I know it will.* He finished climbing over the edge onto the next island before drawing his sword and standing guard as the others made their way up.

They were almost there. Only two more islands and they would be at the top where the islands connected to an opening in the wall. He had seen dungeon monsters fly through, and while the number had concerned him, the amount of Aether they gave off did not. They were all Rank 2 at most on the dungeon scale by their aura, though he would need to do a ritual to know fully. When the last member of his party had made it onto the island, they moved toward the next with their weapons bared and ready.

This island was different from the others, with large pillars decorating the vast majority of it, hiding the edges from view. Cormac took the lead as the strongest member of the group, with Killian following behind. Fiona took up guarding the rear of the party while Eoghan scouted the perimeter cloaked in shadows. They had made their way across the majority of the island before Eoghan appeared in front of Cormac. He held up a finger and the party stilled. Like a whisper, Eoghan's voice carried itself to Cormac's ears, his raspy tone still strange to hear.

"Mice ahead. Possible guardian among them."

Cormac nodded at the words and motioned for him to repeat them to the others. Once he was sure Eoghan had done so, he motioned for him to circle behind the mice to strike once they had engaged the rest. Afterward, he mimed himself attacking directly while Fiona and Killian flanked on either side. After they all nodded in acknowledgment, he motioned for everyone to get moving.

He moved forward cautiously until he saw an end to the pillars in sight. Readying his claymore, he moved to get a look at what he was dealing with before engaging. Standing before its kin was a massive mouse with a large broadsword clenched in one paw and a thick cape of fur that hung around its neck, fashioned with clasps to keep it in place. It was an impressive creature but not threatening when compared to the massive beasts Cormac had fought in the past and certainly less terrifying than the small whale down in the basement.

The other mice around it were even less impressive, though they did have what looked to be needles that they held in their paws like swords. Cormac sneered at the sight. This would be easier than he thought. With a bellow, he charged forth from his spot and leaped into the air, bringing his claymore crashing down on the larger mouse. He smiled even as he reinforced his body with Aether to make sure he hit as hard as possible.

His surprise, therefore, was complete when the blade of the mouse met his and stopped his attack dead in its tracks. He blinked in bewilderment even as he was grabbed by his opponent's tail and slammed into the ground. Hard. He rolled away and rose only to find the creature rushing toward him, its blade whistling through the air. He had no time to notice the battle cries of his party as they joined him in battle. All his old instincts came rushing back as he fought for his life.

Their blades flashed back and forth in a dizzying display, and Cormac found himself respecting his opponent more and more as they dueled. The mouse had talent, but he could tell it was bestowed and not learned naturally. It had the same feel as the humanoid monsters found in deeper dungeons. Slowly, Cormac overcame the larger mouse, and by the narrowing of its eyes, he could tell it knew it too.

With a flair of power, its sword lit up in searing flames that momentarily blinded Cormac. He tried to disengage but the mouse pursued. "*Will of Steel!*" Cormac shouted, activating one of his inheritances. His sword shimmered and shine even as he brought it to bear against the flaming sword. When the two clashed, sparks flew from the contact, but Cormac's sword remained unmarred and whole.

A new kind of duel began as each began using their elements against the other. Cormac weaved, dodged, and parried the flaming blade while also using his earth affinity to create divots and entrapments for the mouse to fall into. Each one allowed him to score minor wounds that soon had the mouse covered in blood from multiple nicks.

Cormac was unable to escape all of the mouse's attacks, however. The flames it controlled would often flare out at inopportune moments, scorching Cormac's skin. Hardened as it was by his life of working with metal, his skin still bore minor burns from the attacks. Back and forth they raged until, as if by mutual accord, they disengaged momentarily. Looking around, Cormac found that his party was doing okay with Killian facing off against two of the mice and Fiona facing the other two.

There was no sign of Eoghan, and Cormac wondered for a moment if he had abandoned them and was about to curse his name when he noticed a flicker of shadow near Fiona's fight. He smiled and raised his sword to re-engage but froze at the expression his opponent gave him. The mouse smiled and the sight chilled Cormac even as he realized his hubris. It was a guardian. Of course, the dungeon would be speaking to it. Not to mention the dungeon was feral, uncontrolled, and entirely willing to throw away honor to protect itself.

The fur cape on the mouse's back blazed with light, and Cormac cursed himself for a fool. Artifacts. How the hell did such a young dungeon have artifacts already?! He opened his mouth to warn his party but could only watch as if in slow motion as the mouse spun and hurled its blade with a speed it didn't have moments ago. Cormac turned to follow it and found Eoghan's expression mirroring his shock as the blade took him through the middle of his chest and sank into the stone pillar behind him. Distracted, Cormac didn't notice as, with a blaze of speed, the mouse's tail flicked out and slapped him across the face, the crack from the empowered whip-like appendage snapping his head back.

His head ringing, Cormac attempted to focus and spoke forcefully, "*Unbreakable!*" Instantly, his pain vanished as the inheritance took it away. He entered a state of being where his body, mind, and spirit were as hard and unyielding as the depths of the earth. He hadn't wanted to use it. It would take months to recover.

Even as he turned to follow the mouse, he knew it wouldn't be enough. He saw Killian brought down by three mice, one of Fiona's mice disengaging to help, as they hounded him with their needles. He saw Eoghan gasp as the mouse ripped its blade from his torso. He saw Fiona... his beautiful fiancée... struggling to survive even as the large mouse turned its blade on her. Cormac was halfway to her before the mouse began his swing, but he knew that he wouldn't make it in time. The blade fell, time stopped, and divinity descended.

Chapter 46

The End of Conflict Part 2

Cormac found himself somewhere else, surrounded on all sides by a white haze. It was familiar in a way he hadn't expected. He turned and sure enough, there he was, the High Spirit of Trickery and Mischief, lounging on a throne.

"How yah been, Cormac?" Trik'Weri said through his smirk. "You seem to have found yourself in a tough spot."

Cormac forced an easy smile onto his face. Of course, the god would latch onto this chance. After the severing of ties with the tall folk, Cormac had also severed ties with the god he had been meaning to devote himself to. At the time, he had lost his faith in the gods of the tall folk and returned to the first deity of his people, the Mother Tree. To this day, he refused to acknowledge the seed planted in him by Trik'Weri, afraid of what it would cost him.

"What do you want?" Cormac asked and watched as Trik'Weri's face darkened even as he rose from his throne.

"What do I want?" the god hissed. "I want what was promised!" he roared. "I crafted a seed of potential for you, and out of spite and anger, you chose to spurn my kindness, and now I am forced to give you another chance." His eyes burning, Trik'Weri stalked back to his throne even as he waved his hand to create a window. Through it, Cormac could see the frozen tableau of his fight in the dungeon.

"No more games, Cormac Torgir, and no more bargains made with half-truths. You have two options before you." Trik-Weri made a motion, and Cormac felt the seed respond to the pull. A golden thread materialized between himself and the god, and the high spirit motioned to it. "You can accept being bound to me for life and after it. In doing so, the seed will reach its full potential, but you will serve me completely and no others." Cormac felt his heart clench at the thought and clench harder at the next words spoken. "If you agree, I will save your party and remove them from the dungeon, including your fiancée Fiona, healed and completely whole."

"Refuse,"—here, Trik'Weri's voice grew cold and frigid—"and not only will I let the dungeon kill you and your party, but I will help it do so and claim that seed from your cold, dead corpse before the dungeon can absorb it for itself."

Cormac shuddered and bowed before the weight of his choices. He was a fool to have come here without the full support of his people. He could see that now. He had been overconfident and overzealous, and it had led to this outcome. But he also knew himself better in this moment than he had before. He didn't want to die. He wanted to live. He wanted to marry Fiona. He wanted to craft masterpieces the world had never before seen. And he wanted power. He let out his breath in a rush and made his choice. The thread between him and Trik'Weri pulsed, and the god smiled.

Valterra watched as the bearded one disappeared along with his party. His anger still simmered beneath the surface at being denied their deaths, but he also knew that he was getting something from the exchange when he didn't have to. Technically, the bargain he had made with the high spirit so long ago had ignited a Divine Spark, and nothing Valterra had would repay that kind of debt. The favor he owed to Trik'Weri was completely open-ended, and the god would have been well within his rights to simply take what he wanted without needing Valterra's permission or giving anything in return.

So, Valterra turned and focused on his survival and the new servant he would hopefully possess after this. He sped through his dungeon, collecting the Aether and Potential of all the fallen invaders. By the time he finished, there was a massive flow of Aether heading toward his funnel and down to his core.

It was the Divine Potential, though, that he was after. Trik'Weri had hinted that it was what he needed, but he was sure that what he had wasn't nearly enough to claim the creature. Even after absorbing the different invaders, he had only gained a little over a thousand Potential. Considering his creator had given him over five thousand, if the price for claiming this Silver Rank invader was even half, then he wouldn't have enough.

He quickly moved to observe the battle, where he found a desperate struggle taking place. The Fomorian Stalkers had gotten involved, and their attacks seemed to slow the creature's regeneration considerably. The Wyvres were doing their jobs as well, holding down the creature and tearing chunks out with their strong jaws.

It was the rats, though, that surprised him the most. They hadn't retreated or scattered. In fact, they had rallied around a singular rat whose eyes sparked with green lightning. He wondered at that even as the rat seemed to gather energy from bundles nearby with a few other rats, sending a beam of crackling green-blue lightning at the invader. The smell of burnt fur pervaded the room as the invader screeched in pain.

Its eyes flared ruby red, and the blood of fallen creatures flowed into its body, healing it at a rapid pace. In the same motion, it punched out with its clawed hands, ripping into the Wyvres around it and absorbing their blood as well. Valterra could figure out the result on his own. The Wyvres were falling as the creature tore their wings from their bodies or threw them against the walls with sickening cracks.

They would heal and regenerate eventually, but only if they could keep their blood. Yet the invader would continue to draw it from them until they

were spent. With their blood supplementing its already enhanced regeneration, the invader would be unkillable. It would only be a matter of time until the rats were killed, and without them distracting the invader, the Fomorians would be next. After that, there would be very little keeping the invader from taking his core.

It was time to act.

The first thing Valterra did was find his third-floor guardian. He found him trying to squeeze his way through the dungeon in between the walls, headed for the invader's path of destruction. Moving to help, he opened a passage through the walls and commanded the snake to enter.

The two-foot snake slithered forward rapidly until he came upon the battle. Commanding his creatures, Valterra watched as they collapsed upon the invader. His three remaining functional Wyvres fell on the creature from above, even as the Fomorians trapped its limbs in shadowy chains. The rats retreated and watched. They weren't his and didn't quite know what was happening. Only the lead rat, the one with the sparking eyes, remained with bundles of spent Aether stones around it.

The final creature to collapse on the invader was the Emerald Adder, guardian of the third floor. He slithered up the invader in a flash of movement before settling in front of it and activating his powers. This was a crucial moment, and Valterra channeled his Aether to funnel into his guardian in order to boost his power.

He sighed in momentary relief as the invader sagged in the grip of his creatures. He took a moment to center himself before gathering his will and pushing his Aether forward to claim the creature. The Aether flooded it like a cresting wave, and he felt it push out the foul, twisted Aether the creature had before. He could feel it within the creature as it mapped out its Aether conduits. He pushed more and more inside, washing away the filth until he slammed into another force coming the opposite way.

The sheer malevolence of the thing stunned Valterra for a moment, but he shook it off and pressed harder. He still lost ground. He struggled to do more, but it wasn't until he really examined the other force that he understood. He was fighting against whatever twisted divinity protected the creature from being claimed.

Gathering his Divine Potential, Valterra used it like a drill and began penetrating deeper, using Aether and Potential both to push the foul presence away. It was strong but lacking in intelligence. Valterra learned more and more as he dove deeper. Whatever this presence was, it no longer existed physically. It was more like a miasma that coated the creature.

It took a long time, but eventually, he reached the source. Where the creature's Aether core should have been was a shattered gemstone. Traces of Spark Essence flickered between the pieces like static electricity, and Valterra realized that the creature's Spark was contained within. The miasma was strongest here, and it lashed out at Valterra's presence like a wounded animal.

Valterra reached for more Potential to drive it out for good but felt his reserves drying up. He had been correct; he didn't have enough to claim it. He growled and attempted it anyway but came up short as the miasma fought him tooth and nail.

The Dungeon Core sighed and reached into the part of his soul where Trik'Weri had left a connection, like a parcel waiting to be opened. He looked at it for a moment before sighing again and opening it. The flood of Divine Potential that slammed into him was staggering, and he quickly directed it from his core to the invader he was trying to claim.

It rushed through the connection he had made before colliding with the miasma clustered around the shards. It gave ground, howling as it went until it was scoured completely from the creature. Its spark fluttered weakly as the miasma left, and Valterra hurried to control the Potential, forcing it to piece the shards back into a full gemstone.

Piece by piece, he rebuilt it until it shone fully complete. He then did what the miasma had done previously and marked it with his presence, signifying that it was his. What he didn't expect was for a massive chunk of the remaining Potential to burst out of his core and flood elsewhere, outside of his dungeon to somewhere nearby.

He pulled out of the creature only to watch it slump to the ground, even as his awareness took in a multitude of signatures outside his dungeon. He flexed his will at them and watched, stunned, as other creatures like the invader stumbled out of the woods around the cabin and entered his dungeon's domain. His System was going insane with notifications, but he really only had eyes for one of them.

Congratulations, Valterra Unok'Davaas!

You have claimed or created your very first sapient lifeform!

The previously Fallen race, the Fomorians, has been claimed as your own.

As a dungeon core, they have been integrated into your dungeon but are connected to you via your divinity. As free sapient creatures, they may disobey your commands but are also subject to punishment if they do so. It is up to you how benevolent of a god you wish to be.

Valterra's eyes widened. His dungeon was partially destroyed, and he had lost many of his creatures, but apparently, he was a god now, and he had survived. *I wonder what the uncles and aunts are going to think about this.*

Epilogue

Wrapping Up

The high spirits watched their adopted "nephew" begin cleaning up his dungeon before turning to each other.

"I think that went about as well as it could," Krat'Imos said gruffly. "He truly is one of us now in the full sense of the word."

"Indeed." Tal'Irieth concurred. "This will cause issues for him down the road."

"Perhaps, but conflict is inevitable, as you all well know." The others nodded in agreement to Ile'Fen's words. His domain wouldn't be nearly as powerful if that weren't the case.

"Now, what are we going to do with you?" Tal'Irieth muttered as they all turned to look at a certain mischievous god who was currently hog-tied on his throne. Trik'Weri gave them all an awkward smirk.

"Ah, you could let me go? I mean, my bargain saved the kid's life."

Krat'Imos guffawed loudly. "Ha! Yeah, and you almost got the lad killed when he was forced to ignite a Divine Spark. No, no, no. I think you and I need to have a chat about the hidden loopholes in my System again. You have a lot of talking to do."

Deep in the woods to the far north, a foul presence woke up. Absolith of the Fallen felt his people ripped from his grasp and roared. He strained at his chains with what remained of his strength but found them as strong as ever. But now he was awake, and now he knew there was a young divinity nearby. He would be free as soon as he could find the key to this infernal prison.

He licked his lips, his long tongue sliding over drooling jaws dripping with miasma. That young Divine Spark would make for the perfect appetizer after he was free—a fine way to soothe his hunger until he went after the high spirits themselves.

He settled in to wait, even as the ache of his missing minions settled in his soul. He had others, of course, Fallen races that had meshed their fate with his. He would bring all of them to bear against the one who had stolen from him. His hiss echoed through the halls of his prison as he began plotting his revenge.

Horace watched as Cormac and four others were surrounded by his men. They didn't put up a fight, and it was clear to see why. They were beaten and tired. They weren't wounded, but then again, why would they be after the display of divine power that had teleported them out and healed their wounds?

Cormac had given his group the slip, and by the time they had left Mother Tree, they had been a day behind. Though the evident losses tore at his heart, Horace couldn't help but be relieved by the fact that Cormac hadn't succeeded. He stepped forward and addressed his former council member in a stern voice. "Cormac Torgir, you are hereby stripped of your seat on the council and are under arrest for betrayal of the Mother Tree. Do you intend to resist or will you come peacefully?"

Cormac's gaze lifted to his, and Horace was shocked at the shame and deep guilt that lay there. His hoarse voice echoed the look in his eyes. "No. No, I will not resist, Horace. Do what you came to do."

"Very well. Men." As his men moved forward and clasped the cold iron around the former council member and his team, Horace turned and surveyed the dungeon and its grounds. He didn't dare enter, but he would wait and see if any of the misguided souls that had joined Cormac could make it out. He doubted it, but he would wait all the same before taking the prisoners back to face judgment.

The Mouse Captain looked upon the column that housed his lord, and then his gaze fell to the scene of war spread out around it. He nodded to the third floor guardian and received a dip of the head in response. He made his way over to the scene of the battle to find his new brother-in-arms resting against a wall.

The former invader simply watched him come, breathing heavily from the rigors of what he had just gone through. The power radiating from him was immense in a way the mouse had never experienced in a monster before. Not even the whales on the fourth floor gave off such an aura.

"Come... closer, little one. I will not bite," the creature said, and the guardian took the offered olive branch.

"What are you?" the mouse asked simply, his muzzle contorting in odd ways to help him speak clearly. The creature leaned its head back and closed its eyes, letting out a breathless chuckle.

"I am what remains of a shattered pact. The shards of a broken race remade. I was Fallen and am now risen again. I made a gamble invading this place, and my gamble has paid off." The creature looked down at him and smiled a tired, toothy grin. "I needed a god to break my chains, and your master has provided. You need not worry about my loyalty."

The Mouse Captain nodded, surprised that the creature had so easily read his intentions in spite of the simplicity of his question. He left the creature to rest with a farewell flick of his tail and moved to the next possible threat.

The rats of the fourth floor were picking through what remained of their dead, spearheaded by the strange rat at their head. They froze when the Mouse Captain approached with his retinue behind him. They moved to stand behind their leader, bristling as the mouse moved closer.

The rats' leader, however, remained impassive. His eyes blazed with sparks as they roved over the mouse and his guard, seemingly encouraged by what he saw. The rat shambled forward to meet the mouse, and they stared at each other for a long moment.

The moment was broken when the presence of his lord fell on them. The rat looked around wide-eyed as if he could feel it too, despite not being a dungeon creature. His lord seemed to want to rectify this, as the rat suddenly shone with the light of his lord. The other rats too shone with light, and the mouse relaxed as the rats refused to fight the claiming. He turned away and moved off, content that each of the remaining threats to his lord were dealt with.

Followed by his retinue, he moved to the spire in the center of the room and looked up. It was time to finish his delve. He climbed the service of the spire, the rock pitted and marked for easy climbing. He entered through the hole in the top and began his descent. The pilgrimage lasted some time as he skirted pools of condensed liquid Aether before climbing down into the lower caverns. But soon, he was greeted by the cool light of his lord. He moved with his entourage, and they spread out to either side of him.
He led them in kneeling before the core, his battle blade held vertical with paws around the hilt. His fellow mice did the same with their needles. They bowed in subservience to their lord who had given them life and Aether. The mouse guardian reaffirmed his conviction. His lord would be protected against all those who would seek to do him harm. He swore it.

Void Sovereign by Zaker Syed

An action-packed apocalypse LitRPG about a feral survivalist who defies the System to live on his own terms.

Aenon abandoned humanity long before the world ended.

Deep in the wilderness, he survives by patience, discipline, and the certainty that weakness carries a price. While others cling to fragile comforts, Aenon has already learned to endure a world that gives nothing for free.

Then the System descends, and the world is dragged into a multiverse of monsters, magic, and trials.

Classes awaken. Power can be earned. Death comes easily.

Where others see danger, Aenon sees opportunity, a chance to seize his freedom even if that path awakens powers once feared enough to erase entire civilizations.

But first, he must survive the System's tutorial.

Perfect for fans of *Defiance of the Fall*, *The Primal Hunter*, and *He Who Fights With Monsters*.

Available now on Kindle Unlimited and Audible!

Thank you for reading a MoonQuill® original novel. More exciting stories can be found at www.moonquill.com.

We would greatly appreciate it if you would take a moment to leave a review. Each one helps the author and supports their ability to continue writing fantastic books for everyone to enjoy!

If you're looking for more great books to read, join our mailing list by scanning the QR code below. You'll get a few ebooks for free!